A Novel Way to Die

A NOVEL WAY TO DIE

KAREN HANSON STUYCK

FIVE STAR
A part of Gale, Cengage Learning

GALE
CENGAGE Learning™

Detroit • New York • San Francisco • New Haven, Conn • Waterville, Maine • London

GALE
CENGAGE Learning

Set in 11 pt. Plantin
Printed on permanent paper.

LIBRARY OF CONGRESS CATALOGING-IN-PUBLICATION DATA

Stuyck, Karen Hanson.
  A novel way to die / Karen Hanson Stuyck.
    p. cm.
  ISBN-13: 978-1-59414-632-9 (alk. paper)
  ISBN-10: 1-59414-632-2 (alk. paper)
  1. Women novelists—Crimes against—Fiction. 2. Drugs—Overdose—Fiction. 3. Murder victims' families—Fiction. 4. Mothers and daughters—Fiction. 5. Women college teachers—Fiction. 6. Criminologists—Fiction. I. Title.
PS3619.T89N68 2008
813'.6—dc22   2007041782

First Edition. First Printing: April 2008.

Published in 2008 in conjunction with Tekno Books and Ed Gorman.

Printed in the United States of America
1 2 3 4 5 6 7 12 11 10 09 08

ACKNOWLEDGMENTS

Once again I want to thank the members of the Tuesday Writers' Consortium for their insightful suggestions and their moral support throughout the writing of this book. Thanks to Irene Bond, Patsy Ward Burk, Julia Mercedes Castilla, Louise Gaylord, Guida Jackson Laufer, Vanessa Leggett, Ida Luttrell, and Jackie Pelham.

Thanks too to the good friends who offered their skilled help in the earliest versions of this book: Lee Herrick, Mary Pat Bolton, and Nancy Holland.

And, as always, my heartfelt thanks to Steve.

CHAPTER ONE

I drove through downtown Houston, glumly listening to the radio while trying to ignore my sense of foreboding. It wasn't as if I was unaware of what terrible things were around the corner; I just didn't know what to do about them. It was almost Christmas, my husband and I were newly separated, our two children were distraught, and my mother, about to arrive for a visit, was still unaware that Alex had moved out. As a woman on the radio sang about her grown-up Christmas wish, I knew exactly what my wish would be: the ability to fast-forward my life to spring.

I could feel the beginning of a major headache as I finally pulled into the driveway of our small brick home near the Texas Medical Center.

My son Will was at the car by the time I opened the door. "Guess what, Mom? My name is in *People*. A girl in my class saw it and brought the magazine to school."

I leaned down to give him a kiss. "So what did this other Will Patterson do to get himself in *People*?"

"He had a famous, best-selling writer for a grandmother," said Annie, my worldly twelve-year-old daughter, from the doorway of the house. "It's a story about Grandma."

I followed both of them to the kitchen where the magazine story was spread out on the table. "See, here we are." Will pointed, then read it out loud: "Katherine March's daughter, Molly Patterson, is a college professor of criminology in

Houston. 'I'm sure she picked up her interest in crime from our discussions of my mystery novels when she was a child,' March said."

Yeah, right, I thought. If I had become a neurosurgeon, an actress or a stockbroker, Mother would have found a way to take credit for my choice of career.

Will was still reading. "Molly lives in Houston with her husband, Alex Patterson, a middle-school teacher, and their two children."

Used to live with her husband, I mentally corrected. And I'd better phone Mother to inform her of that fact before she arrived on Christmas Eve.

Will at least hadn't seemed to notice the error. He kept reading. "Katherine says she adores spending time with her grandchildren, Annie, twelve, and Will, ten." My son looked up, a big smile crinkling his freckled face.

"You're celebrities," I said, reaching down to tousle his always-messy, sandy-colored hair. "Adored celebrities at that." Although Mother would never have used the word "adore"—she was not, by any stretch of the imagination, an adoring woman—she was, I had to admit, a good grandmother. As a grandmother, she could take the kids on wonderful outings, teach them the magic tricks she'd learned when researching her Houdini novel, and then, at the end of the day, send them home. Where someone else could do all the boring, day-to-day parenting.

"Oh, I want to call Grandma and tell her how cool I think this article is," Annie said.

"Sure, go ahead."

As she left to use my bedroom phone, I studied the photos accompanying the article. The most recent one was taken in Mother's office on the third floor of her house in Austin, her garret high above the mundane world. She was typing on her computer, oblivious to everything except her story. Another photo showed her accepting one of her Edgar awards. But the most interesting picture—one I hadn't seen before—was of Mother as a teenager with her parents and younger sister, Charlotte. They sat in a stiff, posed family photo: my grandfather, a book publisher; his elegant wife; and their two attractive daughters, all of them flashing toothy, upper-class smiles.

The article described my mother's realization as a young university librarian that she'd rather be writing novels than helping college students locate them. It told how Katherine, newly divorced, somehow managed to find time to write three suspense novels, continue her library work, and take care of her young daughter (me). After nine years of part-time writing, her fourth novel, *A Stillness After Dark,* hit the best-seller list and later became a movie. The resulting money allowed her to quit her library job and devote herself exclusively to her writing.

Twenty highly profitable books later, she was still going strong, her success a testament to her talent, hard work, and her willingness to sacrifice any semblance of a normal personal life for her writing. (The article called this her "austere, work-dominated lifestyle.") But I, in a rush of surprising bitterness, suddenly remembered playing alone in my room while my mother, as usual, typed away at the kitchen table.

"Wow!" my son said, pointing at the paragraph he'd been reading. "It says here that Grandma just signed a contract for three million dollars for her next three books. She's finishing the first book now, a mystery set in the fifties."

It was the first time I'd heard about the contract or, for that matter, about the novel. But there were a lot of things my mother and I didn't tell each other.

I'd just started dinner—sticking frozen lasagna and French bread in the oven, and dumping ready-to-eat salad greens into a bowl—when Annie returned. "I thought Grandma would be there, but she didn't answer. The last time I talked to her she said she was going to be home all this week. I left her a message that I'd read the article."

"She's probably writing," I said. "She'll call you back eventually. When she isn't too busy." It did not come out as the neutral, purely factual statement I intended.

My daughter pushed her long blond hair out of her face and regarded me solemnly. "You know you are very weird about Grandma."

"What do you mean?"

She shrugged. "A lot of the time you act as if you don't like her very much."

My cheeks suddenly felt hot. "A lot of the time you act as if you don't like me very much. That happens with families sometimes. It doesn't mean we don't love each other." I wanted very much to believe this.

"But it's different with you and Grandma," Annie insisted. "You're grown-ups."

Supposedly. The discussion was cut short when Will came back to see when we were going to eat. "Hey, Mom, I talked to Dad this afternoon and he said he'd take me and Annie to pick out a Christmas tree on Saturday."

"Great," I said, smiling tightly.

"You're going to let him put the tree up here, aren't you, instead of at that crummy apartment?" Annie asked.

I took a deep breath, telling myself that even at the best of times twelve-year-old girls often saw their mothers as the bad guys. "I already told you we'd all spend Christmas here together." Even though I knew it fed the children's fantasies that any day Daddy would be moving back home—just as soon as Mom stopped being mad at him.

Fortunately our dinner conversation revolved around gross behavior on the kids' school busses. Afterward I made sure Annie and Will started their homework and then headed to the study to finish grading papers.

I heard the phone ring. "Mom!" Annie was in the doorway. "The phone's for you. It's Helen Lewis."

I frowned. Why would Helen, my mother's long-time friend and my former second-grade teacher, be phoning me?

I hurried to the kitchen. "Hi, Helen. How are you?"

"Molly, I'm afraid I've got bad news."

I could feel my palms start to sweat.

"It's your mother. The two of us were supposed to go out to dinner tonight. When Katherine didn't come to pick me up, I phoned her, but no one answered. Finally I went to her house to see if anything was wrong. I have a key."

"So what happened to Mother?" I interrupted.

"The house seemed empty. I went inside and called out her name, but no one answered." Helen took a deep breath, as if steeling herself for what came next. "I found your mother . . . in the living room . . . lying on the floor. She was dead." Helen started to cry.

I felt as if all the air had been sucked out around me. My mother—my healthy-as-a-horse, sixty-year-old mother—dead? Surely there was some mistake.

"She can't be," I said. I'd spoken to her only a few days ago. She was perfectly fine, discussing what time she'd arrive on Christmas Eve.

"Molly, I'm so sorry."

For a long moment neither of us spoke. I wanted to hang up and go back to my papers. To blot out Helen's words from my consciousness. "What—what did she die from?"

"The paramedics said it looked like a heart attack."

"Heart attack? But she was too young for that. She was thin. Didn't smoke. No history of heart disease."

"I know, dear, I know." I could hear her sniffling even as she tried to comfort me, and suddenly I envisioned her on the other end of the line, a tiny, gray-haired woman who had expected to spend a pleasant evening dining with an old friend and instead discovered her body.

I tried to marshal my thoughts. "We can be there in three hours. We'll leave right away."

"Tomorrow morning will be soon enough, Molly. You all need to get some sleep."

"But I need to . . ."

"It can wait until tomorrow, dear," Helen gently interrupted. "We'll talk then."

I hung up. Staring at the phone, I felt so very cold.

CHAPTER TWO

My entire family made the drive to Austin the next morning. When Annie, in tears, had phoned her father with the news of Mother's death, Alex had insisted on coming with us.

"That really isn't necessary," I'd told him. "The kids and I can manage."

"Let me do this for you, Molly. I really will be a big help with the kids and all the arrangements that need to be made. If you want, I'll even stay at a motel."

I'd been in no condition to argue with him. "You don't have to stay in a motel. Mother has plenty of bedrooms." Hanging up the phone, I realized I'd used the wrong tense.

But I ended up feeling grateful that Alex was with us. His presence seemed to soothe the kids, who were upset enough about losing their grandmother without also having to worry about their mother and father breaking up. And after a night of insomnia, I was glad I didn't have to drive. Later I would deal with the problems in our marriage, but not today.

We pulled into the driveway of Mother's home around eleven. I expected to feel a surge of emotion when I laid eyes on the three-story stone house where the two of us had lived during my teenage years, but as I unlocked the front door, all I felt was exhausted.

The interior of the house looked the way it always did: sleek, spacious, uncluttered. The residence of a fastidious grown-up who no longer had any children living at home.

While the rest of my family headed for the kitchen I hesitantly walked into the living room, a big, high-ceilinged room with stone fireplace and gleaming hardwood floors. This was where Helen had found Mother's body. Heart pounding, I scanned the hundreds of books in the floor-to-ceiling built-in bookcases, the neat stack of magazines on the end table, the vase of pale pink gladiolas in the center of the glass-topped coffee table.

Moving to the center of the room, I closed my eyes. Someone had once told me that when a close friend of hers had died she was haunted by a heavy sweet smell for days after his death. She knew, she said, that the smell was her friend's presence.

I sniffed, smelling only lemon-scented furniture polish. I took several deep breaths, willing my mother to make her presence known—somehow. To make her death seem real to me, to let me know what had happened, to send me some final message—to tell me something. This was the room where Mother's very last thoughts had played out, where her final images had faded from view. If there was any place where I would encounter her, surely it was here.

But I didn't. Not anymore than I had when Helen had phoned me with the news of her death.

I opened my eyes. In the kitchen Annie was asking if it was okay to turn on Grandma's answering machine. Alex must have said yes because suddenly I heard a female voice saying the electrician was on the way. Had Mother been alive when the electrician got here? Then I heard Annie's recorded voice, full of excitement. "I read the story in *People* about you, Grandma. It was cool. Call me when you have a chance, okay? Love ya."

The next message was from Helen, asking if Mother had forgotten their dinner date. And then Helen called again, her voice sounding anxious as she said, "Katherine, are you there? Please call me the minute you get in."

I closed my eyes, taking deep breaths. Then I heard the next message. I moved closer to the kitchen to hear better. It was my father. "Katherine, it's Ned. We need to talk. Can we forget the first unfortunate conversation and start again?" He didn't sound at all like his usual happy-go-lucky self.

Alex emerged from the kitchen. "What do you think that was about?" he asked me.

"I have no idea. I didn't know the two of them even spoke to each other these days." Years ago, when they'd had to make arrangements for my visits to Wisconsin, their conversations had been short and to the point. "I suppose I need to call Dad to tell him about Mother's death."

Alex nodded. "If you want to make a list of the numbers I can make some calls on my cell phone."

"Thanks, but I can do it myself." I needed a few minutes alone and then I would make the calls.

I moved to the small study at the back of the house, feeling too tired to do anything except stare at the pale yellow walls. Finally, though, I roused myself and phoned my father.

Ginny, my stepmother, answered. "Molly, what a nice surprise!" Her warm, contralto voice brought back memories of lazy summer afternoons in Wisconsin, the two of us in the kitchen baking sugar cookies and chatting while the kitchen filled with wonderful cinnamon smells.

I took a deep breath, then plunged in. "The reason I'm calling is my mother. She died last night. They think she had a heart attack."

"Died?" There was a long silence.

My mother, I remembered, was not one of Ginny's favorite people. "Ginny?"

"I'm here, but what a shock for you, Molly," she said, her voice full of concern. "Are you okay?"

I told her I was. As okay as anyone could be when her mother suddenly drops dead. "So you'll tell Dad?"

"He's right here, honey. You can tell him yourself."

I was a little surprised that my father was home on a Friday morning, but December was always a slow month for real estate agents.

"Molly, sweetheart, Ginny just told me about Katherine. I can't believe she's gone."

"Me neither. I was just talking to her a few days ago." My voice broke. "We—we were making Christmas plans."

"This is terrible for you and for the kids too. What can Ginny and I do to help? We can fly down there today, if we can find a flight."

I envisioned Dad's round, slightly jowly face, his empathetic brown eyes. I loved my dad, had connected with him in a way I never had with my mother. "That's very sweet of you, but Alex and I can handle things."

"Well, if you change your mind, remember we're always here for you."

"I know you are, and I appreciate it." As I was about to hang up, I remembered what I'd wanted to ask him. "Dad, I heard your message on Mother's answering tape."

"She never called me back," he said, as if that was what I wanted to know.

I hesitated, not sure how to phrase it. "I guess I was just surprised that you called her."

"Oh, I read the story about her in *People* and wanted to congratulate her. I thought it was about time that your mother and I let bygones be bygones." He sighed. "Though I guess it's too late for that now."

It was too late for a lot of us who'd always intended to patch up our relationships with Katherine March, I thought as I hung up the phone.

I scanned my mother's address book, not sure who to call next. Although she had always been intensely curious about

16

people, Mother had never been a very social person. I'd often thought that the characters she wrote about—the people in her imagination—were more real to her than any living, breathing person in her life.

I phoned my mother's literary agent, Samuel Pryor, and left a message with his assistant. Then I called Brenda Stein, Mother's long-time editor.

"Oh, God," she said, her voice husky, when I told her the news. "I thought there was something wrong when I talked to Katherine last week."

"What do you mean?"

"She just didn't seem like herself. I asked her if anything was wrong, but she said no, she was only tired. This book was very draining, and she wasn't sure if it was worth finishing. In the nine years I've known her, Katherine never said anything remotely like that."

"But you thought something else was bothering her—besides having problems with her book?"

"Yes. Katherine and I have worked on seven books together and she hit rough patches on all of them. This sounded different—as if something bad was happening and Katherine didn't want to talk about it. I'd heard she was having some kind of problem with her agent, Sam Pryor. I thought maybe she was upset about that. The two of them had been together for a long time."

"What kind of problem?"

"I'm not sure. She wouldn't really tell me, but I gathered she was thinking about getting a new agent."

"She also might have been feeling ill." Perhaps she'd been feeling poorly for a long time and I hadn't even known it.

"Very likely that was it. In any case, I am terribly sorry, Molly. I loved working with your mother. I had enormous respect for her and for her work."

We said goodbye and then I was left staring at the phone. I had not sensed that anything was wrong when I'd talked to Mother only a few days earlier. Had Brenda Stein imagined my mother's distress—a run-of-the-mill bad day magnified, in hindsight, into something ominous? Or had Mother just put on a cheerful front when she'd talked to me, unwilling to expose any hint of vulnerability to her only child?

I needed to make at least one more call. Obviously someone in Mother's family had to be notified. Unfortunately, I hardly knew any of her relatives. Mother hadn't gotten along with her mother and had almost nothing to do with her. Though I didn't really know her either, my Aunt Charlotte, Mother's only sibling, had sent me birthday and Christmas gifts and postcards from the exotic places she visited with her husband, a wealthy businessman. I decided to call her.

A woman with a Spanish accent answered the phone. Could she tell Mrs. Todd who was calling?

A minute later my aunt came on the line. "Molly, how nice to hear from you," she said, her voice low and pleasant.

I pictured the glamorous blond woman I'd met only once, at my great-grandmother's funeral. A young Grace Kelly look-alike, someone had said, and a gracious woman who'd made a point to be kind to her gawky, ten-year-old niece. Would our only conversations concern deaths in the family, I wondered inanely, suddenly remembering the note I'd written her a year ago when her husband died in a boating accident.

I took a deep breath and told her why I was calling.

"Oh!" It was a little shriek.

"Aunt Charlotte?" I was afraid she might have fainted.

"I'm still here," she said, sounding dazed. "Tell me what happened—everything."

I told her what I knew: Helen finding my mother's body, a suspected heart attack, but we wouldn't know for sure until the autopsy had been completed.

"Our father died of heart disease," Aunt Charlotte said. "He had a massive heart attack right after his fiftieth birthday party."

"How terrible." I'd known my grandfather had died when my mother was a teenager, but Mother had never told me any details.

"I can't believe that Katherine is dead. Why, I talked to her just a few days ago. I called to see what she thought of that magazine article about her. She was in good spirits, feisty as ever. Said the article was superficial and badly written. When I said I liked it, she said, 'you would.' " Charlotte chuckled at the memory. "She certainly didn't sound ill."

"I thought she was in good health too. Her death was a terrible shock for all of us."

"Oh, you poor thing," my aunt said sympathetically. "Why don't you let me break the news to Mother. She's in poor health, and I think I should be the one who tells her."

She paused for a minute, and when she spoke again the sadness in her voice was palpable. "When Katherine came to visit Mother this summer, it was the first time they'd seen each other in over twenty years. Katherine told me she guessed she needed to see Mother at least once before Mother died. Who would ever have expected that it would be Katherine who'd die first?"

As I hung up, I could hear Charlotte crying.

By mid-afternoon I'd called everyone who I thought had to be notified. Mercifully I seemed to be operating on auto-pilot, fueled by the ton of coffee I kept drinking.

When I told Alex I had an appointment to talk to a funeral director, he insisted on accompanying me.

"You don't have to," I said. "Maybe you should stay here with the kids."

"The kids are fine, watching those old movies of Katherine's. And I'm coming with you," he said.

I shrugged. "Okay."

It wasn't that I didn't want Alex along. As the two of us listened to an unctuous, bald man describe our options in coffins, Alex was extremely helpful. He asked the right questions, was sensitive to my feelings and backed my decisions. But it was time for me—or soon would be time—to start weaning myself from his helpfulness.

As we made the arrangements I remembered that Mother hadn't known Alex and I were separated. How would she have reacted if I'd told her? I'd never even decided what I wanted to say. The simple, bare-bones version—Alex had cheated on me and I wasn't sure that I could forgive him—wouldn't have been enough for her.

Mother had always been fond of Alex. They regularly exchanged books and e-mailed each other their reviews. I knew she thought he was a wonderful father. But her distrust of marriage, its compromises and accommodations, was very deep. That, as much my dread of a lot of prying questions, was why I hadn't mentioned our separation. I wasn't up to dealing with her cynicism about the institution that for so long had defined a huge chunk of my life. "See?" I imagined her saying. "Didn't I tell you it never works out?"

Alex and I drove back to the house in silence. "Let me take the kids out to dinner while you take a nap," he said as we turned onto Mother's block.

"That sounds great," I said. But then I spotted Helen Lewis's aged Volvo parked in front of the house.

Helen herself was sitting at the dining room table with my children and a big plate of chocolate chip cookies. "Molly, dear!" She stood up to give me a hug.

I smiled down at the small, stocky, gray-haired woman who had once taught me second grade. She seemed shorter than I remembered. Her commanding presence had always made Helen Lewis seem tall.

"I brought over some food," Helen said. "There's a salad and King Ranch casserole in the refrigerator."

"And ice cream and cookies," Will added jubilantly.

"That's very thoughtful of you." I felt compelled to add, "Why don't you stay and eat with us? It's almost dinnertime now." I avoided Alex's eyes.

Helen hesitated for a few seconds, then accepted the invitation. "We do have a lot of things we need to discuss."

I excused myself long enough to splash cold water on my face and take a couple of Advil for my throbbing headache. My exhaustion felt bone-deep, like a bad case of the flu.

Back in the dining room, I let Alex deal with most of Helen's questions. I barely tasted the salad and casserole that she had set on the table.

"Mrs. Lewis," Will said midway through the meal, "how did you find Grandma's body?"

"This isn't a *Goosebumps* book, Will," Alex said, his voice sharp.

I could see Will's cheeks redden at the unexpected rebuke.

"He's just curious, Alex," Helen said. "He has a right to know what happened." Turning back to Will, she told him, succinctly and matter-of-factly, how she'd used her key to get into the house, and, after calling out Mother's name with no results, decided to look upstairs in case Mother was in bed. Instead Helen found her body lying on the living room floor. "I tried to take her pulse, but, unfortunately, she was already dead. Then I called nine-one-one."

Will nodded, seeming satisfied with the explanation.

Helen waited until the kids left to dish up the ice cream to add more details. In a low voice she said, "I wanted to tell you I found the bottom lock—but not the deadbolt—locked. Which surprised me."

"Why?" I asked. "I only use the deadbolt when I leave the house or go to bed at night. If I'm home during the day I only have the bottom lock on." Why would my mother, who'd never been a fearful woman, suddenly want to barricade herself inside her home?

Helen shrugged. "Perhaps your mother was more concerned about security because she was always writing about crime. I do remember her telling me a few months ago how easy it is to break into most houses—how flimsy most locks are. She said she'd just bought new, heavy-duty deadbolts for her doors so that any thief who tried to break in would really have to work at it." She glanced toward the kitchen, making sure the children were out of earshot. "I always suspected that Katherine might have been concerned about that crazed writer who was harassing her."

Her words seemed to yank me from my stupor. "What crazed writer?"

"A would-be mystery writer, Suzanne somebody-or-other. Your mother let Suzanne interview her several times; supposedly she was doing her master's thesis on Katherine's novels. I'm not sure I believe that."

"Why not?" Alex asked. "It sounds like a legitimate thesis topic."

"It wasn't the topic I questioned. It was the woman's attitude. She seemed obsessed with Katherine, wanting to know every detail of the way she worked. What hours did she write? Where did she do it? Did she use outlines?"

The questions seemed innocuous, though I couldn't imagine Mother being patient enough to answer all of them.

"I warned Katherine that Suzanne reminded me of a stalker."

"Did she ever threaten Mother?" I asked. I thought of all the case studies I'd read of obsessed "fans" harassing celebrities.

Some of them were just annoying. But one woman had broken into a famous writer's house, threatening to kill him and his family. Another, a man, had murdered a beautiful young television star.

"She wanted Katherine to help her get published. It was almost as if she believed that Katherine could simply talk to her agent and Suzanne would instantly have a book contract. She was very persistent, quite obnoxious, I thought."

"So did Mother help her?" I couldn't see my mother tolerating such behavior from anyone.

"I think she tried to. She read some of Suzanne's stories and made suggestions. But suddenly Suzanne was acting as if Katherine wasn't doing enough. She said Katherine didn't want her to succeed, that she was jealous of Suzanne's talent."

Alex shook his head. "That's absurd."

Helen's thin lips were pursed in disapproval. "That was the last straw. Until then Katherine had been sympathetic to Suzanne. But I think that after that, even she realized how unbalanced Suzanne was."

Will and Annie appeared in the doorway, bringing in our desserts. "How was she unbalanced, Mrs. Lewis?" Will asked.

Helen, Alex, and I exchanged a look. "Oh, she was just an eccentric woman your grandmother met at a writer's conference," Helen said in a dismissive voice. "Someone she hadn't seen in a long time." Before Will could get in any follow-up questions, she added, "By the way, dear, I meant to invite you to come over to my house tomorrow. I thought you might enjoy playing the computer games I bought for my nephew."

Will's freckled face lit up. "Cool!"

"Terrific," Alex said. "Now who'd like some of these cookies?"

After dinner Annie and Will were assigned to load the dishwasher. As Helen and I walked past the kitchen I heard Annie whisper, "I bet they're all educational computer games, Dufus. And if you'd just shut your big mouth we would have heard all about the crazy woman who was stalking Grandma."

CHAPTER THREE

"Are you the person who found your mother's body?" Dr. Lester, the pathologist who'd conducted my mother's autopsy, asked me on the phone.

"No, a friend of hers did. Why?" What did that have to do with the results of her autopsy?

"Do you know if your mother was being treated for anxiety or depression, perhaps seeing a psychiatrist?"

"No, she wasn't." At least I was sure about that. My mother thought seeing a therapist was a sign of weakness—hardly an enlightened point of view, but Mother was openly contemptuous of any form of what she called "whining." If Katherine March were experiencing anxiety or depression, I was confident she would have ignored it and kept working.

"Perhaps her illness made her change her mind about that," Dr. Lester said. "Most people are anxious when they learn they have cancer."

"Cancer?" What was this man talking about?

"Your mother," he said in the voice of a grown-up addressing a young child, "had an advanced case of ovarian cancer. You weren't aware of this?"

"No." I wondered if Mother herself had known.

"Did this friend who found your mother mention that she'd found a bottle of pills or a syringe nearby? Or a suicide note?"

"No!" I realized I was practically shouting at him. "There was no suicide note, no pills, no syringe. Why would there be a

25

syringe? What are you insinuating—that my mother was taking drugs?"

"I'm not insinuating anything," Dr. Lester said stiffly. "I found a high level of Trifluoperazine—you'd call it Stelazine—in your mother's bloodstream. There was a needle mark on her left arm. The Stelazine could have been injected or taken orally."

"What is this Stelazine?"

"It's used to treat severe anxiety—psychotic anxiety—and some agitated forms of depression. It's a central nervous system depressant. If given in a high enough dose it's lethal."

Surely there had to be some mistake here. My mother hated taking medication—any medication. This was a woman who refused to take aspirin for her headaches. And this doctor who'd never even met her was trying to tell me she'd taken a lethal dose of some antianxiety medication? "Are you sure we're talking about the same person? Perhaps you got my mother confused with another woman you autopsied."

"I'm taking about Katherine E. March, a sixty-year-old Caucasian woman who died Thursday," he said gruffly. "Thursday afternoon, sometime between three-thirty and five-thirty."

"You're saying that my mother didn't have a heart attack?" I asked, trying to make sure that I understood him correctly, trying to make sense of all this terrible new information.

"I'm saying that cardiac arrest was probably induced by an injection of Stelazine," he said curtly. "And I'm notifying the police to that effect."

The church was packed for my mother's funeral. Seated in the front row with my family—Alex and the kids and my mother's sister, Aunt Charlotte—I turned to scan the assembled mourners for familiar faces. I saw only a few people I recognized: Helen, dressed in solid black, her face showing every one of her sixty-seven years; two women my mother worked with long ago at the UT Library; a few neighbors. I nodded at a tall woman with a rather horsy face who'd earlier introduced herself as Brenda Stein, my mother's editor. She was sitting next to Samuel Pryor, Mother's literary agent, a dapper, gray-haired man in an expensive-looking charcoal suit.

My father and stepmother sat directly behind us. Dad and Ginny looked unusually subdued. My dad's face appeared tired and puffy, while my vivacious stepmother seemed uncharacteristically grim.

At dinner last night, when my father was out of the room, Ginny had whispered that Dad had been fired from his long-time job in commercial real estate. He'd been looking for work everywhere, she said. "He even came down here to Texas, but no one seems to be interested in hiring an unemployed fifty-nine-year-old real-estate salesman." Ginny's small face was taut with concern. "Ned tries to put up a good front, but I can tell how depressed he is. And we have so many financial obligations. . . ."

I now flashed a small smile at my dad. He gave his familiar reassuring grin. If I inherited any money from my mother, I intended to give Dad and Ginny a substantial cash gift. It would give me great pleasure to help out these two people who, throughout my childhood, had always been so supportive of me.

I scanned the church one more time, then turned back to face the pulpit. Who were all of these strangers who'd come to mourn my mother's death? They were mainly women, probably the loyal readers who wrote her fan letters and lined up at her book signings to tell her how much they loved the strong female characters in her books. And some of them were probably journalists or plain old curiosity-seekers who'd read the morning's newspaper and were hoping for some juicy revelations about a well-known writer who'd died under mysterious circumstances.

Pastor Thayer, a pale, earnest man with thinning blond hair, walked to the front of the church. He was a new minister, a man I'd met only a few days ago. I glanced around the sanctuary—the church where I'd been confirmed, where Alex and I had been married—remembering sitting next to my mother when I was small, watching the sun stream through the stained glass windows.

At the pulpit Pastor Thayer regarded the congregation with a solemn expression. "Katherine March was a vital, intelligent, and talented woman who has been taken from us in the prime of her life," he began.

I tried to focus on what the minister was saying, but I was having a hard time concentrating. Part of this, I knew, was due to sheer exhaustion. My sleep last night had been fitful and filled with disturbing dreams. In the last one I'd been running through the house, searching vainly for my mother. There was menacing laughter behind me, but I'd awakened, heart pounding, before I could see who it came from.

"Yet Katherine was more than a consummate writer," I heard the minister say. "She was a loving mother, a woman who single-handedly raised her daughter Molly."

"Single-handedly!" I heard my stepmother whisper to my father. "We begged her to let us raise Molly!"

"And more recently," the minister continued, "Katherine was a doting grandmother to Molly's children, Annie and Will. Only a month or so ago Katherine told me how very proud she was of those grandchildren."

On my right I heard Annie sobbing quietly, while Will, seated on the opposite side of his father, slumped down in the pew so no one would see his tears. I groped through my purse for a tissue, but Charlotte, seated on Annie's left, had already handed her an embroidered handkerchief. I was touched by my aunt's ready sympathy.

Aunt Charlotte glanced over at me and I could see that her eyes—those intense blue eyes which reminded me so much of my mother's—also were filled with tears. I remembered what she'd told me this morning when she came to the house, Charlotte reaching out to give me a tight hug. "It took me over twenty years to get your mother back in my life, and now, after only a few months, I've lost her again." How unlike my mother this warm, charming woman in her black couture suit was. Mother had hated to hug. The best she could manage was an awkward pat on the shoulder or a quick kiss on the cheek for her daughter or the grandchildren she was so proud of.

Despite myself, I thought again of the swarm of police officers, evidence gatherers who had descended on my mother's house like a plague of locusts. How often I had mentioned such people in my lectures: the fiber expert, the fingerprint expert, all the crime scene people who photographed, searched, and questioned. Long ago, in graduate school, I'd even taken a criminal investigation course. Never once had I realized how intrusive these people's presence was, what an assault on the newly bereaved—these experts with their messy black powder and their long list of demands.

They'd asked me endless questions. Had any doors or windows been unlocked when I first entered the house? Was anything missing? Had I spotted anything unusual when I walked in?

Getting no's to every question, the police investigator, a homicide detective named John Martinez, then tried another tack. Had my mother seemed depressed lately? Had she perhaps given away some possessions, tried to resolve long-standing issues or said goodbye?

I told him I hadn't noticed any signs of depression. I'd talked to Mother four days before her death. She seemed her usual no-

nonsense, undepressed self, making plans to come to my house for Christmas. "So obviously Mother wasn't planning to kill herself. You wouldn't discuss what time you were arriving on Christmas Eve if you intended to give yourself a lethal injection, would you?"

Detective Martinez, a slight, soft-spoken man, raised his eyebrows. "Maybe not," he said with a look that told me he was just trying to be kind, that said, I don't want to hurt you, but you're heavily into denial here.

I'd taken a deep breath and tried to calmly, rationally convince this man that, even facing a terminal illness, my mother would not have killed herself, not in this way. If Mother chose to commit suicide, she would have left a note. She was a writer, for God's sake; she always wanted to get in the last word. She would have tied up loose ends, made arrangements about finishing her book, canceled the speech she was scheduled to make in January at a writers' conference. And yes, she would have said goodbye.

Pastor Thayer was looking right at me now. I tried to focus, to give him the courtesy of my complete attention. "We need only remember our Father's promise of eternal life for true believers to realize that Katherine March has gone on to a better life."

I hoped so. There were so many things I wanted to believe.

But as the soloist started singing "Amazing Grace" I thought instead of all the things I would have expected my mother to tell me—things any other mother would have told her adult daughter—which Katherine March had chosen to keep to herself: She'd signed a richer-than-God book contract that *People* magazine readers learned about before I did. A crazed writer had been harassing her.

And then there were all my questions. Had Mother known that she had an advanced case of cancer? If so, why hadn't she told me? And why had she taken an antianxiety drug? Would I ever know what actually happened during my mother's last day?

I heard, through tears, the soprano launch into my favorite line: "I once was lost, but now I'm found." The sounds of muffled crying reverberated throughout the sanctuary. The loudest sobs, though, seemed to be coming from directly behind me.

Turning around, I was startled to see my father cradling his face between his hands. I could see the tears between his fingers. And at his side my normally empathetic stepmother was glaring at my mother's coffin.

Afterward, everyone told me how wonderful my mother was. People who loved her books or had met her once at a book signing and felt as if they knew her wanted to offer their condolences. A tall, muscular man in a tweed jacket told me he'd gotten to know Mother when she consulted him on research for her book. "She was an impressive woman with a great sense of humor. I wish I'd had a chance to get to know her better."

No one mentioned suicide or accidental overdoses.

"Katherine was my mentor," a middle-aged woman with wild, curly gray hair and sharp hazel eyes told me, squeezing my hand.

"I'm glad to hear that," I said, smiling the automatic smile I'd pulled out for this line of strangers who all seemed to want to tell me about Katherine March's impact on their lives.

The woman did not let go of my hand.

"You're a writer too?" I asked, for want of anything else to say.

"Yes, I write mystery and suspense fiction. Just like your mother."

"Well, good luck with it," I said, glancing surreptitiously at the line of mourners behind her.

She squeezed my hand harder. Making me focus all my attention on her. "I'm sure your mother told you about me—Suzanne Lang?"

"Suzanne?" I felt as if I'd stopped breathing. I had a sudden urge to shove this strange woman as hard as I could.

I took a deep breath, reminded myself that I was a calm, rational woman. "Are you the Suzanne who was writing a master's thesis on Mother's work?"

"Yes," she said, looking pleased, relaxing her grip.

I yanked my hand free. "It's nice to meet you," I lied, turning to the next person in line, my mother's long-time neighbor, Mrs. Benjamin.

"Molly, I'm so sorry," the white-haired widow said, giving me a hug. She looked frail, but a very welcome bastion of normalcy. "I'm going to bring over some brownies I baked for your children."

I smiled and said the kids would appreciate that. When I turned to the next mourner Suzanne was there in front of me again.

She held up her palm to the woman who was at the head of the line. "I'll just be a minute," she said with a cold-eyed smile that seemed more a warning than an apology.

"It's imperative that I talk to you about your mother," she told me, her voice loud, self-important. "I'll phone to set up an appointment."

She shot me that eerie, aggressive smile then vanished into the crowd.

CHAPTER FOUR

Will ripped off the Christmas paper and held up his new computer game. "Thanks, Santa." He rolled his eyes at Alex and me. "Just what I wanted."

I smiled, trying my best to look cheerful. It was a miserable Christmas for Will too, and he was being a very good sport.

Annie, who'd already opened her big gift from us, a mauve pullover sweater she'd coveted, smiled politely as she opened a box containing two CDs. "This is great."

She too was on her best behavior after blowing up last night at me—the person who'd made her beloved daddy move out of the house. "And don't think, Mom, that I don't know about that English teacher who Dad was seeing; I heard all about it at school. But this is what you don't get. Dad was only trying to help the woman. She was a pathetic, weepy basket case and not even pretty at all. So why don't you just get over it and stop ruining everyone's lives?"

Alex, who'd gone with us to Christmas Eve services, had walked in on the last part of Annie's tirade and coldly told her that she didn't know what she was talking about. This was a matter between her mother and him, and when we figured things out, we'd let her know.

Annie had spent the rest of the evening sulking in her room. Will and Alex and I played Scrabble, trying to pretend that everything was okay. Afterward I'd sobbed in the shower, where no one could hear me, not sure if I was crying about the loss of

33

my mother, my once-good marriage, or my daughter who, for the moment at least, hated me.

This morning, glimpsing all the glum faces around the Christmas tree, I was reminded of my wish to fast-forward our lives into spring.

In addition to everything else, it was a very skimpy Christmas, even by our frugal standards. After we got back from Austin Alex and I had dashed out among all the other last-minute Christmas shoppers to pick up a few things. But lack of shopping time was only one of the reasons for the children's paltry supply of presents. We'd had too many other expenses this year to spend much money on non-necessities. Alex's twelve-year-old car had required numerous repairs and paying the student loans for my graduate school still took a hefty chunk of my paycheck. And shelling out the extra money for Alex's garage apartment hadn't helped either.

I saw that Alex and the kids had saved until last opening my mother's Christmas gifts, traditionally a book and one other gift for each of us. They must have felt as awkward as I did to be unwrapping the package of someone who was no longer with us. Someone who was supposed to be here right now while we opened her gifts.

I took a deep breath and tore off the wrapping on the book my mother had chosen to give me this year. It was *Little Women* by Louisa May Alcott, an old edition with a faded cover and a faint musty smell.

Annie looked puzzled. "Why would Grandma give you *Little Women* when you've already read it? She knows we have a copy."

I shrugged. "It was my favorite childhood book, and Mother loved it too. She read it to me, a chapter a night, when I was in second grade."

I opened the cover and saw an inscription: "To Katherine on her eighth birthday, I hope you will enjoy these stories about another March family." It was signed, "Affectionately, Margaret O'Ryan."

"Oh, this was Grandma's book that she got when she was a little girl," I told my children.

"Who is Margaret O'Ryan?" Annie asked, reading over my shoulder.

"I don't know. Maybe she was a friend of their family." I myself was more curious about why my mother had chosen to give me this book now, a copy I'd never seen before. If only she were here in my house, the way she intended to be, so I could ask her.

"I hope that Grandma didn't give me one of her old books," Will said as he ripped open his gift. "Hey, it's two books—one on magic tricks and one on learning how to program the computer. Cool. I told Grandma once that I wished I knew how to program games."

Annie's gift was a boxed set of *Jane Eyre* and *Wuthering Heights*. She made a face; reading the classics was not high on Annie's priority list.

Alex got the latest John Irving novel. "Great," he said, "it's just the book I wanted."

Now all that was left were my mother's non-book gifts. This year the boxes were bigger than usual. Mother had phoned in early December to say that since her gifts were quite bulky this year, she was going to send them all rather than bring them with her on the plane.

"You first, Mom," Will said.

I opened the largish box. Inside was a corduroy study pillow. Another reminder of my childhood. I'd always done my studying in bed, propped up by just such a pillow. Had my mother turned sentimental in her old age?

Will peered over my shoulder. "There's some more stuff in the box. Hey! It's a laptop! Will you let me use it?"

"Sure." I pulled out the remaining items in the original box: a pile of notebooks, tied together with a ribbon, and a short note from my mother.

"What does the note say?" Alex asked.

I read it to him. " 'Molly, dear, it's time to branch out with your writing. To write *your* book. You can do it. You have the talent. All you need is the desire. And, of course, something you want to write about. I'll think of you, propped up in your bed, creating. Have fun. Mother.' "

"She gives you a laptop and me a collection of the boring Brontës," Annie grumbled.

"Why don't you open your other gift from her?" I told her, glad for the opportunity to focus my attention on someone else. I wasn't sure how I felt about my gift. I hadn't especially wanted a laptop. And who said anything about writing a book? Certainly not me!

I watched Annie unwrap her gift. Looking supremely bored, her current favorite expression, Annie slowly removed the wrapping paper, as if all the effort was too much for her. But her expression changed as she caught sight of the writing on the package inside. In less than a minute her small, heart-shaped face registered indifference, surprise, and then, finally, awestruck incredulity.

"What is it?" Alex asked, as curious as I about what item could have wrought such a transformation.

"It's a ten-disk CD player," Annie gasped. "And speakers. The really expensive kind." Annie reached into the box and pulled out an envelope. "And look at this. There's a hundred-dollar gift certificate so I can get a bunch of CDs. Grandma thought of everything!"

It certainly looked that way, I thought, as I watched my daughter peer at her gifts as if she couldn't quite believe they were real.

Annie leaped up. "This is so awesome. I need to call Katie. She won't believe it!"

"Don't you want to see what I got?" Will asked, ripping off the wrapping paper. "Wow!" he yelled. "Wow! My own computer." He scanned the writing on the box. "A great computer." He looked up at Alex. "This baby has one hundred twenty-four more megs of RAM and six more gigs of memory than our old one. And it comes with tons of cool software."

"Wow," Alex said in a much more subdued voice. We exchanged looks.

"I'll probably let you guys use it too," our magnanimous son said.

"Thanks," Alex and I said together.

"Open your present, Alex," I said as Will continued to examine the gift of his dreams.

Alex held up a tiny box. "No computer for me," he said, shaking his head in mock disappointment. "Looks more like a ring box."

I watched him open it. Saw his face grow visibly paler.

"What is it?" I asked.

He held up the keys to a car.

"It can't be," I said, more to myself than to anybody else.

Alex also got a note from Mother. He read it silently, then looked up. "She bought us a new car," he said, in a shocked voice. "A Ford Explorer. The note says she had the dealership park it right outside."

The three of us rushed to the window. There was indeed an Explorer parked in front of our house. A pale greenish-blue one, gleaming in the oblique morning light.

Alex stared at it. "My God," he said softly, "my God."

"Is it a brand-new car?" Will asked. For as long as he could remember, we had always bought used cars.

"The note says it is," Alex said.

I felt tears well in my eyes, then start cascading down my face. Nobody noticed. Hearing all the noise, Annie had come running from the kitchen, and now she too was standing at the window admiring our new sports utility vehicle.

Alex, his voice full of boyish excitement, asked who wanted to take the Explorer for a test drive. I turned away so he wouldn't see my face.

"Give me a rain check, okay?" I said. "I'm going to take a shower."

Alex followed me to the bathroom. Turned me around so I was facing him. "Tell me," he said quietly.

I didn't know how to explain it. My mother had obviously tried to give each of us the object we most wanted in the world. Our dream-come-true gift. In my case, the gift was what Mother thought I ought to want, but she'd managed to tap into everyone else's wish list.

"It is overwhelming," Alex said. "Mind-boggling is perhaps the word I'm searching for here."

I shook my head. "Don't you see? This is Mother's happy ending. She always said the first and the last chapters were the most important parts of a book. The beginning had to grab the readers' interest, but the end had to leave them smiling, satisfied that they got what they'd paid for. And that's what she tried to do with us too." Except, in my case at least, she hadn't succeeded.

Helen called early in the afternoon. By that time we'd all gone out for a drive in our new car. Annie had phoned every one of her friends to tell them about her new sound system and the Explorer. Will and Alex had set up Will's new computer and Will, wearing a died-and-gone-to-heaven expression, had spent hours playing his new computer games. A Christmas only a

Madison Avenue copywriter—or my mother—could have invented.

"Merry Christmas, dear," Helen said when I answered the phone. After I returned the greeting, she added, "Molly, you'll never believe what your mother gave me for Christmas," her voice ripe with excitement.

"A new car?"

She gasped. "How did you know?"

"A lucky guess. We got a Ford Explorer. What did she give you?"

"A Volvo, what I always drive. A pretty blue sedan."

"Was there a note with yours too?" Mother's note to Alex, which I read later, told him what a good husband and father she thought he was. It also mentioned that it was time we got a new car.

"Yes. It thanked me for being a loyal friend to her throughout the years. Katherine said she'd always meant to tell me that but never got around to—" Helen's voice broke. "It's almost as if these are Katherine's last bequests. As if she didn't want to bother with lawyers and probate and she was going to do this on her own."

"Yes, I thought of that too." I hesitated, then asked the question I'd been wanting to know for days. "Helen, did Mother tell you that she had cancer?"

"No." My old teacher's voice was thick with sadness. "At first I told myself that Katherine didn't know either. From what I've read, ovarian cancer has very few symptoms and she was the kind of person who just ignored her aches and pains. But now I think she must have known. Look at these Christmas gifts and these notes of appreciation. Certainly they have the ring of finality about them.

"And I keep remembering how tired she looked the last months. She seemed drained of energy. When I asked her if she was ill she insisted she felt fine, that she was just having trouble writing her new book and wasn't sleeping well. I only wish she had confided in me." Helen paused, as if to compose herself. "I would have liked to help her."

"Me too," I said. "I wish she'd told me." And a new car, CD player, and computers didn't offset the fact that she hadn't, I thought as I hung up the phone.

CHAPTER FIVE

The next morning I left for Austin, glad for the opportunity to be alone with my thoughts. Alex had offered to come with me; he and the kids, he said, could help me sort through Mother's belongings. But I'd insisted that they stay in Houston. Most of what had to be done were solitary tasks, and there was no need for them to waste the last days of their vacation on such boring activities.

"Well, at least take the new car," Alex said.

"No, that's okay. You and the kids keep it." Since you all seem to like it so much.

In my old Toyota, I headed out on Highway 290. I knew Alex was upset that I was leaving. He'd wanted us to meet again with the marriage counselor we'd consulted before my mother's death and to make time to "talk things through." But I wasn't up to talking anything through right now, least of all our marriage problems.

Maybe some time alone would help me to see the situation more clearly, adjust to all the sudden upheavals in my life, and regain my equilibrium. Or maybe not.

I forced my mind to go blank as I turned on the classical station on the car radio and sped down the highway to Austin.

The phone was ringing when I walked into my mother's kitchen. I picked it up, expecting to hear Alex's voice or one of my kids'. They were the only people who knew I was here.

"Molly, I'm glad I caught you," a deep male voice proclaimed. A genial, vaguely familiar voice with a New York accent. "This is Sam Pryor," he quickly added. "Your husband told me you'd be there."

I pictured the elegant, gray-haired man, my mother's literary agent, whom I'd met for the first time at the funeral. He'd been charming and, I thought, genuinely upset by her death. But I'd also seen the way those assessing gray eyes had taken in everything around him and remembered what her editor Brenda Stein had said about him: Mother was thinking about getting another agent. "Hello, Mr. Pryor. What can I do for you?"

He chuckled. "I was hoping to tell you what I could do for you."

"And what's that?" I kicked off my shoes, wanting him to cut to the chase.

He seemed to sense my impatience. "I realize how over-whelmed you must be right now with everything you have to do to settle Katherine's affairs. I'll be brief. She was finishing a novel when she died. The working title was *The Summer That Changed Everything*, but she was talking about revising it. I'm hoping you can find the manuscript and send it to me. Even if she hadn't completed her revisions, I might be able to find someone to polish it a bit and salvage the book."

"I'll look for it." I jotted the title and his phone number on a notepad Mother kept in the junk drawer near the kitchen phone. "Is this the book Brenda Stein said Mother was having so much trouble with?"

"It is. Katherine told me that too. But both Brenda and I liked the early chapters Katherine sent us. The novel seemed less plot-driven than some of her others, more of a character study. And your mother was always her own harshest critic. The fact that she found problems in the book doesn't mean that anyone else will."

"I'll look for it," I repeated. Maybe not today, but eventually. "If I find it, I'll call you."

"If you find any other works in progress, I'd be interested in seeing those too. I know her readers will be eager to read virtually any writing of Katherine's that hasn't been published yet."

"Maybe her readers would like it, but I doubt Mother would have," I said, not bothering to hide my annoyance. "She was very particular about what she allowed to be published."

"Oh, I'm not suggesting that we publish anything that isn't up to snuff," he said quickly. "It's just that Katherine's standards were so high there may be some little gems in her files you'd be proud to see published."

I was suddenly tired of talking to him. "I need to go, Mr. Pryor. If I find any gems, I'll let you know."

Not sure of what to do next, I walked through the house. It seemed intensely quiet—a thick, heavy silence—without my family there, banging things in the kitchen, calling to someone in another room. But this was the way it had been when Mother lived here: silent, solitary, an immaculate, self-enclosed world.

I'd never liked this house, and I liked it even less now. Mother and I had moved here when I was twelve, Annie's age. We'd left a tiny stone bungalow near the University of Texas campus, on a street where children played in their front yards in the early evenings. I'd had lots of friends there, children of graduate students or UT instructors who couldn't afford pricier neighborhoods. The move to this house in affluent Tarrytown, on a quiet, tree-shaded street with mainly elderly residents, seemed like a trip to a soundless tomb. But a spacious and luxurious tomb where my mother could retreat to her third-floor office while I holed up in my bedroom and phoned old friends to complain about my life.

Without paying much attention to where I was going, I wandered up to the office—her garret, she called it, her garret with a computer. I found the file cabinet where she kept her manuscripts but didn't see any folder labeled *The Summer That Changed Everything.* Maybe Mother had decided to change the title. Or maybe she hadn't printed out the whole manuscript yet.

I flipped through the box of computer disks on top of her desk with no luck, then looked in the two-tier divider on her big walnut desk. But the only thing I found of interest was a master's thesis by Suzanne Lang, titled "The Fiction of Katherine E. March: A Critical Analysis." Maybe tomorrow I would read that and come back to look more carefully for Mother's manuscript. Right now I wasn't in the mood to do either.

I wandered down the stairs to Mother's bedroom. It was a small beige room with the only splashes of color provided by the red and blue jackets of two books on the night stand. How could she have chosen to live in such a bland, austere room? I thought of my own cluttered bedroom, with the bright prints on the wall, the vivid lavender comforter, and the piles of multicolored pillows that Alex and I used—or at least used to use—to prop ourselves up while watching TV in bed. If I ended up inhabiting that bedroom by myself, would I eventually turn it into a monastic cell like this—a room where I slept but didn't want to spend too much extra time?

I moved downstairs, through the dining room and into the big, high-ceilinged living room. The room where Helen had discovered Mother's body lying on the floor.

Although I'd already done this—and Alex and the police had as well—I picked up each of the sofa cushions and looked again for some clue to how my mother had died: the syringe that had injected her or the prescription bottle of the Stelazine she'd swallowed. Once again I found nothing. Getting down on the floor, I checked underneath the sofa. Nothing there either.

I'd thought a lot about what could have happened to the

Stelazine, trying to figure out why no one had seen it. Helen hadn't spotted pills or a syringe the night she found Mother's body, although she admitted she'd been so shocked that she might not have noticed them. Alex and I, who'd looked throughout the living room, in all the bathroom medicine cabinets, and even in all the wastebaskets, never saw them.

I'd come up with three possible conclusions: My mother had received the injection or swallowed the pills somewhere other than in her house. Someone had come to the house to give her the pills or the shot, then left. Or Mother had given herself the injection or swallowed the pills at home, but then had made a point to destroy all evidence of the act in hopes of convincing everyone that she'd died of natural causes.

My inclination was to doubt the third explanation. It seemed cowardly and totally unlike my mother to commit suicide but try to hide it as a natural death. Wasn't this the woman who'd always preached to me that I had to take responsibility for my own actions? And Mother had done too much research on forensic pathology to believe that any reputable pathologist would miss the high level of Stelazine in her body.

Which left the first two explanations. Could she have received the injection or taken the pills somewhere else? A doctor's office, perhaps? Maybe someone—an inexperienced nurse or an exhausted intern—had accidentally given her the wrong dose of the medication. Perhaps whoever had given the injection wasn't even aware that my mother had died. Or maybe he or she was too frightened to come forward for fear of being sued or even arrested for criminal negligence. I needed to phone Mother's doctor, to at least see if she'd had an appointment on the Thursday she died.

As for the second scenario, someone coming to the house, the question, of course, was who. Could Mother have been so ill or so distraught that she'd persuaded some medical person to come to her house? Did anyone make house calls anymore?

A major problem with the medical bungling/accidental overdose theories was Mother's Christmas notes. If she had assumed that she'd be alive and celebrating with my family at Christmas, why had she sent my family and Helen those notes with our gifts? Notes that told Alex he was a fine husband and father, told Helen what a loyal friend she'd been, told me to write a book. Not only did her Christmas gifts this year seem like final bequests to her loved ones, the accompanying messages also sounded very much like farewells.

As much as I wanted to believe that my mother's death was due to some medical mistake she had no part in, all the evidence seemed to point to the opposite conclusion: Mother had indeed committed suicide. The fact that we didn't have the pills or the syringe seemed only a minor issue, an irrelevancy. Possibly Mother had merely disposed of the pills or the syringe with no intention of being secretive. She was, after all, an almost obsessively neat person. She would never have left a syringe lying on a table or pill bottles cluttering up the place if she could have helped it.

I suddenly was tired of thinking about it: how Mother had disposed of the Stelazine, why she hadn't waited until after she saw us at Christmas before killing herself, why she hadn't told us—told me—that she was sick. I needed to stop thinking and do something—anything—that would make me feel less hurt and angry that my mother had shut me out of her life.

I marched to the kitchen, grabbed a box of plastic garbage bags and ran up the stairs to that pristine, beige bedroom. I threw open the door of Mother's closet and pulled her clothes off their hangers: the long gauzy skirts and flowing tunics—the artsy costumes she wore to book signings and public appearances. Next I grabbed the simple silk blouses and tailored slacks and skirts, the clothes she wore when she wasn't being a famous writer. Then the baggy sweat suits, in an array of colors, which she wore when she was writing. I shoved them all into plastic garbage sacks. Tomorrow I'd drop the bags off at Goodwill.

I worked quickly, furiously, shoving clothes and shoes into bags, feeling—what?—satisfied? vengeful? I didn't want to stop long enough to evaluate the feeling. I only wanted to keep going, to maintain the adrenaline rush.

Finished with the closet, I moved to the bureau drawers, tossing sweaters, scarves, nightgowns into the bags for Goodwill, emptying the underwear drawer into a bag for the trash. I continued in the bathroom, shoving toiletries and Mother's few items of makeup from the medicine cabinet into a trash sack. I opened the drawers underneath the bathroom sink and scooped out the contents.

But then, suddenly, I stopped. Far back in the bottom drawer, behind the extra rolls of toilet paper, was a brown plastic prescription bottle. With shaking hands, I picked it up and studied the label. It wasn't Stelazine, but another drug, Percocet. The label had Mother's name on it and the directions, "Take every six hours as needed for pain."

I pulled out the phone book in the night stand. The Dr. J. Albright listed on the bottle had an office downtown. Taking a deep breath, I phoned the number.

"Dr. Albright's office," a chirpy female voice answered.

"I wonder if I could speak to Dr. Albright," I began.

"I'm sorry. He's seeing patients now. Perhaps you'd like to speak to one of the nurses?"

I hesitated. "I'm not sure who I need to talk to. My mother, Katherine March, was a patient of Dr. Albright's. I want to find out what her diagnosis was, how often she came for treatment, what medication she was taking. Perhaps someone could find her chart and read it to me."

"We can't give out that information—it's doctor–patient

confidentiality," the woman said, making it sound as if I'd just asked her to reveal military secrets.

"My mother is dead. I can't get the information from her." Then, realizing that she might think I was gathering ammunition for a malpractice suit, I added, "I'm trying to reconstruct what happened in her last days, to find out what was going on. I—I live in another city and hadn't seen Mother for a while. Her death was a terrible shock to me and to my family."

"I'm sorry, but—"

"I would really appreciate your help," I interrupted. "Could you make an appointment for me today with Dr. Albright? I only need a few minutes with him."

"Hold on." Abruptly taped music played in my ear.

I waited for what seemed like an eternity before a no-nonsense female voice came on the line. "This is Anne Benton, Dr. Albright's nurse. How can I help you?"

I explained the information I needed.

"Just a minute. I'll take a look at her chart."

I was put on hold again, for a sufficiently long enough time for me to contemplate what I hoped to gain by this.

When the nurse came back she said, "Dr. Albright saw your mother only once, on July second. The chart says that she had ovarian cancer, stage three. She refused any of the treatment options Dr. Albright proposed—surgery, or chemotherapy. All she wanted was palliative treatment—drugs for the pain, to keep her as comfortable as possible."

"But why would she refuse treatment?"

"I don't know. The chart doesn't say." The nurse's voice seemed a tad less stern when she added, "Your mother's cancer was very advanced. The prognosis would not have been good. Perhaps she thought that treatment was futile and decided she'd rather live the time she had left outside the hospital."

I felt suddenly, unexpectedly, weak-kneed. I sank onto

Mother's bed. Took a deep breath.

"How much time did she have left?" I asked.

"I don't know. It's very hard to tell. It's only in movies that a doctor tells a patient she has six months to live." When I didn't respond she said, "Is that all?"

"One more thing," I said. "This palliative treatment you talked about. Does it say what drugs Dr. Albright prescribed for her?"

"I think so. Here it is: Percocet. That's an opioid with acetaminophen that Dr. Albright often prescribes for cancer pain management."

"There wasn't a drug called Stelazine?"

"No, only the one I told you."

I could tell she was about to hang up. "Just one other thing," I said quickly. "Are you sure that my mother didn't come to your office on Thursday, December twelfth?"

"She only came once, on the second of July. I'm afraid I need to go now, Ms. Patterson. I'm very sorry about your mother." She hung up.

I was left sitting on the bed, staring at the receiver in my hand. So my mother had known that she had cancer, advanced cancer. She'd refused surgery or chemotherapy, had only accepted a prescription for pain pills—the pills I now held in my hand.

I held the bottle up to the light. It seemed almost completely full. The label said there were sixty in the bottle. I poured all the pills into my hand, then counted as I dropped them, one by one, back into the bottle. There were fifty-nine left. Did that mean that Mother had not been in much pain? Or that suffering, she'd taken a pill and, when it didn't help, decided that she needed a more permanent solution to her discomfort?

Suddenly I was overcome with exhaustion and a hopelessness so profound it felt bone-deep. Trudging downstairs to the kitchen, I found a half-full bottle of Chablis. I took it and a wine glass to the small den at the back of the house.

There, sitting in a brown corduroy arm chair, my feet propped up by an ottoman, I stared into the growing darkness and steadily drank to dull my own pain.

I must have fallen asleep. When I awoke the room was totally dark. But something—some sound—had awakened me. Still groggy, I heard a noise from the vicinity of the kitchen. It sounded as if the back door were being opened.

No, it must be some other noise, perhaps the wind blowing against the screen door. But then I heard it again: the unmistakable sound of a key turning in the lock.

I sucked in my breath, my heart hammering in my chest. Who could it be? Who, besides me, had a key to the house?

Helen! Yes, of course, it had to be Helen. She had a key. She didn't know I was here because I'd parked my car in the garage, and all the lights in the house were off.

"Helen," I called, not wanting to startle her by marching unannounced into the kitchen. "I'm here. It's Molly."

I waited. Only silence—a thick, menacing silence—filled the air. "Helen?" Perhaps she hadn't heard me.

Or perhaps it wasn't Helen at all!

The relief I'd felt only seconds earlier changed swiftly into panic. The phones were in the kitchen and in Mother's bedroom upstairs. Whoever was opening the back door would, any second now, be entering the kitchen. Which left only the second floor phone.

Swiftly now, protected by the darkness, I needed to run up the stairs, lock myself in Mother's bedroom, and phone the police. And just pray that the intruder—the intruder who I'd just alerted to my presence—was as eager to avoid me as I was to avoid him.

I dashed down the hallway to the stairs. One foot was on the bottom step when I heard it: the sound of the back door closing quietly, the key turning in the lock.

Heart pounding, my breath loud and ragged in my ears, I stood on the stairs, waiting for another noise, waiting for a clue to what was happening. But there were no other sounds.

On shaky legs I walked to the kitchen, turned on the overheard light. No one was there.

I peered out the window that overlooked the driveway, then moved to the dining room window that looked out on the front sidewalk. No one was in sight. The street was empty, without even a parked car in view.

CHAPTER SIX

When I was finally able to think straight I phoned Helen. She answered on the third ring.

"Helen, it's Molly. I'm at Mother's house. You weren't by any chance over here within the last fifteen minutes, were you?" When I said the words, I realized how stupid they sounded. Only if Helen had run from the back door to her car, then hot-footed it to her own house, three or four miles away, would she have been able to get home in time to answer my phone call.

"No, I wasn't," Helen said calmly. "But why are you asking? Has something happened?"

I told her what I'd heard. "I thought it was you because you have a key," I finished weakly. I'd hoped it was Helen because then I wouldn't now be sitting alone in a dark house in danger from an unknown intruder.

"I can't imagine who else would have a key," Helen said, the calmness now gone from her voice. "Did you give one to a real estate agent to put the house up for sale?"

"No, I haven't given one to anyone."

"What about that extra key that Katherine kept on the nail on the back door frame? You think somebody might have used it to get into the house?"

"No, I have that with me. It's on my keychain."

"Have you called the police?"

"I don't know what good that would do. I didn't see anyone; I just heard a lock turn. And when I looked outside there was no one in sight." I pictured the expressions of the police officers I knew from my classes if someone said, "Well, I think I heard the door open, officer, but of course I'd been asleep and, before that, I'd drunk quite a bit of wine. . . ."

"Molly, you can't spend the night alone in that house," Helen announced in her brooking-no-nonsense schoolteacher voice. "Either you come sleep over here tonight or I'm coming there."

I was surprised at the rush of relief that washed over me—I, who only a few hours ago had been so eager to spend time by myself. "I don't want to put you out," I said without much conviction. But even more I didn't want to be alone in this big house straining to hear another lock turning, another door being eased open.

"You're not putting me out at all," Helen said firmly. "I'd be a lot less worried about you if I knew you weren't alone. Now do you want to come here or me to come there?"

I suddenly realized how lightheaded I felt. Driving over to Helen's did not seem like a smart move. "If you don't mind, maybe it would be better if you came over here." *If you don't mind putting yourself in jeopardy from a potential burglar with a key.*

"Of course I don't," Helen said briskly. "Whoever was trying to break in was probably scared out of his wits to learn someone was home. With several people in the house, he won't dare try again."

The mental image of us two tough broads, one of us in her late sixties, fending off the skulking prowler made me burst into giggles.

I could hear the edge of disapproval in Helen's voice as she added, "I'll bring some food when I come. You sound as if you could benefit from something to eat."

I hung up the phone, asking myself the same question I'd pondered when I was in Helen's second-grade class: Could this woman read my thoughts?

She was at the house within half an hour, loaded down with an overnight bag and a grocery sack of food. I'd had enough time to sober up a bit and grow embarrassed. What kind of scared-of-the-dark wimp was I, needing my old elementary school teacher to come babysit me?

"I've been thinking things over, Helen. It's silly for you to spend the night. Why don't you just visit a bit and then go back home?"

"Don't be ridiculous," she said, walking past me into the kitchen. "I want to stay." She pulled out a plastic container and loaf of French bread from her sack. "I brought some of my chili. Are you hungry now?"

I realized suddenly that I was ravenous. The last time I'd eaten was at lunch, a good nine hours ago. "I'd love some. Will you eat with me?"

She shook her head. "I eat dinner early most nights, but I'll have a cup of coffee with you."

We sat at the kitchen table together while I scarfed down her delicious chili.

"I read somewhere that burglars often read obituaries and then break into the house of the deceased," Helen said.

"That's certainly a possibility. He could have read about Mother's death in the newspaper and waited until we'd left town to break in. But how would such a person get a key to the house?"

"I wonder if someone were picking a lock if it would sound like a key turning," Helen said.

"Maybe." I tried to convince myself that the nameless, faceless intruder had not arrived with a key to my mother's house, merely lock-picking tools. It made the incident seem less spooky or at least more understandable.

Helen sipped her coffee, then peered at me over the rim of

the mug. "Nevertheless, first thing tomorrow I think we should call a locksmith to change all the locks just in case there's someone out there who got hold of Katherine's keys. I know it's a big expense but it seems worth it if you're planning to spend a lot of time alone in this house."

I wasn't sure how much time I'd be spending alone here and wasn't up to thinking about it now. Instead I told Helen about finding Mother's prescription for pain pills and my phone conversation with the nurse.

Helen sighed. "So Katherine did know. After those extravagant Christmas gifts I assumed she did, but . . ." She left the sentence unfinished. I didn't have anything else to say either.

We sat in silence for a few minutes. Finally Helen added, "Those weren't the pills that Katherine used to—"

"No," I said. "We've never found that—the Stelazine."

Helen shrugged. "Well, maybe that will show up too."

"Maybe." Stranger things had already happened today.

"Oh, I know what I meant to tell you," Helen said as I stacked dirty dishes in the dishwasher. "I was talking to your mother's editor, Brenda Stein, at the reception after the funeral. She told me that Katherine used Stelazine in one of her novels, *With Malice Towards One,* the book about the evil psychiatrist. The psychiatrist killed a patient with an injection of Stelazine and then said the man had had a heart attack during the therapy session."

"My God." I stared at her, horrified. I'd read that book. I just hadn't remembered the name of the fatal drug. "Was Brenda saying that she thought Mother injected herself with Stelazine?"

"Not really. She did say that Katherine had researched it and decided to use Stelazine rather than another drug because a large dose of it could be fatal and, if injected, death would be almost instantaneous. Also, of course, it made sense for a psychiatrist to know about an antianxiety drug."

"But it sounds so unlike Mother to want to make her suicide look like a heart attack," I said, feeling suddenly sick to my stomach.

"Maybe that wasn't her intent," Helen said quietly. "Maybe it was just a drug she was familiar with, one that she knew worked quickly and effectively."

"There's also a chance that someone else got the idea about the Stelazine from that book." Perhaps someone who'd extensively studied Mother's fiction for her master's thesis? I was surprised that I, who a few hours ago had been totally convinced that Mother killed herself, could now even consider the possibility that she'd been murdered.

"Maybe," Helen said. But the expression on her wrinkled face told me that she doubted it.

Soon after that we went to bed. Or rather Helen went to sleep in Mother's bedroom and I, wide awake from my nap, headed to my old room to read Suzanne Lang's thesis on the fiction of Katherine March.

I didn't learn much, or at least I didn't learn what I had hoped to. In her discussion of *With Malice Towards One* Suzanne did not mention the Stelazine. In fact her analysis of the book, which she considered one of Mother's weakest, was conspicuously shorter than her critiques of Mother's other novels. Overall the thesis was not particularly insightful or well-written.

Bored by my reading, I finally fell into a fitful sleep around two-thirty. No suspicious noises, no keys turning in the lock disturbed my sleep. The only sound I heard was Helen getting up in the middle of the night to use the bathroom—a comforting noise which reassured me that I wasn't alone.

A knock on my bedroom door woke me the next morning. I peered groggily at the alarm clock—it was already nine-fifteen, hours later than I usually slept—as Helen walked in carrying a cup of coffee for me.

"I didn't know if I should wake you," she said apologetically, "but we have the appointment with the lawyer at ten-thirty."

I took a sip of coffee. "Ms. Ivins called you too?"

"Yes." Helen glanced at her feet. "Apparently your mother has left me something in her will."

I'd embarrassed her and I hadn't meant to. "Of course she would," I said quickly. "I'm glad I'll have some company."

The attorney's office was near the state capitol, in a small, older stone house converted into two offices, a folksy kind of place that would have appealed to my mother. The lawyer who came out to greet us was a tall, big-boned, middle-aged woman with intelligent gray eyes and a generous smile. She introduced herself as Pat Ivins and ushered us into her office.

A profusion of plants, floor-to-ceiling bookshelves, and a grouping of antique wing chairs in front of her mahogany desk made the room seem more like a study in a lovely old home than a law office. She gestured for us to sit in the chairs, then sat down across from us.

"First of all let me say how sorry I was to learn of your mother's death," she told me. When I thanked her she added, "When I updated this will for Katherine I never dreamed that I'd be reading it to you so soon."

"When did Mother update it?"

"Last July. It was July third. I remember we talked about the fireworks that would be taking place at Zilker Park the next night."

The day after Mother consulted the oncologist! I envisioned her walking out of the doctor's office and immediately heading for a phone to make an appointment with her lawyer. A focused, task-oriented woman, this Katherine March.

With an effort, I tried to turn my attention to what the attorney was telling us. Although Helen seemed to be paying rapt attention, I only managed to pick up the main points. I was to be my mother's literary executor, which essentially meant that I would be responsible for overseeing her unpublished literary works. I also inherited her house and the remaining financial assets after all other bequests were distributed.

Mother had established two trust funds for my children's education. The attorney looked at me. "Each fund contains five hundred thousand dollars."

I gasped. I hadn't realized Mother had so much money.

Helen beamed at me. "You certainly won't have to worry about how to pay for Annie's and Will's college expenses."

"No," I said in a weak voice. "I guess not."

The lawyer turned to Helen and read from the document in her hand, " 'And for my dear friend Helen Lewis I leave one million dollars as a token of my appreciation for her years of loyal friendship.' "

"Oh, my," Helen said softly, her hand flying up to touch her lips. "I had no idea she was going to leave me so much. It's too much."

"No, no," I reassured her, though I too was a bit shocked. How much money did Mother have?

As if she could read my thoughts, the lawyer looked at me and added, "The stocks and bonds you inherited, Ms. Patterson, are worth roughly three million dollars."

I could only stare at her, too stunned to speak. "Are you sure?" I finally asked.

"Yes, I checked with your mother's stockbroker yesterday afternoon."

Afterward Helen insisted on taking me to lunch. She frowned slightly when I ordered a frozen Margarita, but didn't say anything except to state her order for an iced tea a bit loudly.

She paused until the waiter left and then said, "Your mother's generosity—" and stopped. "Well, I don't know what to say.

Katherine knew that I had a lot of debts from my mother's hospital bills. She wanted to pay Mama's bills, but I said no, I could manage. Katherine told me then that she'd left me some money in her will. But Molly, I never imagined that it was a million dollars."

"Me neither," I said. "I mean I didn't realize she had that much money."

"Well, she was always a frugal woman. Her house was really the only expensive thing she ever bought."

Our drinks came then and I gratefully took a large gulp of my Margarita.

"I feel as if I'm taking money that rightfully belongs to you and your family," Helen said, looking miserable.

"That's ridiculous. For the first time in my life, Helen, I have more money than I know what to do with." I patted her hand. "I'm glad Mother gave you that."

"Well, it's generous of you to feel that way," Helen said. We ate our taco salads in comparative silence, both of us, I thought, too shell-shocked to talk.

After lunch I dropped off Helen to pick up her car. Then I took the bags of Mother's clothes to Goodwill, stopped at a grocery store for a few items, and, on a whim, just drove around Austin. I drove past the stone bungalow where Mother and I had lived for most of my childhood, then over to my grade school and my junior high. After that I headed for the graduate student apartments where Alex and I had lived when we were first married. We'd been so happy there in our tiny rooms furnished with furniture we'd picked up at garage sales. Today the complex looked rundown and depressing.

I wasn't sure why I was doing this driving tour. Maybe by visiting these sites from my past I was trying to make some sense out of my present. Or maybe I just didn't want to go back to that empty house.

I didn't get back to Mother's until almost three. Damn, I thought, as I unlocked the back door. That was what I'd forgotten to do: call a locksmith to change the locks. I'd promised Helen that I'd get the locksmith over today.

I stepped into the kitchen, feeling unaccountably nervous. What did I expect—that the intruder had come back and was waiting to jump out at me from behind the refrigerator? Setting my groceries on the counter, I listened for any suspicious sound. Nothing. The only noise I heard was the humming of the refrigerator. I glanced quickly around the room. Everything seemed to be exactly where I left it this morning.

The jangling of the telephone made me jump. I grabbed it on the second ring.

"Molly, this is Sam Pryor," the now-familiar voice with the New York accent announced. "I don't mean to be pressuring you, but I wondered if you were able to locate your mother's manuscript."

"Oh, you're not pressuring me at all," I said, suddenly happy to be talking to him. "I didn't see it when I looked in her office last night, but I intended to search more carefully today. Do you remember what her alternate title was? She might have filed it under that name."

"Something like *Vengeance*." He sounded disappointed. "Did you check on her computer?"

"I looked in the box where she keeps her disks, but I didn't see anything. I'll look again under the new title. If you want to hold on, I'll run up there right now. I can grab the portable phone upstairs."

I was afraid he was going to say, "No, I'm too busy. Call me if you find anything," leaving me alone with my fears. But instead the agent said, "Fine, I'll wait."

I ran up the stairs to my mother's bedroom and picked up her phone. "By the way," I told him, "I found out today that

I'm Mother's literary executor."

"Great," Sam boomed, perking up considerably. "I hoped you'd be the one she chose."

I was at the door of Mother's office now. I flipped on the overhead light and headed to the file cabinet while Sam chatted happily about foreign rights to her books.

"Why, I can't believe it!" I exclaimed.

"Can't believe what?"

"The manuscript—it's here. Filed under the S's for *The Summer That Changed Everything.*"

"Terrific. Now you'll send me a copy right away?"

"Sure." I stared at the thick folder in my hands. Was it possible that I'd just overlooked it yesterday?

CHAPTER SEVEN

Now that I was Mother's literary executor, I was curious about this new manuscript I'd finally located. Before I sent it to Sam Pryor, I wanted to read it.

Sitting in Mother's big leather desk chair, I skimmed through the first chapters. The story was narrated by a precocious teenaged girl, her version of the summer that ripped apart her family. Even from the few pages I read I could see what Sam meant; this was not the kind of book Mother usually wrote. The pace was slower than many of her other novels, with the focus on the book's characters rather than the plot. I sensed that something bad was about to happen in these people's lives but that was all.

I'd read the novel tonight when I'd have the time to give it my complete attention. But before I set it aside I turned to the last page. Sure enough, on the bottom of page three hundred eighty she'd typed the words "The End." Good. I couldn't tell from what I'd read so far what draft this was. Usually Mother wrote multiple ones, sometimes substantially changing the novel from one version to the next. I just hoped I could figure out whether she meant for this to be her final effort—the manuscript she was ready to send out into the world—or if this was an early version she'd intended to keep working on.

The portable phone that I'd laid on Mother's desk rang. "Hello?"

"Molly, it's Helen. I just wanted to see if you'd been able to find a locksmith who'd come out today."

"I was about to call right now."

"I'd be happy to spend the night again if you can't find anyone. I don't like the idea of you being alone there without the locks changed."

"That's very sweet of you, but I'm sure it won't be necessary." Last night I'd needed the company, but today the lure of the solitude I'd come to Austin for seemed suddenly irresistible.

It took several calls, but I found a locksmith who was willing to come over in half an hour. "It'll cost you time and a half if I have to work past five," he groused.

"Fine. I need to get the job done by tonight." It was worth a lot more than time and a half to me to be able to spend the night safely alone in this house.

The phone rang the moment I hung up. "How are things going?" Alex asked. "I expected to hear from you."

I took a deep breath. Only a few months ago I would never have let a day go by without phoning him if one of us was out of town. "Sorry. I've been out all afternoon, and Sam Pryor called just as I walked in the door." There was no point in mentioning my possible intruder. Hearing the story, Alex would either want me to drive home immediately or else he'd round up the kids and come here to spend the night with me. "What have you and the kids been doing?"

He told me about Annie's shopping spree, Will's afternoon working on his new computer. "So what did you do?" he asked. "Isn't this the day you were going to see the lawyer?"

"Yup. She read Mother's will to Helen and me. Mother made me her literary executor and set up two trusts to pay for the kids' education."

"Terrific," Alex said. "You'll be great at that. You have good literary instincts as well as a sense of what Katherine would want. And it's nice that she left money for the kids' college. The Patterson Higher Education Fund is badly in need of capital."

"There's five hundred thousand dollars in each trust."

Alex's voice was a croak. "One million dollars? Tell me you're not kidding."

"I'm not kidding."

"My God."

"Helen also inherited a million dollars and I inherited Mother's house and a portfolio of stocks and bonds. The lawyer said they're worth about three million."

Alex whistled. "I think I need to sit down."

"I know what you mean. And I've had a few hours to let it all sink in."

"The kids could go to school anywhere. Harvard, Yale, then law school or medical school or grad school."

"Well at least it won't be lack of money that will keep them from going to Harvard."

He chuckled. "You have a point."

I thought suddenly of what else the money would have meant to us, just a short while ago: being able to go on an expensive family vacation, to take a few summers off from teaching, to remodel our house the way we'd always wanted to. Would we ever do any of that, ever return to a time where we delighted in doing anything together?

"I was thinking that since I'm the literary executor I need to go through Mother's old files and the computer disks to see what's here. I have no idea how much unpublished work she has. I'm going to have to stay here a while longer than I planned."

"How long?" Alex asked. "Remember we have that marriage counseling session the day after tomorrow."

"I'm not sure, probably just a few extra days. Could you cancel the therapy session? We can reschedule when I get back. I'm—I'm just not up for it right now."

From downstairs I heard the doorbell ring. Probably the

locksmith arriving. "Listen, there's somebody at the door. I need to go. Give the kids my love."

"Sure." He paused, then said, "We miss you."

"See you soon." I hung up and hurried down the stairs.

But it wasn't the locksmith waiting impatiently on the front porch. Suzanne Lang—Suzanne-the-Stalker—stood there wearing a long black cape that somehow made her bright hazel eyes look more sinister. She smiled defiantly at me. "I knew you'd be here."

"This really isn't the best time," I said, wishing I hadn't opened the door. "I'm expecting someone any minute."

She seemed not to hear me, or, more probably, she just didn't care what my plans were. "Your mother had my master's thesis," she announced. "I want to get it back."

I found it hard to believe that she'd given Mother her only copy. Nevertheless the prospect of getting rid of her simply by returning her thesis was appealing. "I saw it in Mother's office. I'll go get it for you." I wasn't going to tell her that I'd read it. I didn't want her asking me what I thought of it.

"I'll just wait inside," Suzanne said, marching past me into the living room.

I didn't like having her in the house, but I didn't see how I could get her to wait outside on the porch either. Reassuring myself that the locksmith should be here any minute, I hurried up the stairs. "I'll be right back."

"Take your time," she said, moving over to the living room bookshelves to read the titles of Mother's books.

I raced upstairs to my bedroom, picked up the document from the nightstand, and headed back down.

Suzanne was standing in the middle of the living room, looking as if she were trying to memorize every detail of the room. I handed her the thesis.

"I'm going to use this as several chapters in the book I'm

writing about your mother," she said.

I stared at her. "What kind of book?"

She smiled. "I like to think of it as the definitive biography on Katherine March, an analysis of both her work and her life. My thesis will be the basis for the book."

Good luck, I thought. Reading Suzanne's thesis had literally put me to sleep last night.

As if she knew what I was thinking, Suzanne added, "Of course I'm also going to include much more about Katherine's personal life: her struggle to establish herself as a writer when she was a single working mother with a young child, and, earlier, her conflicts with her family. I'll tell the story of how a smart, protected young woman from a wealthy New England family broke off all ties with her relatives and built a life of her own."

She made it all sound like the jacket blurb to a rather sleazy biography. "How do you know all that?"

"Your mother told me when I interviewed her," she said in an isn't-that-obvious voice.

"Did she say why she broke off from her family?" I was embarrassed to ask her but even more intent on learning the answer to a question I'd always wondered about.

Suzanne's smile was not a pleasant one. "Katherine loathed her mother and adored her father," she said in a soft, obscenely conspiratorial voice. "But after he died, the summer after she graduated from high school, Katherine couldn't even bear to be in the same room with her mother. From what I gather, she left home shortly after her father's funeral and never went back."

The most information I ever managed to get from my mother on the subject was, "Your grandmother and I don't get along."

"I intend to interview Katherine's family for more information. You would have known this"—she sent me an accusing look—"if you ever returned any of my phone calls."

I did not take the bait. "You're going to interview my grand-mother?"

"Not her. But Charlotte, the sister, is willing to talk to me. She, in fact, seems quite pleasant." When I didn't respond, she added, "I understand you also had a turbulent relationship with your mother when you were a teenager. History repeating itself, you might say."

I stared at her. Had my mother told her that—my mother who never told me anything about her past personal life? "I certainly wouldn't call our relationship turbulent. As the mother of an adolescent daughter, I'd say it was quite usual."

"Then you didn't want to go live with your father and his wife instead of with Katherine?"

I had no intention of sharing my feelings about my mother with this odious woman. From everything she'd said so far I could already see the way Suzanne was envisioning her book: the real-life, never-before-told struggles that shaped the reclusive, best-selling novelist. Katherine March, who hated cli-chés and worked hard to expunge them from her fiction, deserved a better biographer.

I took a deep breath. "Like most teenagers I was often ir-ritated by my parents. And since Mother was the parent I lived with, she was the one who took the brunt of my hostility. It was just typical adolescent rebellion."

"That isn't the way I heard it from your stepmother," Su-zanne said with a smirk.

So it was Ginny who was feeding her this information! A stay-at home mom, Ginny had always viewed my mother as a compulsive workaholic who selfishly neglected her only child. But as a parent myself, I now suspected that if I'd lived with Dad and Ginny for the entire year, not just for vacations, they probably would have stopped being my fun parents and turned into resented taskmasters, just like my mother. I said as much to Suzanne.

She did not look convinced, but fortunately the buzz of the doorbell interrupted whatever she was about to say. I hurried to the door and beamed at the waiting locksmith.

"I'm sorry I don't have any more time to talk," I pointedly told Suzanne.

"Changing the locks?" she asked with interest.

I told myself I was imagining the malice in her smile, the knowledge of why I needed to change the locks. "Yes."

She waited for me to offer an explanation. When I didn't, she said, "I'll be in touch after I talk to your aunt. You'll probably want to know what Charlotte has to say." Since you know so little about your mother, her tone implied. "We can set up a time for our interview then."

I opened my mouth to say I wouldn't be having any interview with her—not now, not ever—but Suzanne breezed past me out the front door, black cloak swirling around her.

The locksmith was a welcome change, a loquacious, aging hippy with his gray hair tied back in a ponytail, a real Austin kind of guy. Watching him work, I could feel myself calm down a bit and stop my ruminating on the withering comments I should have said to Suzanne. While he tinkered with the front door locks, I peered out the living room window to make sure she was gone. Then I watched to make sure these new locks would keep her out.

"You're sure that someone won't be able to pick these dead-bolts?" I asked as he finished with the kitchen door.

"Your average burglar would give up on locks like this," he said. "Too much effort. And these are good solid doors—can't kick them in the way you can with some of those cheap, flimsy jobs." He turned around, surveying the room. "Though I don't know about your windows."

I sighed. "Let me write you a check."

Not finding a pen in my purse, I opened the junk drawer under the telephone to rummage for a pen.

The locksmith turned when he heard me gasp. "Something wrong?"

With a trembling hand I held up what I'd found at the back of the drawer: my mother's house keys and a syringe with traces of liquid still in the vial.

CHAPTER EIGHT

I stared at the once-missing keys and the empty syringe. Should I call the police officer who'd come to the house to question us after Mother's death? Forensic tests could determine what the liquid in the vial was and whether there were any identifiable fingerprints besides mine on the syringe.

No, I just couldn't face that right now. I didn't want to know what the tests would undoubtedly prove: that my mother had killed herself with an injection of Stelazine. She probably had given herself the shot in the kitchen, then unthinkingly tossed the syringe into the junk drawer, the place where she dumped stray items that had no other assigned place in her life. She must have been on her way to the living room couch when she collapsed.

I considered calling Alex or Helen with the news, but I wasn't up to that either. Instead I started sorting through the junk drawer, wondering what other secret items I might find. Unfortunately, nothing very interesting: a few pencils, a notepad, some coupons and a half dozen business cards, mainly for home maintenance people. I glanced at the cards, then pulled out one for Eric Nielson, Ph.D., a clinical psychologist. I vaguely remembered seeing that name on her appointment calendar. Could this be the person who'd given her the Stelazine?

I punched in the printed phone number, realizing too late that it was already almost six; no one was likely to be at the office. But as I was about to hang up, a man answered, sounding impatient. "Eric Nielson."

"Uh, this is Molly Patterson. I'm Katherine March's daughter. I found your business card in my mother's desk."

"Oh, yes. I met you at your mother's funeral." He sounded a tad more pleasant. "What can I do for you?"

I hesitated, then blurted it out. "Were you my mother's therapist?"

He laughed. "No. From what she told me, I gathered Katherine was not a big fan of psychotherapy."

Despite myself, I smiled. "She certainly wasn't."

He saved me from having to ask my next awkward question. "I met Katherine after a speech I gave. She was interested in research I'm doing about psychological profiles of violent criminals, and we met a few times to talk about it. I liked her and was very sorry to hear about her death."

"Thank you. I appreciate the information." Even though it's led me to another dead end.

"What were you trying to find out?"

Maybe it was because he said he liked Mother or maybe I was just ready to talk to anyone who might give me some answers. In any case I found myself telling him, a perfect stranger, about the drug that was supposed to have caused my mother's death and the empty syringe I'd discovered. "I just have so many questions about what happened and what was going on with her those last weeks. I didn't even know she had cancer."

"I didn't either," he said quietly. "I sensed that something was bothering her, but she never talked about it. For what it's worth, I can't imagine any reputable therapist prescribing Stelazine for her. It's for psychotic anxiety, and Katherine certainly wasn't psychotic."

I considered what he'd said. "Maybe it was someone who wasn't so knowledgeable about the different drugs for anxiety, like a family practitioner who just noticed that she was upset."

"I suppose that's possible, but I think most family practitioners would prescribe something more common, like Valium. I'm not a psychiatrist; I don't prescribe drugs but I try to be knowledgeable about ones that might be helpful to my patients. The first time I ever heard of Stelazine was in your mother's novel."

I forced myself to ask the last question. "She didn't happen to mention if she had any Stelazine in her possession, did she?"

"It never came up." He hesitated, then said, "Listen, I have to see a patient now, but if you'd like to talk some more about this, I have a dinner break at seven." When I didn't immediately reply, he added, "I'll be at Luigi's on Guadalupe. If you'd like to join me, I'd enjoy the company." He said goodbye before I could figure out an answer.

I told myself I'd gotten all the useful information from him that I was likely to get. I'd planned to spend the evening reading Mother's new novel, and after my big lunch, I wasn't even hungry. Dr. Nielson would just have to eat dinner by himself.

At six-forty-five, I decided I needed to follow up all leads, no matter how improbable. I got into the car and drove to Luigi's.

When I walked into the crowded restaurant, it occurred to me that I didn't even know what this Eric Nielson looked like. But fortunately the woman at the reservation desk was able to point out the table where a broad-shouldered man with wind-blown brown hair was eating a bowl of pasta.

He looked up when I walked over. "I'm glad you decided to join me," he said with a smile. "Let me call the waiter."

Sitting down, I started to say I wasn't hungry but then ended up ordering a salad and a glass of wine. "I remember you from the funeral," I said. The tall man in the tweed jacket. He had a pleasant, lived-in kind of face, and up close he seemed older than I originally thought, maybe in his late thirties or early forties.

For one awful moment I revisited the first minutes of blind dates I'd had in my youth, when the only thought in my head was, Why in the world did you put yourself in this awkward position? Then I remembered why I was here and got a grip. "I realize this is rather unorthodox, talking to a total stranger about someone you probably didn't even know very well, but I'm really desperate for information about what happened to Mother."

He nodded. "I can understand that. I'm not sure how much I can help, but I wanted to tell you one thing I didn't have time to say over the phone. I saw your mother the day before she died. We had lunch together."

I stared at him. "Did she seem upset? Did you get the sense that she was suicidal?"

He met my gaze with deep-set blue eyes that seemed to reflect my pain. "No. I've been thinking a lot about it, and I didn't pick up anything like that. She was pleased about finishing her book. She said she was looking forward to being with you and your family for the holidays. She mentioned that she'd been Christmas shopping."

I could feel my eyes well with tears. Why would Mother, the most straightforward of people, tell this man she was looking forward to seeing my family if she planned on killing herself the next day? She might have felt compelled to say that to me, but not to a disinterested party. It didn't make sense unless—"Did she seem to be in a lot of pain?"

He considered the question. "She looked worn out, but no, not in serious pain. I asked her one other time if she was ill— she looked pale and exhausted—but she brushed off my questions, said she was just tired from working so hard on the book."

"That's what she told her editor too." I sighed.

We ate in silence—actually he ate and I drank my wine—until he looked at his watch. "I'm sorry, but I'm going to have to leave in a few minutes. I don't know how much help I've been to you."

"At least you don't think she killed herself," I said, feeling once again close to tears. "I didn't really think she did either. If Mother chose to commit suicide, she wouldn't have done it like that."

I took a large gulp of wine. "Of course now I'm left with the question of who actually did this to her. Was it some kind of medical bungling, an accidental overdose? Or was it someone who set out to kill her? And what kind of sick person would commit murder like that?"

He grimaced, the pleasant face contorted with anger. "A sly, arrogant one who wants to prove how superior and clever he is. The killer read her novels and probably was envious of her success. He didn't just want to get rid of Katherine—if that's all he wanted, he could have shot her when she opened the door—he had to show her up too. It's as if the murderer was saying, 'You thought you were so damn smart, but who's the smart one now, Katherine?' "

"That's"—I struggled for words—"an interesting interpretation."

He shook his head, looking rueful. "Sometimes I get carried away. You're right—it only is an interpretation, just one possibility."

He insisted on paying the waiter for both of our meals and then pulled out a business card from his wallet and scribbled something on it. "I wish I could stay, but I have a group in a few minutes." He handed me the card. "If you want to get hold of me, I've written my cell phone number and e-mail address."

He reached down to grasp my hand. "I'm very sorry for your

loss, Mrs. Patterson. And I hope you find the answers to your questions."

As I drove back to the house, I mentally ran over all the things the psychologist had just told me. An opinionated man, this Eric Nielson! But were they informed decisions or just some off-the-cuff shrink theories unsupported by any real evidence? I wasn't sure. His guesses about the psychology of my mother's killer reminded me of the criminal-personality profiling done by the FBI to track down serial killers.

Students in my classes, many of whom had read John Douglas's popular books about how he profiled serial killers and assassins, were fascinated with the subject. But the cops in my class always seemed more skeptical about these profiles. "Half the time their guesses are wrong," one said. "But they're like those psychics who 'see' a crime scene. You only hear about the times when they guess right."

Maybe it was because, like my mother, I was a psychotherapy cynic. Dr. Nielson's ideas about Mother's murderer reminded me too much of a parlor game: "I accuse Colonel Mustard in the billiard room with the lead pipe." And unlike Special Agent John Douglas who carefully examined each crime scene and every detail of the case, Eric Nielson was making a lot of assumptions from very few actual facts.

Still that didn't mean he wasn't right. It was certainly likely that Mother's killer had at the very least read her novel featuring a syringe of Stelazine as murder weapon, and common sense told me that anyone who managed to plan and carry out this crime was likely to be sly and clever—it was certainly no impulsive crime of passion. The part about the killer's envy and wanting to show up Mother I wasn't so sure about.

But as I pulled into the driveway of Mother's big, silent house all of my carefully honed analytic skills and my professor's detached intellectuality seemed to desert me. Once again I felt on the verge of tears. Despite all of his unsubstantiated speculations, Eric Nielson had convinced me of one thing: Mother had not committed suicide. He knew it and I knew it too.

First thing tomorrow I would phone the police and hand over the empty syringe I'd discovered. And then, if the Austin police still persisted in their belief that Mother had killed herself, I would find her killer myself.

In the kitchen I made myself a pot of decaf and kept reminding myself that, thanks to the expensive new deadbolts, I had no reason to feel scared in this house. Then I took my coffee and Mother's manuscript to the study and settled down to read *The Summer That Changed Everything*.

Perhaps because I wanted so desperately to be distracted the novel sucked me in with the first pages, into an unhappy, upper-middle class New England family during the 1950s. On the surface the Page family is beautiful and accomplished, the father a successful book publisher, the mother an elegant Junior Leaguer, one teenage daughter a great beauty and the other—the older, more serious one—the valedictorian of her high school class. But beneath the picture-perfect exterior is a loveless marriage between two incompatible people and growing friction between the parents and their daughters.

Jane, the older daughter and the book's narrator, is eager to leave home for college. A bookish girl who can barely tolerate her controlling mother, she's intent on establishing an intellectual, career-oriented life. The younger daughter, rebellious, boy-crazy Emily, is furious that her father is threatening to send her to a strict, all-girl boarding school in the fall. Nathaniel, their father, has decided to leave his wife to marry a young editor. Their mother, Anne, has been having an affair of her own, but her lover, the club golf pro, is not her idea of marriage material. In her world a divorce from Nathaniel would signal a major drop in status, and Anne is not about to let that happen.

I read until hunger pangs made me stop. After eating a bowl of Helen's chili, I went back to the manuscript. I read on, about the parents' screaming fights and Jane's foreboding that something terrible is about to happen. Anne insists on giving her husband a big fiftieth birthday party even though he doesn't want one. The party is a lavish ordeal of forced gaiety and too much alcohol. Jane spots both her father's and her mother's lovers among the revelers.

The next morning a maid finds Nathaniel dead in his bed. A doctor rules that he suffered a fatal heart attack, but Jane is convinced her father was murdered. The next chapters detail her attempts to find evidence to convict her mother of a crime that only Jane believes has been committed.

Around midnight I set the manuscript down. I still had about seventy pages left, but I was too tired to read any further. It was a disturbing book, a portrait of a teenaged girl's obsession with punishing a mother she despised. But was Anne a killer? At this point I wasn't sure. Immediately after the party Anne had left with her lover to spend the night at his apartment. If Nathaniel had indeed been killed, how was it done? Even Jane couldn't find any evidence of foul play, and since no autopsy was performed, there was no medical proof for her suspicions.

Was it possible that this was my mother's portrait of her own family? Her father, a book publisher, had died of a heart attack the summer after Mother's graduation from high school, Aunt Charlotte had told me. Certainly that summer of her life could have qualified as one that changed everything. And if what Suzanne Lang had told me was true, that Mother loathed her own mother, there were even more real-life similarities in this book. Anne Page, the mother in the novel, was indeed a loathsome woman, tyrannical, stupid, and totally self-involved. Very seldom had Mother created a character with fewer redeeming traits.

As I checked to make sure that all the new deadbolts were

locked I wondered: Could Mother have actually thought her mother murdered her father? Of course authors often use a real-life event as a starting point for their novels, and no one said the book was anything other than fiction. But why had Mother made the characters in her book so closely resemble their real-life models?

I fell asleep in my old bedroom thinking of all my unanswered questions and awoke at six the next morning wondering how the novel was going to end.

Padding down to the kitchen, I drank a cup of coffee and then phoned Detective Martinez, the man who had come to the house to investigate Mother's death. He wasn't in, but I left a message for him to call me.

Then I resumed my reading. An hour and a half and several cups of coffee later, I finished the book. Anne indeed had killed her husband. Jane manages to piece together what happened: Anne had returned to her house and sneaked into the bedroom where her husband slept. She'd killed Nathaniel by injecting an air bubble into his heart, causing a fatal heart attack.

The evidence, though, is skimpy. Jane finds a box of hypodermic syringes in the medicine cabinet. In the drawer of her mother's nightstand she discovers a dog-eared copy of *Unnatural Death*, a Dorothy Sayers novel in which the killer injected air bubbles into her victims' main arteries, causing embolisms and heart failure.

Jane goes to the police with her evidence. The officer tells her she's read too many mystery novels. Her father, a man with a known heart condition, had obviously died of natural causes.

Jane has to settle for confronting her mother with her knowledge that Anne is a murderer. Furious, Anne orders her out of the house. Jane departs for college, knowing that she's leaving her mother and her old life for good.

It was an unsatisfying ending. I'd expected one of Mother's

surprise plot twists—if not an unexpected killer, at least some startling revelation—but none occurred. Instead *The Summer That Changed Everything* ended with a thud, a promising book that limped to a predictable conclusion. I wondered if Mother was ill when she wrote the last chapter. Or perhaps her determination to write what had really happened to her father—or what she believed happened—forced her to write an ultimately dull novel.

I found it hard to believe that she hadn't intended to do some rewriting. Without those revisions, though, would she still have wanted the book to be published?

And there were other issues to consider as well. Some reviewer or journalist was sure to see the similarities between the book and Mother's life. But maybe that was what Mother intended. Perhaps she wanted the media to rehash her father's death. If what she wrote was true, this book could be her final attempt to bring her father's killer to justice—or at least public condemnation.

But what if the book was totally fictitious? Was it fair to Mother's remaining family—her elderly mother and her sister—to publish a novel that strongly suggested that my grandmother, Elizabeth March, had murdered her husband over forty years ago and gotten away with it?

I wanted very much to discuss the book with someone knowledgeable about publishing. The obvious choice was Sam Pryor. But I could already predict what the agent would say: "Just send me the manuscript, Molly. We'll check with an attorney on the libel angle." Brushing aside my concerns like crumbs from his morning bagel.

What I really needed to know was what Mother was thinking. Was she satisfied with this novel? Had she intended to portray her real-life mother as a murderer?

I found her address book and punched in the phone number

of the person most likely to have some answers: Brenda Stein, her editor.

She answered the phone at the first ring, sounding rushed, but assured me she'd be happy to answer any of my questions. "I don't know how much I can tell you, though. I haven't read the whole manuscript."

"I did. I just finished it."

"And what was your reaction?" she asked, her deep voice full of anticipation.

"Well, at first I loved it. It was beautifully written, the characters were intriguing, and Mother did a great job of evoking the underlying tension in this Waspy family in the fifties."

"Yes, I thought that too in the chapters I read," Brenda said.

"Unfortunately I found the ending, the last two chapters, disappointing, very predictable. I'd hoped that you'd read the book or talked to Mother about it."

Brenda sighed. "All I can tell you is Katherine said she was having trouble with the book and was thinking of giving up on it—something I'd never heard her say before."

"Maybe she knew that she wouldn't have the time to do the rewriting it needed." Or perhaps she was having pangs of conscience, second thoughts, about setting up her family. "Did she tell you what it was that she disliked about the book?"

"I remember she said she was having problems with the last third of the book and she was concerned that the character of the mother, Anne, was perhaps too one-dimensional. The story, of course, is told through the eyes of a teenaged girl, and she sees her mother as a total bitch. Still, Katherine didn't want to portray Anne as a vacuous socialite cliché."

I felt a small surge of hope. So maybe this book was not my mother's final hatchet job on her mother. Maybe it was just a story. "Uh, did Mother ever mention if she was basing this story on any real-life people or incidents?"

"No. When I complimented her on how well she evoked that specific time and place she did say that she'd grown up in that area. But she never said anything about the characters being based on real people. Why do you ask?"

"I just thought there were a lot of similarities to Mother's own life." I listed a few of them.

"Oh dear. Katherine never let on at all that the book was about her own family." She hesitated, then said, "Could you perhaps ask your relatives if there was ever any talk that Katherine's father might have been murdered?"

I hesitated. "I suppose I could ask my aunt." Even though I barely knew the woman.

"Good. We need to know what we're dealing with here."

The minute I hung up I phoned Aunt Charlotte. This time she answered the phone herself. "Molly, what a nice surprise!"

I thought about how easy it would be to just chat. Abruptly, before I could reconsider, I plunged into my reason for calling. "I realize how difficult this must be for you, but I don't know who else to ask," I ended lamely.

"Actually, I'm glad you called me," she said. "I would hate to have heard about this from some tabloid reporter. The answer to your question is no, there was never any talk of Father dying from anything other than a heart attack. He'd had a milder one the year before, and we all knew his health was not good."

"Someone told me that Mother did not get along with Grandmother when she was a teenager. Is that true?"

"To put it mildly. But even Katherine, much as she disliked Mother, never suggested that she killed Father. I suspect Katherine thought that the stress from our parents' arguing brought on his heart attack. She blamed Mother for their fights, but Katherine always was a daddy's girl."

"You got along better with your mother?"

Charlotte chuckled. "Both Mother and Katherine were

extremely strong-willed, stubborn women; they both always wanted to have their own way. So did I, but I was more covert about it. I at least pretended to do what Mother wanted. It didn't help either that she and Mother had almost nothing in common. Mother loved parties, shopping, and gossip, and Katherine was totally uninterested in any of that. Instead she was very cerebral and bookish, like Father, and Mother was never interested in books."

How strange, I thought, that a woman who disliked books would have married a publisher. But there were more pressing matters to consider now. "So you're saying that Mother's novel is not really autobiographical?"

"I guess I'd have to read it to say. I can't believe that Katherine didn't tell me anything about this book. I do hope the sister character isn't a bore."

I grinned. "Not remotely boring." So perhaps the book's murder was nothing but a plot device. "I'll make sure that you get to read the manuscript before it's published. And thanks for telling me about the family history. Mother never discussed her childhood, so I know almost nothing about her past."

"How odd," Charlotte said, "but Katherine always was secretive, even when she was a little girl." She paused. "You know, Molly, it's such a coincidence that you'd call today. Yesterday I was telling Mother about you and she said how much she'd like to see you. The last time she laid eyes on you, she said, was when you were ten."

I was touched that this grandmother I didn't know had remembered our brief meeting. "I'd like to see her too."

"How about next week?" Charlotte asked.

"Oh, I doubt I can come that soon."

"Well, think seriously about it," Charlotte urged, her voice animated. "You could stay with me. I know we'd have a wonderful time. And after you meet Mother, you can decide for yourself whether Katherine's book is an autobiography."

CHAPTER NINE

It was time to do a little detective work, I told myself after lunch. Maybe if I talked to all of Mother's neighbors, one of them might remember seeing someone come to visit her on the afternoon she died—a visitor who hadn't seemed especially noteworthy at the time but now might be our best chance of identifying Mother's murderer.

I was well aware that finding such an eyewitness was definitely a long shot. Not many people these days noticed who went in and out of their neighbors' homes. It was also extremely likely that such a well-prepared killer had made a point of arriving and leaving as unobtrusively as possible. Still, eyewitness testimony sometimes provided invaluable leads and, as far as I knew, the only people the police had interviewed were Helen, me, and the electrician who showed up for a scheduled appointment at four-thirty but said no one answered the door.

Unfortunately no one was home for me either at the first two houses I tried, those on either side of Mother's. Long-time neighbors lived there, Mrs. Benjamin, the elderly widow who'd come to Mother's funeral, and the Clarks, a retired couple who traveled a lot.

I didn't know the people in the two houses across the street, but I decided to talk to them anyway. No one answered my knock at the first place, a stone Tudor. I sighed. I hoped this didn't mean that the whole neighborhood had been gone for the entire month of December.

I moved to the next home, a sprawling, brick ranch-style. To my relief, a red-haired woman in jeans and a black sweater answered the door. "Yes?" She regarded me suspiciously, as if she were looking for an excuse to slam the door in my face.

Quickly I explained who I was and why I was there.

"Sorry, I didn't see anything. I was at work that day." She shook her head. "Almost every waking hour I seem to be at work."

"Well, thanks anyway."

She started to close the door. "You know who you should talk to is Mrs. Benjamin, in the gray house across the street. She's always home, and she keeps an eye on the neighborhood."

I nodded. "I already tried her house, but she didn't answer the door."

"Oh, I forgot. She's at her daughter's for the holidays."

Great. I thanked the woman again and turned to leave.

"Mrs. Benjamin told me that someone else was asking her the same thing—if she saw anybody at the house the day your mother died."

I swiveled. "Did she say who asked her that? Was it the police?"

The redhead smiled apologetically. "I'm not sure. Could have been. All I remember is that she said it was a woman. Apparently Mrs. Benjamin was a little confused about which day she saw the different people at your mother's house."

My heart began to race. "Then she did see somebody the day Mother died?"

"I think so, but you really need to ask her. If I remember right, she saw two men and two women come and go from your mother's sometime that week. But that's all I know. Sorry I couldn't be more help."

"No, no, you've been extremely helpful. Thank you." I waved to her as I started back to the house. It was probably too much to hope that one of the women Mrs. Benjamin had seen was Suzanne Lang, but stranger things had happened. Mother once said that Marion Benjamin was a one-woman neighborhood crime watch. Now if only she'd spotted a tall woman with wild gray hair enter Mother's home on the day she died . . .

When I got back to the house Detective Martinez had left a message. I returned the call and this time was connected to him. "I think I've found some evidence that pertains to my mother's death," I told him.

"What kind of evidence?"

"A syringe, a used syringe with a little liquid still in it. Although Mother died of an overdose of Stelazine, we never could find any sign of the drug—an empty prescription bottle or a vial or syringe—in the house."

"Where did you find it now?"

"In a drawer in the kitchen, under a lot of papers. Of course I don't know for sure that it's Stelazine in the syringe. Maybe it's something entirely different." A grim possibility I'd tried not to think about. Maybe the syringe contained traces of pain medication or extra-strength vitamins that had nothing to do with her death.

"We'll send it to the lab to see what it is." The detective said he'd come to the house within the next hour.

He arrived just as I was sitting down with a cup of coffee. A quiet-spoken man with pock-marked skin and thinning dark hair, Detective Martinez was as careful and methodical as I remembered. Immediately after stepping in the door, he asked to see where I'd found the syringe.

I took him to the kitchen and opened the drawer where the syringe still lay. "Unfortunately, my fingerprints are probably on it. I was digging through the drawer for a pen and inadvertently touched it," I said as he carefully lifted it with a tissue and placed the syringe in an evidence bag.

He accepted a cup of coffee and we sat at the kitchen table to talk. "My husband and I looked all around the house for a pill bottle or a syringe, but we didn't find a thing. I thought we looked in the junk drawer too, but apparently we didn't look closely enough."

Or maybe someone placed it in the drawer weeks after we'd looked! My God, why hadn't I thought of that before?

"What is it?" the detective asked.

I stared at him. "I—I just realized how the syringe could have appeared in the drawer after we'd looked a few weeks ago and found nothing." And how a manuscript which was missing from Mother's office the first time I checked was suddenly—magically—tucked neatly in her file cabinet the very next night.

His dark eyes narrowed. "Tell me your theory."

I wanted to shout, "Look, I figured it out. This is how she did it." But I knew, from long experience with the police officers in my classes, that was absolutely the wrong approach. I needed facts and evidence, neither of which I had much of at this point. All I had now was a theory.

I took a deep breath and then began, as dispassionately as possible, to explain about how Suzanne Lang, a would-be writer upset with Mother for not launching her publishing career, had turned into something close to a stalker when Mother refused to see her. I related my own experiences of the past few days: someone, thinking no one was in the house, unlocking the kitchen door but quickly leaving when I called out; Mother's missing manuscript miraculously reappearing the next day—a manuscript that would be very useful for the biography Suzanne was writing; then Suzanne showing up at the house last night, supposedly to retrieve her master's thesis. "And while I was upstairs getting it, I think she put the syringe and Mother's house keys in the junk drawer."

Martinez took notes, but he didn't give me a clue to his reaction. "But if Suzanne killed your mother, why would she not have left the syringe in the drawer in the first place? Why return it now?"

"I think she learned about the Stelazine from Mother's novel, *With Malice Towards One,* and thought that, like in the novel, everyone would think Mother had died of a heart attack. But I guess she wasn't counting on the autopsy, which determined the death was due to a Stelazine overdose. Suzanne must have decided then that she'd have to make it look as if Mother had injected herself. Which of course leaves the question of what happened to the syringe she used. Suzanne probably figured if we found it in the messy junk drawer we would have thought it was there all along but we'd just overlooked it."

"You're saying that while you were upstairs looking for her thesis, Ms. Lang planted the syringe and returned the manuscript she'd stolen earlier?"

I took a deep breath. No, of course that didn't make sense. "I'm guessing that Suzanne took the manuscript and house keys on the day she killed Mother. She tried to return the manuscript on the night I came to Austin, but when I called out, she just left fast. Probably she came back with the manuscript the next day when I was out, and it's possible she returned the keys and syringe then. But she showed up at the house last night to discuss the book she was writing about Mother and try to convince me to let her interview me."

Detective Martinez's sad, dark eyes inspected me. "Why didn't you tell me before about this woman who was bothering your mother?"

"Because I didn't think it was important. Because it never crossed my mind that someone might have killed Mother."

Martinez said nothing, but his expression said, That remains to be seen.

"Someone told me today that a neighbor, Mrs. Benjamin

who lives next door, saw two women and two men come to Mother's house around the day she died," I said, leaping in to fill the silence.

His head shot up. "Is this Mrs. Benjamin home now?"

"No, she's out of town visiting her daughter. I heard there was some other woman who already asked her questions about this. Was that a police officer?"

He looked puzzled. "Not that I know of."

Could it have been some journalist, doing a feature about Mother's death, nosing around the neighborhood looking for some juicy tidbits to report?

The detective closed his notebook and stood up. "It will probably be at least four or five days before we get the lab results."

I wanted to blurt out, "Will you be questioning Suzanne Lang this week? Was I able to convince you that my mother didn't take her own life?" But I knew exactly how well that would go over. None of the officers I knew enjoyed being told how to do their jobs.

Instead I said, "You'll let me know when you get the results?" Not that there were likely to be any big surprises. If Suzanne had indeed planted the evidence, there would be no fingerprints other than mine on the syringe and the liquid inside it would be Stelazine.

"If there's anything to report, I'll let you know, and if you find any more evidence in the meantime, you call me." He nodded to me and left.

Staring at the closed door, I felt a wave of depression wash over me. What I had to do now was something I'd always been terrible at: sit patiently and wait.

CHAPTER TEN

Two days later I drove back to Houston and my family. When I walked into my house Alex and Will were sitting at the kitchen table eating sandwiches. "Mom!" Will yelled when he saw me, jumping up to give me a hug—a display of affection he probably wouldn't have allowed himself if his big sister had been in sight.

I hugged him back, mussing his sandy-colored hair. "Maybe I need to go away more often if this is the kind of reception I get when I come home."

Alex's smile was a bit strained. "I'm glad you're back. We missed you."

I avoided his eyes. "Me too. Where's Annie?"

"Over at Katie's house," Will said. "It was great to have her gone. Dad and I went out to Fuddruckers for lunch, just the two of us."

"Sounds like fun," I said.

Alex glanced at the cardboard box filled with stacks of notebooks and manila folders that I'd set on the kitchen counter. "Are those your mother's unpublished manuscripts?"

"I think some of them are, but I haven't read everything yet."

"Did you ever find the novel that Katherine was working on—the one that literary agent was so eager to get?"

"Yes, I mailed copies to her agent and her editor." Had I forgotten to tell him that I'd discovered the lost manuscript?

"So what did you think of the book?" Alex asked.

I told him. When I got to the part about the similarities between the characters in the book and Mother's own family, he whistled. "That does make things more complicated. I can't remember your mother ever using any overtly autobiographical details in her novels before."

"Maybe it's not as autobiographical as it seems. When I phoned Aunt Charlotte to tell her about the book, she said there was never any talk that her father had been murdered. That no one—not even Mother—thought he'd died from anything other than a heart attack."

Alex raised his eyebrows. "Talked to everyone, haven't you?"

But I hadn't talked to him, the man who, until a few months ago, had been my best friend, my confidant. I could see the hurt in his expressive brown eyes and felt guilty at my unintentional snub. "I brought home a copy of the manuscript. Why don't you read it? I'd be interested in your opinion." Trying to say, See, I value your input. It just took me a while to ask for it.

"I'd like to read it." He glanced again at the stacks of papers in the cardboard box. "Did you get a lot done in Austin?"

"Not as much as I'd hoped," I said, trying not to sound defensive. "Everything took a lot longer than I thought it would."

"That's certainly understandable," Alex said in a soothing voice.

The kind of voice one used with a difficult or irrational person. I was spared having to respond by Will running up to me, his freckled face bright with excitement. "Mom, you've got to come see all the awesome things my new computer can do."

"Sure, honey." I turned away from Alex and followed Will to his room. What was getting into me, I wondered as I pretended to be fascinated by Will's computer. Why was I feeling so irritable? Yes, things between Alex and me were tense and unresolved, but this seemed more than that. I'd always loved spending time with my family, just hanging out together and talking, but right now the only thing I really wanted was to be back in Austin by myself. Was this one of those predictable stages of grief? If it was, I wanted to get over it—fast.

To ease my guilt feelings, I insisted on fixing one of the kids' favorite dinners: spaghetti and meatballs, garlic bread, a green salad, even a cheesecake (store-bought) for dessert. The cooking made me feel a little better, more like my old self.

I had just set the pot of spaghetti sauce on the stove to simmer when Annie walked in the back door. "Oh, you're back," she said when she spotted me, not sounding thrilled.

"Hi," I said brightly, "did you have a good time at Katie's?"

"It was okay." She walked past me to the refrigerator. After a brief inspection of its contents, she pulled out a can of Diet Dr Pepper. "Did you bring me back Grandma's jewelry and some shawls the way you promised?"

"I promised?" I asked stupidly. When had I promised her that?

"The day we were coming home from Austin. We were getting in the car and I said how much I always loved Grandma's silver jewelry, especially those long, dangly earrings, and those cool shawls she always wore. You said I could keep some of the jewelry and a couple shawls as a remembrance of Grandma."

Oh, God. I had said that. I tried to think. Had I given away all the shawls, taken them with all the other clothes to Goodwill? Yes, unfortunately I had. I could remember shoving them, a pile of them, into a plastic garbage bag. The shawls were history. Fortunately, I hadn't touched the jewelry.

"I remember now," I said carefully. "The jewelry is still at Grandma's house. The next time I go to Austin I'll bring it all back and you can pick out what you want."

"What about the shawls?"

I took a deep breath. "I'm afraid the shawls were with the

clothes I gave away to Goodwill. I'm so sorry, Annie."

"What?" Annie's face was incredulous. "You gave away my shawls? The shawls you *knew* I wanted?"

"I am sorry, Annie. I forgot that you wanted them."

"You forgot? How could you forget? You promised me! I wanted to go back into Grandma's house and get some shawls before we left Austin. But no, you said we had to get back home. Leave the shawls for later."

I took a deep breath, willing myself to be patient. She was right. If I'd let her go back when she wanted to, she'd have the shawls now. And her reaction was about more than lost shawls. Grief over her grandmother, general anger with her parents, especially her mother, and raging hormones were all mixed in.

Two vivid red splotches were spreading over Annie's pale face. "The only person you ever think about is you," she screamed. "And why would you throw away Grandma's beautiful shawls? It's because you hated her, isn't it? You didn't want to keep anything to remember her by, so you didn't keep anything for me either. But I loved Grandma and she loved me. You can't stand that, can you?"

"That's enough, Annie." Alex stood in the doorway, his face stern.

Annie turned on him. "And you—you always take her side."

"Go to your room, Annie. Now."

She glared at her father, but went. Seconds later we heard her bedroom door slam.

I sighed. "I can't believe that I forgot she wanted those shawls," I told Alex.

He patted my arm. "Give yourself a break. You've been under enormous stress and have a lot of other things on your mind. Annie can still have the jewelry. She'll get over this."

I turned back to my spaghetti sauce. "I hope."

But she was still not over it by dinnertime. "I'm not hungry," she said when I came to knock on her door to tell her we were ready to eat.

"Honey, I'm sorry about the shawls. Even if you're not very hungry, come sit with us. I haven't seen you in days."

She refused to look at me. "No thanks, I'd rather stay in my room."

"Fine." Even before I closed her door the volume of the rock music she'd been listening to escalated dramatically: Merry Christmas from Grandma.

Dinner was subdued. Neither Alex nor Will said anything when I explained that Annie wouldn't be joining us.

After dinner Will wanted to go to a bookstore to buy a computer magazine. Alex and I took him and afterward the three of us drove around looking at Christmas decorations. I'd always loved our family drives to find the best Christmas decorations, but tonight seeing the bright, multicolored lights and remembering how much I used to savor this family ritual only made me feel sad.

When we got back I decided to try to talk to Annie again. Yes, she'd acted like a brat, but I was at fault too. I headed for her bedroom.

Annie's door was still closed, but I could hear her talking to someone. She must have taken the portable phone into her room to talk to a friend. I was about to knock when Annie's voice grew louder.

"She was jealous of Grandma," my daughter was saying. "That's what the problem was. Here Grandma was, this famous, best-selling novelist, and nobody ever heard of Mom except a few college students. I mean she has a Ph.D., but she makes almost no money. And her mother was rich and in *People* magazine and had thousands—millions—of people who loved her books. Mom always hated it when people used to say how great it must be to be Katherine March's daughter."

Lowering the hand I was about to knock with, I took a deep breath. How many hundreds of hours, I reminded myself, had I, as a teenager, spent on the phone complaining to my friends about *my* mother? I was hurt by Annie's assessment of me, but it wasn't as if she hadn't said basically the same things to my face.

Annie had stopped talking, but then, as I turned to walk away, I heard her say, "Yes, Mrs. Lang, I'll tell her."

Mrs. Lang? Suzanne Lang? Could my daughter possibly be saying those terrible things to the crazy woman who was writing a lurid book about my mother?

I hurried to the bathroom where, sitting on the toilet seat with the tap water running, I burst into tears. Afterward I took a shower, letting the hot water rain down on me like a benediction. By the time I got out my skin looked shriveled, but I was feeling a little better.

I padded to the kitchen in my bathrobe to make myself a cup of tea. Annie was sitting at the table eating a sandwich. Apparently she'd regained her appetite.

"Did I get any phone calls while we were out?" I asked her in a carefully neutral voice.

I thought she looked surprised, but when she answered her voice was flat, betraying no emotion. "Yeah, you got a call from Suzanne Lang, that writer who knew Grandma. She wants you to call her. I wrote down the number."

I hadn't returned any of Suzanne's calls to my mother's house. She'd left repeated messages on the answering tape saying she wanted to set up a time for our interview. Since I clearly didn't want to talk to her, had Suzanne "interviewed" my daughter instead?

I turned to Annie. "Is that all she said?"

"That's the gist of it," Annie said. When she looked up from her sandwich her eyes were filled with hostility.

CHAPTER ELEVEN

Just like old times—except different, I thought on New Year's Eve as Alex and I drove to the house of our friends Lisa and Sean Adams.

The four of us had spent the previous New Year's Eve together too, and I suspected that Lisa, my good friend and teaching colleague in the University of Houston Criminal Justice Department, had suggested this outing in hopes of encouraging a reconciliation. "The two of you are too good together to break up over a moronic one-night stand, Molly," she'd said with typical bluntness. "You have to at least make an effort to work things out with Alex."

But right now I was having second thoughts about the wisdom of this dinner. While it would be fun to go out with Lisa and Sean, the amount of time that Alex and I were spending together seemed to be confusing our kids. Our trial separation was almost no separation at all.

Will and Annie had both been visibly upset when Alex, after being at our house since Christmas, moved back to his garage apartment when I returned from Austin. And I was the one the kids blamed for Alex's exile: "Hey, I thought you let Dad move back, that everything was back to normal, and now you make him leave again?"

What I'd seen as flexibility—and, to be fair, also Alex's generosity in helping me out after Mother's death—was coming across to everyone concerned as an on-again-off-again separation instigated by a wronged wife who didn't really know what she wanted. I probably should have turned down Lisa's invitation and spent New Year's Eve alone with a good book.

Still I could feel my dour mood improve as we pulled into the driveway of Lisa's lovely two-story colonial in West University Place. Tomorrow, in the new year, I could sort out my feelings about my marriage. Tonight I'd try to just have a good time.

"Great vehicle," Sean said as he and Lisa got into the back seat of our new Explorer. "My mother, by the way, gave me an ugly plaid bathrobe for Christmas."

Alex chuckled, but I didn't. Lately nothing seemed very funny.

As we drove to the restaurant Lisa leaned forward to talk to me. She was a tall, enviably skinny woman with straight, chin-length blond hair and large, appraising eyes that missed nothing. Lisa had worked as a model to put herself through grad school, but I liked her anyway. "Is Annie still mad about you giving away your mother's shawls?"

"I phoned one of Mother's friends in Austin, and Helen rushed over to Goodwill this morning. Thank God she was able to find two of the shawls. She even went to Mother's house and got some of the jewelry that Annie wanted, and mailed everything to us."

"That's great. So has Annie forgiven you?"

I sighed. "Sort of. At least she was happy she was getting the shawls and the jewelry."

Alex pulled into the crowded parking lot of a new restaurant Sean had read about.

"You did make reservations, didn't you?" Lisa asked her husband.

"A week ago."

I turned around to see Lisa lean over to kiss him. "Oh, you're so anal," she teased.

Sean chuckled, then leaned in to nuzzle his wife's neck. I jerked forward in my seat, not wanting to watch or to remember when Alex and I also had been affectionate with each other.

The restaurant was wood-paneled and dimly lit, divided into several small dining rooms. After the waiter took our orders and Sean and Alex were busy talking to each other, Lisa said, "You never told me about your trip to Austin. Was it productive?"

"Oh, I got some things taken care of, but there's still a lot to do." Another day I'd tell her the longer version of the days I'd spent at Mother's house.

"Did you ever hear anything more from that strange writer who talked to you at your mother's funeral?"

"As a matter of fact she showed up at Mother's house while I was there." I told her about Suzanne's visit to pick up her thesis and her announcement that she was writing a biography of Mother.

"A scholarly book analyzing your mother's novels?" Sean asked.

"That's not what Suzanne has in mind. She wants to write a sleazy profile that digs up all the gossip she can find. I'm just hoping no one will publish it."

"Sleazy gossip?" Lisa asked. "I always thought your mother spent all her time writing."

"She did," Alex said, "but a lot of the gossip is going to come from the novel Katherine was working on when she died. Molly brought the manuscript from Austin, and I just finished reading it. Suzanne would have a field day with that book. It seems to be autobiographical with a lot of parallels to Katherine's own family, except in the novel Katherine's mother kills Katherine's father."

Sean whistled and looked at me. "How in fact did your grandfather die?"

"A heart attack right after his fiftieth birthday party—just like the father in the book seemed to. And no," I added before he could ask, "there's no evidence that he was murdered."

"But you're afraid this Suzanne will speculate that the novel was true?" Sean asked.

I took a large gulp of my wine. "It's not just that. I—I think she may have killed my mother."

The shocked silence at the table made me wish fervently that I'd kept my suspicions to myself. Talk about squelching a party!

Sean's fork, full of pasta and Italian sausage, stopped in mid-air. "Suzanne killed your mother so that she could write her biography?" he asked, his voice incredulous.

I shook my head. "It's just a theory, Sean. I have no proof. Let's talk about something else. You haven't told us about your trip to Cancun."

"Later." He smiled at me. "I'm a research scientist, Molly. I love considering hypotheses. Tell me yours."

"I want to hear too," Lisa said.

I took a deep breath, marshaling my arguments. "Okay, Suzanne apparently was stalking my mother. She was a high-strung, unpublished writer, and here was Mother, a successful novelist, a woman who had everything Suzanne wanted. She seemed to have this fantasy that Mother could wave her magic wand and make her a successful writer too. When that didn't happen, Suzanne turned on her. Stalkers do that: 'I love you, I hate you, it's all your fault that my life is so miserable.' The stalker who was shot trying to break into Madonna's house was yelling that he wanted to 'marry the bitch or slit her throat.' "

"But you don't know that Suzanne isn't anything more than a desperate wannabe writer who's simply jumping at the chance to turn her master's thesis into a biography," Alex said. "Just because she's obnoxious and overly aggressive doesn't mean she's a killer."

"That's exactly what I thought. But then I started thinking

about how Mother's missing manuscript miraculously reappeared the next day, right after I spent hours away from the house. And how Mother's house key and the syringe suddenly turned up after I left Suzanne alone while I went upstairs to get her thesis. We checked that drawer, Alex, when we were looking for the syringe."

He nodded. "But there was a lot of stuff in the drawer. The syringe and the key could have been under all those papers and coupons."

I knew he had a point. It was only because I'd been hunting through all the papers for a pen that I'd found the syringe and keys.

"It's also quite possible that Suzanne did steal the manuscript but had nothing to do with your mother's death," Sean said. "That makes more sense if Suzanne really was so obsessed with becoming a published writer."

"But stalkers aren't rational." Lisa jumped into the discussion. "That's the point. Mark David Chapman, the guy who killed John Lennon, worshipped Lennon. He collected all of Lennon's music, he had relationships with women of Asian descent, like Yoko Ono. From what I read, he killed Lennon because he wanted to be linked forever to his idol. And also because he was jealous of him."

Lisa turned to me. "I did a lecture on stalkers a few months ago. I remember reading about this man in L.A., Gavin de Becker, who developed a computer model which can evaluate how dangerous a stalker is to a celebrity. He said that rejection-based stalkers were the ones most likely to kill or harm a famous person. Their motivation was often revenge for what they perceived to be the celebrity's rejection of them. Suzanne might well have interpreted your mother's behavior toward her in that way."

"Exactly. Helen said Mother finally refused to talk to Suzanne because she realized how crazy Suzanne was."

"She was afraid of Suzanne?" When I nodded, Lisa added, "Did she notify the police?"

"Unfortunately, she didn't. She probably figured she could handle Suzanne and there was no reason to get the police involved."

"Too bad. It would be easier to build a case against her if there was some record of a previous threat."

I sighed. "Tell me about it."

"There's still the syringe," Alex said. "You said the police are testing it for traces of Stelazine. If they find it and if Suzanne's fingerprints are also on the syringe, wouldn't that be proof that she killed Katherine?"

Lisa and I looked at each other. We might have only academic knowledge of police work, but we knew that it was seldom that easy. If Suzanne hadn't thought of wiping every surface before she returned the syringe, if I hadn't destroyed her print when I pulled it from the drawer, maybe there might there be some useful forensic evidence.

"Only if we're very, very lucky," I said, stabbing my fork into my chicken Marsala. I had the unpleasant suspicion that would-be mystery writer Suzanne Lang had been very clever about covering her tracks.

After dinner we went back to Sean and Lisa's for dessert and champagne. At midnight we all kissed and wished each other "Happy New Year."

At 12:10 Alex and I left. It had been fun to get out, good to see Lisa and Sean, but watching our old friends tread so carefully through our marital minefield, trying so hard to be pleasant and avoid sensitive topics, made me feel sad.

We drove in silence for a few minutes, hearing New Year's firecrackers exploding somewhere nearby. When Alex pulled the Explorer into our driveway, he turned to me. "I can't go on like this, Molly."

All I could think was no, not now—not when I was half-drunk and the only thing I was sure I wanted was to crawl into bed and sleep for a very long time. "Alex, I'm exhausted, and this is too important to discuss when I'm so out of it."

"You don't have to discuss. You just have to listen, to understand what I'm feeling. I can't stay in this limbo much longer, waiting for you to decide what you want to do. I know you feel betrayed and angry, and I can only tell you again how sorry I am to have hurt you. I know I've said this before, but I don't think you believe me. I never loved her. I wanted to help her, be a friend when she was so upset by her divorce, but things just got out of hand. It had nothing—absolutely nothing—to do with my feelings for you."

I started to say something, but he resolutely kept talking, like an earnest schoolboy determined to finish his dreaded speech. "The only thing I can tell you now is what I want: I want to be married to you, Molly, I want to live with you and the kids, and I'll do whatever needs to be done to make that happen. If you think that counseling will help, maybe we should go back to that marriage counselor."

"You mean that you agree with Annie, that you've suffered enough, the Time Out is over, and now we should return to our old life?" I asked, suddenly not at all sleepy.

"No, I mean that now it's time for you to decide what you want," he said in that calm, reasonable voice that always drove me crazy when I wanted to fight. "And then you let me know."

He got out of the car and walked over to my side to open the door. It was less gallantry than an effort to extricate me, but I reminded myself that I was the one who'd wanted to postpone this argument for another day.

He followed me to the door, waited until I unlocked it. "Goodnight, Alex."

He leaned in and kissed me on the forehead. "Happy New Year, Molly. Call to tell me what you decide."

Chapter Twelve

I woke up early the next morning, feeling hungover and headachy. It was time, I decided as I massaged my temples, to get my life in order.

First I phoned Alex. I was nervous about what I had to tell him and was half relieved when he didn't answer. But I was only postponing the unpleasantness. I left a message on his answering machine asking him to call me.

Then I got out a yellow legal pad and wrote "Suzanne Lang— Things We Need To Know" at the top of the page. I'd start with Helen for dates and specific stalking incidents.

But when I phoned her, Helen said, "I'm not sure I'd characterize Suzanne's actions as stalking, Molly. I know I said that before, but now I think that was unfair. Suzanne was more of a pest than a threat."

"But didn't you say Mother was frightened of her?" I knew from the literature that a stalker's intense interest—which the victim correctly perceives as obsessive and dangerous—often looks innocent or even flattering to others.

"I don't know if Katherine was frightened, but she certainly was annoyed. Suzanne is a very insistent woman. When she told your mother that she wasn't doing enough to get Suzanne published, Katherine washed her hands of her."

"Do you know when that was?" I asked, making notes.

"September or October, I think. Suzanne kept phoning Katherine and writing her letters. Your mother stopped answering her phone, letting the answering machine take the messages. But then Suzanne confronted Katherine after some speech she gave at a writer's conference last November."

"What happened?" I asked, writing as fast as I could.

"Well, I'm not entirely sure. I think Suzanne came up to her after the speech and said Katherine was treating her very badly. Katherine said she was sorry Suzanne felt that way, but she was very involved in writing her new book now and didn't have time for anything else."

The classic brush-off, which, ironically, was also the truth. When Mother was involved in writing a book, she had no time for anything—or anyone—else. "Did she say how Suzanne reacted?"

"I don't think Katherine mentioned that."

I felt a sharp stab of disappointment.

"But Molly, why do you want to know all this now?"

I gave her a bare-bones account of my suspicions about Suzanne.

"I hope you're not jumping to conclusions. Just because you found the syringe after she was in the house doesn't mean Suzanne put it in the drawer. Anyone could have put it there, even Katherine. I found her body near the kitchen."

What she was saying was reasonable enough. But something else bothered me, some undercurrent in Helen's voice. "How come you've changed your mind about Suzanne?"

"I've met her now and talked to her about Katherine. And, well, she just doesn't seem like the dangerous, unstable woman I thought she was."

I couldn't believe it. "You're letting that woman interview you for her so-called book about Mother?"

"Yes." Helen had the grace to sound embarrassed. "I thought about it, Molly, and decided that if I wanted her to give a fair and accurate portrayal of Katherine in the book, I should talk to her. I wanted to tell Suzanne what a good friend Katherine was to me throughout the years."

"I doubt that it will make any difference what you tell her," I said angrily, "since the book will probably never be published."

"I think you might be wrong about that, dear. Your mother's agent, Mr. Pryor, has agreed to represent Suzanne, and he's quite optimistic about finding a publisher. Suzanne said she's writing a proposal for him now."

I stared at the phone. Sam Pryor was trying to get Suzanne's book published? The very same Sam Pryor who only last week was telling me how happy he was that I was my mother's literary executor? Was he happy because he figured I was so naive that I wouldn't mind that he was also hawking a sleazy "biography" about her?

"I've got to go now, Helen. I'll talk to you later."

The phone rang the minute I hung up. "Hello?"

"What's wrong?" Alex asked. "You sound upset."

"Helen has decided that Suzanne Lang was never a stalker, and she's letting Suzanne interview her for her book. And—get this—Sam Pryor is Suzanne's new literary agent."

Alex whistled. "Maybe Suzanne's book isn't as bad as you think."

"Or maybe the only thing Sam is concerned about is making money."

"That's a possibility too. Is that what you called to tell me?"

I took a deep breath. "I've been thinking about what you said last night, but I'm just not ready yet to make any decisions."

"What about trying marital counseling again? We really didn't give it a chance."

I thought of the terminally perky therapist who spent our one session urging Alex and me to "keep talking and negotiating."

"I don't want to do that. At least not now. I—I'm so confused, Alex. I feel as if I can't think straight. The only thing I seem to be able to concentrate on is Mother's death—wanting to find out what happened, who killed her."

"I can understand that. But don't you think you could find out with me living in the house? I could help you."

"No, I don't think so. Your moving back would only confuse the kids more than we have already, particularly if I'm not sure what I want."

"You mean in case you decide that you want to throw me out again?"

I didn't blame him for being hurt and angry. "Alex, you've been so helpful to me after Mother died, and I truly appreciate it. I don't know how I would have gotten through it without you."

"But this appreciation doesn't extend to wanting to live with me."

"I don't know!" I said, feeling on the verge of tears. "All I'm trying to say is when I asked you to move out I wanted to have some time on my own to think things through. But Mother's death kind of derailed that plan. I feel as if I have to find out what happened to her—to get some kind of closure on that—before I can go back to focusing on us."

I waited for him to argue or tell me how unfair I was being, but he didn't say anything. "I'm sorry," I said. "Really sorry. Are you—are you okay with that?"

"I don't see that I have a lot of choice in the matter, do I?" he said, sounding more resigned than bitter. "And Molly?"

"Yes?"

"Do what you have to do. I'll be here."

I hung up the phone, feeling like a world-class bitch. How could I be so selfish and high-handed and well, totally unreasonable? All of the labels that Alex hadn't used I now stuck on myself. Still, everything I'd told him was the absolute truth. I needed to find out who killed Mother before I could resume any kind of normal life.

Grimly I returned to my research, listing questions I wanted answered. On the chance that Mrs. Benjamin had returned from the visit with her daughter, I phoned her in Austin. No one, unfortunately, answered.

Will arrived, carrying his sleeping bag. I kissed his pale, tired-looking face. "Hey, honey, Happy New Year. Did you have a good sleepover?"

"Yeah, we didn't go to sleep until two this morning. I want to go to bed." He headed for his room.

Annie appeared a few minutes later, looking both more alert and less friendly than her brother. Her night had been fine, she said. She wasn't hungry and she was going to her room to get ready for school. I did remember that it started tomorrow, didn't I?

I sighed. When the phone rang again, I answered it, assuming the call would be for Annie. Instead I heard Lisa's voice. "So what's going on?"

I knew she meant what was happening between Alex and me, but I wasn't going there. I said that Alex and I had had a nice time last night. Then I told her about my phone conversation with Helen.

Lisa moaned. "Sometimes it seems as if the public expects them to wear a sign saying, Hey, I'm A Stalker. But it is a surprise that Helen let Suzanne interview her."

"And now she thinks Suzanne is just a bit pushy! Even before I thought she'd killed Mother, I found Suzanne threatening. She radiates menace! I can't believe any friend of Mother's would let Suzanne interview her."

A small noise from behind me made me swivel around. Annie, white-faced, was standing behind me. I told Lisa I'd call her back then turned my attention to my daughter. How much had she heard? "You need something, honey?"

"Do you really think Suzanne Lang killed Grandma?"

How could she—my child who never seemed to hear me when I was talking directly to her—have overheard my phone conversation from another room? "I don't know," I said, "but I think it's possible."

"Somebody killed Grandma?" Will asked, coming out of his room.

Oh, God.

"But she told me that she was a good friend of Grandma's," Annie said.

"You talked to her?" Will asked his sister. "When?"

"She phoned the night Mom came back from Austin and you all went out. When I told her Mom wasn't home, she said she'd just as soon talk to me anyway. She was writing a book about Grandma and she was interested in what I had to say." Annie looked as if she was about to cry.

I leaned forward to pat her hand. "It's okay that you talked to her, honey. You didn't know who she was." And you were too busy being angry with your mother to give much thought to who you were confiding in.

Annie pulled her hand away. "It's okay that I talked to my grandmother's murderer?"

I tried very hard to sound like the resident adult. "We don't know that she's a murderer. Suzanne's behavior is just suspicious. The police are investigating things."

Annie did not look appeased. "So why do you think she did it?"

I took a deep breath, wishing that Alex, the calm, patient parent who spent all day with volatile adolescents, were here. "From what I understand, Suzanne was angry with Grandma for not helping her more with her writing career. But there's no proof yet that she did anything."

"She was that crazy stalker Aunt Helen was telling us about?"

Will asked excitedly.

Annie, wild-eyed, looked at him, then burst into tears.

Eventually I managed to get everyone calmed down. Annie, her eyes red and swollen, drove with me to pick up a pizza, while Will took a nap at home.

"Did this detective you talked to believe you when you told him about Mrs. Lang?" Annie asked.

I hesitated. "It's too early to say. If the evidence supports my theory, he'll believe me."

"What kind of evidence?"

"Fingerprints on the syringe or a prescription of Stelazine issued to Suzanne. Or maybe a neighbor who saw her go in or out of Grandma's house."

Annie nodded, her face grave. "And if they don't find evidence like that, Suzanne Lang will get away with it."

Which was exactly what I was afraid of.

The next morning, the first day back to school, my twelve-year-old daughter emerged from her bedroom wearing my mother's large gold hoop earrings.

I tried not to stare. The earrings had looked good on Mother, a tall woman, with a long, sharp-planed face; she'd looked bohemian in her dramatic jewelry and her flowing, gypsy skirts. But Annie was six inches shorter than her grandmother, small-boned with a little, heart-shaped face that made her appear younger than her age. I thought—but did not say—that the big earrings made her look like a child playing dress-up with her mother's jewelry.

I kissed my children goodbye and assured them I would not have too good a time today or in the remaining week before I had to go back to my classes.

Usually I would have savored my time alone. There were very

few days when I had the whole house to myself. But today I just felt edgy.

I finished my coffee then started collecting the dirty laundry. I walked into Annie's bedroom and gasped.

Overnight Annie had constructed a shrine to my mother. I moved closer to inspect it. My daughter had replaced the photos of her friends and the certificate she got for being the best sixth grade English student with photos of my mother and her various writing awards. There was a nice snapshot of Mother, Annie, Will, and me in front of our Christmas tree two years ago and a photo of Mother proudly holding baby Annie, her first grandchild. Next came the professional accolades: Mother's two Edgars and a framed copy of the first New York Times' bestseller list to include a Katherine March novel, which Annie must have retrieved from the boxes I brought back from Austin.

I took a deep breath. Was it so unusual for a child to want to cherish the memory of her beloved grandmother? Admittedly, all of this—the display of awards and photos, wearing her grandmother's jewelry—seemed a bit extreme. But adolescents were, by nature, extreme creatures. This was—I hoped—just Annie's way to grieve.

Resolutely I turned on the washer and started the top task on my to-do list. By noon I'd written all the thank-you notes for flowers or charitable contributions made in Mother's name, sent checks for her bills, and finished a syllabus for a new course I would be teaching this semester. And I still felt edgy.

I made myself a peanut butter-and-banana sandwich and considered how I wanted to spend the afternoon. What I really wanted to do was phone Detective Martinez and find out if he'd talked to Suzanne Lang or if, by some miracle, the lab tests had come in on the syringe. But I settled for phoning Mrs. Benjamin again. After ten rings I hung up.

I just needed to wait, to be patient: two things I had never been good at. But in the meantime I felt ready to scream with frustration. The sound of the mail dropping through the door slot made me jump.

What I needed to do was distract myself: go take a walk, call Lisa, or run some errands. I scanned the mail: three bills, a *Newsweek*, and two letters addressed to me. One was a bulky-looking letter from Aunt Charlotte. The second, from a town I didn't recognize in New York, had originally been sent to me at Mother's address in Austin; the post office had forwarded it here.

I ripped open the second envelope and pulled out a piece of paper covered with rather shaky handwriting.

Dear Molly,

You don't know me, but many years ago I was your mother's nanny. Katherine came to visit me this summer and told me all about you. How proud she was of you and of your precious Annie and Will!

I was saddened to read of your mother's death. Please accept my deepest condolences. Your mother was a wonderful woman.

There is something that it is of paramount importance I must tell you. Because I'm not sure if this letter will reach you I don't want to write it here. Please contact me as soon as you receive this. This matter is urgent.

Sincerely,
Margaret O'Ryan

Margaret O'Ryan, the woman who'd given Mother the copy of *Little Woman* on her eighth birthday! What matter of such urgency could this woman want to tell me? Curious, I phoned the number at the bottom of the letter. I let the phone ring a dozen times, but no one answered. Nor did any answering machine click on. Today certainly was not my day for solving mysteries over the phone.

Feeling disappointed, I opened the letter from my aunt. Her note was short, handwritten on engraved stationery. She was sending an open-ended roundtrip plane ticket to New York City in hopes of persuading me to come soon to visit. "Mother seems to be getting more frail every day," she wrote. "Please come to see her before it's too late."

I reread the two letters, the two appeals for my immediate presence in New York. Why not? I asked myself. While I was in New York visiting my aunt and grandmother, I could meet my mother's old nanny. I could also talk with Sam Pryor about Mother's novel and Suzanne Lang's proposed biography. What better distractions could I ask for?

CHAPTER THIRTEEN

Looking chic in a black cashmere skirt and sweater, Aunt Charlotte was waiting for me when I got off the plane. "I'm so glad you've come, Molly." She leaned down to kiss my cheek, enveloping me in a cloud of Joy.

"Me too," I said, surprised at how glad I felt.

After we picked up my suitcases she led me to her black Mercedes convertible. "So how are you holding up?" she asked me in that soft, intimate alto voice.

"As well as can be expected, I suppose." Never mind that I was having trouble sleeping, having problems concentrating, and much of the time felt so anxious I wanted to crawl out of my skin.

"It's very difficult when your mother dies," Charlotte said. "Even tougher when she kills herself. My therapist says there's all these layers of guilt and anger when there's a suicide in the family. And if I'm reacting so strongly to Katherine's death—a sister I barely saw for forty years—I can imagine how dreadful you must feel."

"Yes," I admitted, "I feel pretty awful: tired all the time and then suddenly crying for no reason at all." I looked at her. "But I don't think Mother killed herself."

"What do you mean?"

I sighed. "I don't have proof of anything. It's just that it seemed so unlike Mother—no goodbyes, no explanation, no canceling of the speeches she was scheduled to give." I didn't want to mention my suspicions about Suzanne Lang until I learned what Detective Martinez had uncovered.

"I thought that too at first," Charlotte said. "It seemed so incomprehensible that Katherine would kill herself. But when you told me she'd been diagnosed with cancer, that at least was an explanation. As for not saying goodbye, Katherine always had trouble expressing emotion. Perhaps she just couldn't bear to face you."

I swallowed hard. But Mother had said a goodbye of sorts in her Christmas letters to me and my family and to Helen. She'd done it her way, in writing, but she had, in fact, left a final message for each of us.

Charlotte leaned over to pat my hand. "My therapist suggested that I attend a grief support group for people with a family member who died recently. You might want to consider that too. Dr. Daniels said many people find it enormously helpful."

I waited until she backed out of the parking space. "You went into therapy because of Mother's death?" I asked, wondering if it was too personal a question. My own mother, if she had ever allowed herself to feel vulnerable enough to step into a psychotherapist's office, would probably not have admitted the fact under torture.

Charlotte smiled grimly. "No, I went into therapy shortly before my husband died—when I realized that Edward was having an affair with a twenty-four-year-old who was a dead ringer for me thirty years ago. I was having problems dealing with that. And then when Edward died suddenly, I was astonished at how grief-stricken and depressed I felt. So you see," she said, her voice sardonic, "I have an assortment of issues to work on."

I didn't know what to say. My aunt had probably told me more personal information in two minutes than my mother had told me in a lifetime.

We drove in silence while Charlotte zoomed in and out of traffic like a race car driver. "Why don't you just tell me what you're thinking," she finally said.

"I'm thinking that I can't imagine you being my mother's sister. The two of you are so different. Mother was so close-mouthed about her personal life—her childhood, her marriage, her feelings about almost everything except her career. And she always told me, 'One does not wash the dirty linen in public.'"

"Oh, I heard that line too," Charlotte said. "It was probably one of the few pieces of advice Katherine ever took from Mother. I resisted that message, at first from adolescent rebellion and then later because I decided that it kept other people from knowing me." She glanced sideways at me. "And I'm not, by the way, this revealing to everyone—only to people who I like and sense I can trust."

"Thank you." My smile faded as Charlotte abruptly switched lanes, missing a huge moving van by what looked like inches.

"Don't worry," she said. "I never have accidents."

I wasn't reassured. "Uh, how is your mother?"

"She has good days and bad. On the good ones she seems like her old self. But on the bad days I'm not even sure that she knows who I am. I thought we'd go visit her now, if you're not too tired."

"Oh, yes, I'd like to see her." I just hoped that today was one of Grandmother's good days. "By the way, I meant to tell you. Just before I left I got a condolence note from Margaret O'Ryan, Mother's old nanny."

Charlotte looked surprised. "Miss O'Ryan? I haven't heard from her in years. That was sweet of her to write you. She and Katherine were always close."

"Yes, she mentioned that Mother had visited her when she was here last summer."

"Did she tell you that she was the one who encouraged Katherine to become a writer?"

I shook my head. "It was a very short note. She didn't say much of anything except to please contact her."

"Did you?"

"I phoned, but no one answered."

"Well try again while you're here. I'd be interested to hear how she's doing. Miss O'Ryan must be almost eighty by now, a little younger than Mother."

Charlotte exited the freeway. "It might be better if you don't mention Miss O'Ryan to Mother. She always thought that Father's and Miss O'Ryan's long discussions of books in the library involved more than the sharing of ideas."

We reached a tree-lined road that led to a huge stone mansion. "That's the nursing home," Charlotte said.

"It looks as if it was once a private home."

She nodded. "It was built in the early 1900s. The Vanderbolten family lived there for years until the later generation decided it was too expensive to maintain. The nursing home added the newer building in the back, but Mother insisted on being in the original home. I think she likes to pretend this was the lifestyle to which she'd always been accustomed. Except she, of course, wouldn't have been so tacky as to sell the family homestead to a nursing home conglomerate."

She parked in a gravel lot and we walked inside. A large scarlet and navy oriental rug covered the gleaming wood hallway which led to a dramatic curving staircase.

A young, apple-cheeked nurse approached us. Charlotte introduced us, then asked the woman how my grandmother was doing today.

"Pretty well. Mrs. March was complaining about her arthritis this morning, but aside from that, she seemed fine." The nurse smiled at me. "She was telling me about your visit. She's waiting for you in her room."

I followed Charlotte, remembering the autocratic woman I'd met only once, when I was ten and my mother took me to her grandmother's funeral. The old lady who sat in a chintz chair near the window had the same ramrod-straight posture as the impeccably groomed woman I recalled, but she was smaller, almost skeletal looking, in her blue sweater set and tan wool skirt, her face more wrinkled, her blond hair now white. But the eyes, blue and fierce, were the same.

She turned them on me, assessing me. She offered a wrinkled hand, which sported a large diamond ring. "You do not look at all like your mother."

"No, everyone says I look more like my father."

"I never met him." She motioned for me to sit down on a chintz loveseat across from her.

She'd never even met her own son-in-law? I sat down, thinking, How Mother must have hated her!

My grandmother turned her cheek for Charlotte to kiss. "That length hair is flattering on you, Charlotte, but you must tell your stylist to darken your color a bit."

Charlotte, to her credit, looked only amused. "I heard your arthritis was bothering you this morning."

"It always bothers me. I told the kitchen I'd like tea served when you arrived. Would you tell them to bring it?"

"Certainly." As Charlotte walked by she winked at me. "I'll be right back."

My grandmother turned her attention back to me. "I understand that you're married to a teacher and that you have a son and daughter."

"Yes, Annie is twelve and Will is ten."

"And you are a college teacher?"

"Yes, I teach criminology."

"So you're interested in crime, like your mother." Her thin lips pursed in distaste.

"We approach it in different ways. I think most people would find Mother's mystery novels a lot more interesting than my journal articles."

"I never liked Katherine's books," the old lady announced in a too-loud voice.

"Which books did you read?"

"I forget. I don't read much. My husband used to say I had an extremely short attention span. He, of course, was an avid reader. He was a book publisher, you know."

I nodded. "Was Mother a lot like him?"

"Oh, yes, both of them were intellectuals, talking all the time about books. They both hated parties. Terrible introverts, no fun at all, though Warren could be quite charming, particularly to pretty young women."

I wondered if Margaret O'Ryan had been one of the pretty young women my grandfather had charmed. Had flirtation really been the basis of their conversations in the family library? Or had bookish, introverted Warren just wanted to get away from an overbearing wife who couldn't abide books?

A heavy woman in a white uniform arrived then, pushing a cart containing a tea pot and a platter of cookies.

"Set up over here, Mary," my grandmother ordered. She turned to me. "I had hoped to offer you something more elaborate, but this apparently was the best the kitchen could manage at short notice."

"I ate on the plane, but this looks wonderful."

"Yes, it does look wonderful," Charlotte said from the doorway. "Thank you, Mary, for all the extra effort."

My grandmother sent her daughter a peevish look. "How is your son handling his new job?" she asked as Charlotte poured the tea. "Is he working in the business office?"

"No, Andrew is working in the advertising department."

"Advertising? Any young man who wants to make his mark

should be working on the business side. I'd think Andrew would have learned that much from his father's example."

"His father's example is seldom far from his mind, Mother." Charlotte sounded bored by the topic.

Grandmother raised her eyebrows. "One would never guess that by observing his behavior. Don't make excuses for the boy, Charlotte. Too many spineless people these days choose to view themselves as helpless victims."

Charlotte turned her intensely blue eyes on her mother. For a second, watching those flashing eyes, I saw the resemblance between the two of them. When she spoke, Charlotte's voice was hard. "We all need to have our behavior excused sometimes, Mother. Every one of us."

To my astonishment, splotches of red spread across my grandmother's wrinkled cheeks.

Charlotte smoothed things over so quickly that I wondered if I had imagined my grandmother's embarrassment. Smiling, my aunt turned to me and started describing her mother's activities at the nursing home.

Grandmother rejoined the conversation a few minutes later. Her hands shaking a bit, she said to me, "I saw Katherine only a few days ago. She was asking me too many questions as usual, wanting to see my old scrapbooks. I always told that girl that asking so many questions was going to get her into trouble some day. And I was right."

"What—what do you mean?" I glanced questioningly at my aunt. Up until this minute Grandmother had seemed perfectly rational.

"Well, she's not around now, is she?" my grandmother asked, her voice suddenly loud.

Charlotte touched my shoulder. "I think it's time to go. I'm afraid we're wearing you out, Mother."

She stood up and kissed the old lady's cheek, and I told her goodbye.

"When will you be back?" Grandmother asked.

"Soon," Charlotte said. "But we need to go now."

"You know she doesn't look at all like Katherine," the old lady proclaimed as we walked out the door.

"I'm sorry you had to go through that," Charlotte said as we walked down the hall. "But that's the way she is—fine one minute and then suddenly she's totally confused."

In the hallway she stopped to talk to the nurse we'd spoken to earlier. "Mother is getting agitated again," I heard her say. "Maybe you should go look in on her."

Chapter Fourteen

My aunt and I arrived at Margaret O'Ryan's small frame house at ten the next morning. When Aunt Charlotte heard that I was planning to take the train to White Plains, she'd insisted on driving me. "It will be faster for you and I'd love to see Miss O'Ryan."

The woman who opened the door seemed surprised to see us. "Yes?" she asked, looking from me to Charlotte with a confused expression on her face. She was a tall woman with sharp features, no makeup, and bushy gray hair that looked as if she'd recently been running her fingers through it.

I wondered if we'd come to the wrong house. "We're here to see Margaret O'Ryan," I said. "She's expecting us." Or at least after our phone conversation last night, she was expecting me.

She nodded, staring at us with vacant brown eyes.

"Margaret," a female voice behind her said, "is there someone at the door?" Another tall woman, but younger and heavier, appeared at the doorway. "May I help you?"

This time Aunt Charlotte explained. "We've come to visit Miss O'Ryan. I'm Charlotte Todd. Miss O'Ryan was once the nanny for my sister Katherine and me. And this is Katherine's daughter, Molly Patterson."

I smiled hesitantly at the bushy-haired woman who the second woman had called Margaret.

She stared at me. "Katherine," she muttered under her breath.

"Yes, Margaret, this is Molly Patterson, Katherine's daughter," the second woman said slowly and loudly. "Remember? You told me she was coming to visit today."

Was Margaret hard of hearing? But surely when I talked to her on the phone she hadn't seemed to have any trouble understanding me.

"Of course." Margaret O'Ryan's face turned scarlet. "Forgive me. My memory has been playing nasty tricks on me lately. Won't you come inside?"

We followed her into a tiny living room. The middle of the room held two straight-backed wooden chairs facing a somewhat faded tan couch flanked by two tables with reading lamps. Bookcases lined the walls, all of them crammed with books.

The younger woman introduced herself—"I'm Margaret's sister, Mary Casey"—and motioned for us to sit on the couch. She and Margaret sat on the wooden chairs.

"Margaret was very eager to meet you," Mary said to me with a big smile. "Did you have a good trip from Texas?"

"Yes, a fine flight. I just arrived yesterday."

"How long will you stay?" she asked.

"I'm leaving the day after tomorrow."

"Unless I can persuade her to stay longer," Charlotte interjected with a smile.

"But I'm sure you must want to get back to your children," Margaret said, speaking in a strong voice quite different from the hesitant way she'd spoken at the door.

"Yes." I smiled at her, relieved that she now sounded like the woman I'd talked to on the phone. "They're not really at an age where they need me much anymore, but I like to keep an eye on them."

"That's wise. From my experience teenagers often require more supervision than younger children."

Charlotte chuckled. "That's also been my experience. And I suspect that some of Miss O'Ryan's wisdom about adolescent mischief was acquired from supervising me."

"Oh, how long were you Mother's and Aunt Charlotte's nanny?" I asked Miss O'Ryan. I'd assumed she had been with them when the sisters were very young.

I could see her hesitate, then glance at her sister.

"Margaret worked for the Marches for almost eleven years, I think," Mary said.

"She started out as a nanny for Katherine and me when we were young," Charlotte told me. "But in the later years she was more of a tutor for us, though Katherine didn't really need tutoring."

Miss O'Ryan nodded.

"I drove you wild with my lack of math aptitude," Charlotte said to her. "Unfortunately, my son seems to have inherited my math gene."

Miss O'Ryan smiled sweetly at Charlotte. "Now who are you, dear?"

Charlotte told her in a gentle voice.

"I see," Miss O'Ryan said, nodding.

Mary stood up. "Why don't you come with me, Molly? I'd like to show you the photos Margaret pulled out for you."

I followed her to a wood-paneled kitchen, leaving Charlotte to chat with Miss O'Ryan about the unseasonably warm weather.

"I'm so sorry you came all the way out here," Mary said in a low voice. "Margaret has early-stage Alzheimer's disease. She's taking some drugs for it, but I can't see that they're helping much."

"But yesterday when I talked to her on the phone she seemed fine."

Mary nodded. "Sometimes she almost seems like her old self, but on the bad days, like today, she's very confused. She didn't even remember you were coming."

"Mary," Miss O'Ryan's voice called from the living room, "did you find the pictures?"

"Yes, dear, I'm just showing them to Molly." She picked up a large envelope. "These are photos of your mother that Margaret thought you'd like. She intended to tell you some stories too, but I don't think that's possible today."

"She wrote me that she had something very important to tell me," I said. "I think it was something about my mother. Do you know what it could be?"

Mary shook her head. "All she said was that she wanted to tell you about your mother's early life and give you these photos. Maybe that's what she thought was important. Margaret was always very fond of Katherine. And so proud that she turned into such a fine writer."

"Mary," her sister called again.

"We're coming, dear." Mary handed me the photos. "She gets upset sometimes when she doesn't know where I am."

We returned to the living room. "Thank you so much for the photos," I told Miss O'Ryan. "I don't have any others from Mother's childhood."

Margaret stared at the envelope, then turned to her sister. "Are they going now?"

Mary blushed and started to say something, but Charlotte quickly interjected, "Yes, I think we should be leaving. Don't you think so, Molly?"

Nodding, I stood. "It was kind of you to see us. And thanks again for the pictures."

Mary stood when we did and walked us to the door. Margaret O'Ryan lingered in the living room while her sister talked to Charlotte at the door.

I turned to say goodbye to her, but to my surprise, she motioned for me to come closer. I walked back.

She gripped my arm, the bony hand tight on my wrist. "Call

me," she whispered, "when *she* isn't around."

At that moment the two women at the doorway turned to look at us.

"I will," I promised. Her hand dropped from my arm.

I walked to the door, wondering which of the two women waiting there was the "she" who Margaret O'Ryan didn't want to overhear our conversation.

"I wish you could have met Miss O'Ryan when she was younger," Aunt Charlotte said as we drove back to Manhattan. "She was such a bright woman. Her family couldn't afford college so she educated herself." Charlotte shook her head. "Sometimes the diseases associated with aging seem like a cruel joke, taking away the things we most value about ourselves."

"Yes," I said, remembering Margaret O'Ryan's red face when she said, "Forgive me, my memory has been playing nasty tricks on me lately." Was her memory tricking her into thinking that another woman—Mary or Charlotte—must not overhear whatever she wanted to tell me? Had her impaired mind perhaps made her view her sister as her prison guard? Or could it be that plump, smiling Mary actually was not so friendly when guests weren't around?

Of course it was also possible that Miss O'Ryan had been referring to Charlotte: "Call me when *she* isn't around." Charlotte, after all, had told me on the drive over that the two of them had not gotten along that well. Didn't people with memory impairments often remember the past more distinctly than recent events?

I wondered what kind of visit my mother had had the previous summer with her old nanny. Had that day been one of Miss O'Ryan's good days? "Mother didn't tell you that Miss O'Ryan had Alzheimer's?" I asked my aunt.

Charlotte shook her head. "She didn't mention Miss O'Ryan

at all that I can remember. Katherine did talk quite a bit about the past. I think she was trying to get the details right for her book: what kind of clothes people used to wear, the slang from our teenage years, that kind of thing." She glanced at me. "Of course she never told me that she was researching a book. She didn't tell me much of anything about herself."

"She didn't tell me either, if that makes you feel any better," I said.

"Katherine always was secretive, even as a girl. But Father was like that too. He was kind enough, but also very remote. I wish you'd known my father, Molly. Katherine was so much like him. They both loved to talk about books and hated to discuss their feelings. Both of them were exceptionally curious about people, about what makes them tick, but also had an equally intense aversion to getting too close to any one of them."

I pulled out a photograph from the envelope the nanny had given me. Many of the pictures she'd sent were Mother's school photos from various years. They showed a dark-haired, serious girl with large, sad eyes. I held the only photo in which Mother had actually looked happy. She and Charlotte stood with a tall, dark-haired man. While Charlotte, a beautiful child of about eight, grinned at the camera, Mother gazed adoringly at the man who smiled back at her with open affection.

I held the photo so Charlotte could see it. "This is your father, isn't it?"

She nodded. "They even look alike, don't they? You can see from the picture how Katherine felt about him. I always thought Father was the only person in our family who Katherine really connected with, and his death was the biggest tragedy of her life."

"Maybe that's why she wrote her last book about him."

Charlotte looked at me. "I think it's high time that I read this book. I want to decide for myself if Katherine was writing about our family."

CHAPTER FIFTEEN

An hour later I left my aunt stretched out on her sofa reading a copy of Mother's manuscript while I took a taxi to my lunch with literary agent Sam Pryor.

Sam had picked the Tavern on the Green for our meeting. In a different mood I would have enjoyed its over-the-top ambiance, a restaurant that looked like a fairy-tale Victorian cottage, crammed with brass, mirrors, glass and chandeliers.

He was already there, a thin, gray-haired man with slightly stooped posture wearing an expensive-looking dark-gray suit. He greeted me warmly.

"I think frequently about your mother, Molly," he said after a waiter took our order. "Katherine was one of my first clients. She was a college librarian when I sold her first novel. We were together for a long time."

"Yes, you were," I said, wondering why, after such a long association, my mother had considered getting a new agent. Though perhaps she'd just told Brenda that after some minor argument with Sam she'd forgotten about by the next day.

"Katherine was the most disciplined and professional writer I've ever met. No matter what happened in her life she kept writing. And writing damn well."

I raised an eyebrow. "You've read all of *The Summer That Changed Everything*?"

He nodded. "It's different from her other novels, but I found it compelling, a lyrical book."

"You didn't find the ending rather weak?"

Sam's watery gray eyes studied me. "It didn't bother me, but Brenda Stein found the last section rough. I suspect that Katherine was intending to rewrite it before she"—he coughed—"died."

Before she killed herself, he'd started to say. But Katherine March, the consummate professional who never let her life interfere with her writing, certainly would have waited to commit suicide until after she'd finished her revisions. The fact that she had left behind only a rough draft of what she knew would be her last book was still more evidence that her death had not been a suicide.

I was so wrapped up in my own thoughts that I only caught the end of Sam's sentence: "but Brenda thought a book doctor could fix the problems."

"A book doctor?"

"Someone who specializes in rewriting and revising—strengthening—an author's manuscript."

I waited until the waiter set down our entrees and left. "My mother hated book doctors. She felt that using them was dishonest, like having an unacknowledged collaborator on your book."

Sam, I thought, had the uneasy look of someone being forced to deal with the emotionally unstable. "But it will still be Katherine's book, Katherine's writing," he said in a soothing voice. "All that will be done is some editing and polishing, fixing the problems that Katherine didn't have time to fix. Certainly you can't object to that."

I sighed. "The issue for me is what Mother would have wished. I'm quite certain that she wouldn't want someone else messing with her work. I reread the manuscript right before I came to New York, and I keep coming back to my feeling that Mother would not have wanted it to be published as it is either. It's not good enough; it doesn't meet her high standards."

Sam stared at me. "Surely you're not serious? This is Katherine's last book. An intriguing book, different from her others. The problems can be corrected—they're minor flaws in a strong book. You don't want to deprive her devoted readers of savoring the last Katherine March novel, do you?"

Or deprive you of your commission, I thought but did not say.

"This is a novel," Sam continued, "that your mother cared about very deeply."

"Why do you say that?"

Sam blinked several times before answering. "Katherine talked a lot about how much trouble she was having with it, but when I suggested that she forget this book and start another, she was vehement that she needed to finish this novel—'even if it kills me,' she said."

"She knew she was dying. She didn't have time to start a new book."

"But it was important to her to finish this one," Pryor said. "Knowing that she was dying, she could have just given up on it. Who would have faulted her for that? But she didn't choose to take the easy way out."

It was a good point. "No, she didn't."

"Why don't you talk to Brenda Stein about the kind of revisions she has in mind? I'm sure she doesn't want to alter your mother's book any more than you do."

"I'll talk to her," I promised, suddenly tired of the topic. "I do want to speak to you, though, about the biography of my mother that Suzanne Lang is writing."

He nodded. "Yes, it certainly seems the right time for a biography. It can only help the sale of Katherine's novels."

I glared at him. "You think Suzanne's sleazy gossip would make anyone want to read Mother's novels?"

The agent looked puzzled. "The part I read wasn't sleazy at

all. Maybe even a little dry. Your mother, rest her soul, didn't lead the most eventful life. She spent most of her adult years holed up in her office writing."

I studied him through narrowed eyes. "Suzanne wasn't drawing parallels between *The Summer That Changed Everything* and Mother's life?"

"I don't recall her even mentioning that book in her proposal. I was going to suggest that you give her a copy of the manuscript so she could include it in the discussion of Katherine's novels. She told me she intended to interview you for her book."

"I have no intention of talking to her or giving her the manuscript." But if Suzanne had stolen the copy of *Summer,* why would she need one from me? Maybe Sam had not read her proposal carefully. Or maybe Suzanne was still gathering information about the real-life parallels to Mother's novel.

"This woman," I said, trying hard to keep calm, "was virtually stalking my mother. From what I understand, Mother initially cooperated with her, letting Suzanne interview her for her master's thesis. But then Suzanne became more demanding, more irrational. Mother eventually had to cut off all contact with her."

"I didn't realize that," Sam said, his expression solemn. But he didn't say, "Well, in that case, I won't try to get Suzanne's book published."

"And from what I read of her master's thesis on Mother, she is a really lousy writer. Pedantic. Boring."

Pryor said nothing, but something in his expression, a sudden hyper-attentiveness, made me suspect that I'd hit a bull's eye. Sam Pryor might not care if he was representing an unstable or dangerous woman. He did care that she couldn't write.

"The last time we talked on the phone," he said after a few minutes of silent eating, "you were about to look through your mother's files for any unpublished manuscripts."

"I brought her files back to Houston, but I haven't had time to read all of them. There do seem to be a lot of short stories. I'd guess that some of them were never published."

Sam's expression brightened. "Perhaps we could put together a collection of her short stories."

I sipped my water. "I'd have to think about that. And it might be a while before I can go through all the files. My classes start in a few days."

"I'd be happy to help. If you'd ship me all the manuscripts, my staff and I could do the reading for you."

I smiled. "That's very considerate of you, but I don't want to neglect my duties as literary executor."

"Of course," Sam said, not looking happy about it.

The waiter appeared then to inquire if either of us would like coffee or dessert. We both declined.

As we were saying our goodbyes, Sam said, "I hope you'll let me know what you decide about those stories. I'm thinking I might be able to sell Brenda on the idea of accepting a short-story collection as one of the contracted books."

Oh, yes, the well-publicized three-book, three-million-dollar contract. I nodded. "Thanks very much for lunch, Sam. Talking to you has been very interesting."

He shook the hand I offered. "I'm glad we had a chance to chat. I'm going back to the office and reread the book proposal for that biography of Katherine. Perhaps it was not as strong as I'd originally thought."

"I'll phone you as soon as I read those short stories."

"You do that," Sam Pryor said, his lips smiling, his eyes cold.

I'd told my aunt I'd meet her at the Guggenheim Museum at four. I decided to walk to the museum. I needed both the exercise and some time to think. I felt as if in the last twenty-four hours I'd been given little bits of information, tantalizing nuggets, that only led to more questions. Had Margaret O'Ryan ever intended to tell me something important about Mother or was her impaired mind playing tricks on her? Was it possible that Suzanne had not stolen the manuscript of *The Summer That Changed Everything* and, in fact, had never laid eyes on it? Had my mother really wanted to replace Sam Pryor as her literary agent?

I reached the Frank Lloyd Wright building housing the Solomon Guggenheim collection of art twenty minutes early. From the outside the building did indeed look like a big wedding cake tilted to one side. I entered the museum, deciding to make a phone call before I met Aunt Charlotte.

I found a pay phone and punched in the number. The phone rang four times, five. Perhaps, once again, Margaret O'Ryan wasn't home. Or maybe she'd already forgotten that she'd asked me to phone her when I was alone.

"Hello?" The voice was Miss O'Ryan's alto.

"Hello, Miss O'Ryan. This is Molly Patterson, Katherine March's daughter." The question now was if she'd recall what she wanted to tell me.

"Yes, thank you for calling me. Are you alone?"

She sounded lucid enough. A bit paranoid perhaps, but not confused. I glanced behind me at the museum goers wandering by. "I'm at a museum, but no one is nearby."

"Good. I want to tell you what I told Katherine. I first told her when she was eighteen. That time she followed my advice. But when I told her again last summer—warned her—she ignored me. Perhaps she thought I was a silly old woman. Or, more likely, she thought she was strong enough now to handle them."

"Handle who?" I asked. She was talking so quickly and not explaining herself.

"Her family," Miss O'Ryan said, sounding impatient. "The

Marches." She made the name into a derisive epithet. "I told Katherine to get as far away as she could from them and not come back. And I'm telling you the same thing. They are dangerous people, Molly. Evil people. I could tell when I was working there."

"What do you mean?" What could she tell? Surely my mother at sixty knew her own family better than a former nanny who hadn't seen the people involved for years. Could this possibly be some kind of delusion brought on by Alzheimer's disease?

Someone tapped me on the shoulder. I jumped. When I turned around Aunt Charlotte was there, smiling at me.

"Well, thank you very much for the information," I said into the phone. "Goodbye." I hung up.

"Who were you talking to?" Charlotte asked. She had changed into a pale gray suit with a double strand of pearls at her neck. She looked very elegant and very rich.

"Oh, I had a question for Mother's editor," I said, pretending to dig in my purse for a handkerchief. "I got here early and thought I'd phone to ask her about Mother's book."

CHAPTER SIXTEEN

"Ready to face Mother again?" my aunt asked as we finished our breakfast of scones, raspberries and coffee.

Not really, but I reminded myself that the reason for my visit was to see my grandmother. "I am if you are."

As we walked to the car, I asked, "Did you have a chance to finish Mother's novel?" When we'd come home from an off-Broadway play last night, Charlotte had said she intended to finish the book before she went to sleep.

"I did. I have to admit I didn't care for it. The book seemed too much like Katherine's revenge against Mother."

"But when we talked about the book on the phone you told me that the story wasn't like your life."

"When you told me the plot, I didn't think it sounded like what actually happened. For one thing, there was never any question of Father having been murdered. But when I finally read the book, there were enough surface similarities to our real lives to make it appear to be autobiographical—even though it isn't. Mother was hardly a Donna Reed–type parent, but she was nowhere near as awful as the mother in the book. And I would like to think I was not quite as vacuous as the younger sister. Reading that novel is like seeing our rather pathetic little family distorted by a fun-house mirror into something monstrous."

Charlotte's large blue eyes flashed. "It was cruel of Katherine to do this to Mother. I know she blamed Mother for Father's death. She told me once that the stress of their constant arguing and the birthday party Mother insisted on giving over Father's objections probably brought on his heart attack that night. But that isn't any excuse for portraying Mother as a cold-blooded, calculating murderer in a book that thousands of people will read."

Before I had a chance to reply she added, "I was so upset that I phoned my attorney this morning. He said the chances of stopping publication are slim at best. Because the book is a novel, not nonfiction, it probably isn't libelous. I just hope that some reporter doesn't choose to view it as a roman à clef."

I studied her. "You're saying that publication of this book will be humiliating to you?"

"Not to me," she said as she unlocked her car. "I'm not so sure about Mother. She's spent her entire life trying to make her family look good to other people."

I got into the Mercedes. "I don't want to hurt Grandmother either." It bothered me that Mother would be so vindictive. It was one thing to personally confront her mother with her grievances, another to portray her as a murderer in a widely read novel—particularly if, as Charlotte said, there was no factual basis for the accusation. And Mother must have known that she was not likely to be alive when the book was published. She wouldn't have to face Grandmother's wrath or reporters' questions. "And I've been having my own doubts about publishing this book."

From the driver's seat Charlotte turned to face me. "Molly, don't stop publication on my account—or Mother's. I phoned my lawyer because the book made me angry. But even if he'd been more optimistic about taking legal action, I probably wouldn't have gone through with it. This is Katherine's last book, and I don't want to be the person who censors literature because I personally don't like it."

I shook my head. "I would be a lot less inclined to stop publication if I thought the novel was personally offensive but good literature. But I'm not even sure that it's a good book. Mother was such a perfectionist about her work, I keep thinking that she wasn't finished with the manuscript, that she intended to write another draft. Would she want a sub-standard book published just because it was what she was working on when she died?"

Charlotte glanced at me. "I didn't think it was up to Katherine's usual high standards either. But I want you to know that whatever decision you make, I'll support you."

I smiled weakly. "Thanks, that's very generous of you."

Outside the day was cold and gray. "I phoned to see how Mother was doing today," Charlotte said as she drove. "The nurse said she'd had a bad night, not sleeping much. I think she was trying to warn me that Mother is not in the best of humor. So brace yourself. If she's especially cantankerous, we'll make it a very quick visit."

I thought about my aunt's relationship with her mother as we pulled into the nursing home parking lot. Charlotte openly admitted that her mother was a socially pretentious tyrant. But unlike Mother, Charlotte seemed quite tolerant, even amused by Grandmother. She didn't let the old woman's criticism and unsolicited advice get to her.

I wished I could say the same for myself. As we walked into her room the gaunt, white-haired woman propped up in bed glared at us, looking more angry than ill. "I had almost given up hope on you," she scolded.

"Well this is exactly the time I told you we'd come," Charlotte said lightly. "I understand you weren't feeling well last night."

"I still am not feeling well. And no one seems to be doing anything about it. I hardly ever see my doctor."

"He hasn't been to see you today?" Charlotte's eyes narrowed. When her mother said no, she added, "Well, I'll have to talk to someone about that."

"I wish you would." Grandmother watched Charlotte leave the room, then turned her attention to me. "What have you been doing since I last saw you?"

I mentioned going to the Guggenheim and to a play with Charlotte and my lunch with Mother's literary agent.

"It's good that you're seeing Katherine's old friends. I'm sure they want to relay their condolences in person. You need to make these social calls while you're here. I hope this literary agent isn't the only person you saw."

It was her imperial, Miss Manners tone that made me say it. "No, I also visited Margaret O'Ryan."

Her cold eyes narrowed into wrinkled slits. "I didn't know that she was still around. She must be very old now."

Younger than you, I thought. "She wrote me a very nice note about Mother. When I phoned her she asked me to come visit." Never mind that when I arrived for the visit Miss O'Ryan didn't remember who I was.

"Did you know that Margaret O'Ryan had a nervous breakdown when she was working for us?" my grandmother asked, not bothering to hide the malice in her voice. "I believe she was in a mental hospital for quite a while. A very unstable and paranoid woman—always thought people were plotting against her. I wanted to fire her, but Warren insisted she stay. She had a brilliant mind, he said, even if she was high-strung. Warren was sympathetic to Margaret, but, of course, he would be, wouldn't he? The two of them were so similar."

"In what way?"

She scowled at me: another question-asker, just like my troublesome mother. "They were both weak. Too sensitive for their own good, both of them much happier with books than with real people. In our marriage Warren was the smarter one, but I was the stronger. I was the one who could face life, which is more than I can say for my late husband."

I looked into her hard blue eyes and wished I could tell her what Margaret O'Ryan had to say about her. Though I wasn't sure that Grandmother was actually evil, she certainly was a thoroughly detestable woman. My mother had run away from Grandmother's tyranny, her small-mindedness, and her total disregard for anyone except herself. But how could this frail old lady have been a threat to Mother last summer? Mother was no longer a young girl, dependent on her parent for financial or emotional support. It was hard to envision her expecting much of anything from this shrew.

So why had Margaret O'Ryan warned Mother and me about the "evil Marches"? Was Charlotte, in Miss O'Ryan's mind, contaminated by association with her awful mother? Probably the warning was the confused message of a mind clouded by Alzheimer's, her early dislike of the overbearing matriarch and her rebellious teenage daughter turned into something much more sinister.

"Oh, Mother," Charlotte said from the doorway, "are you badmouthing that poor, sweet man again?"

"Everything I've said is true," her mother said tartly. "While Warren may have occasionally been sweet, he was also, unfortunately, a weak man. A quitter. I wish I'd realized that before I married him."

Charlotte sighed. I bet she'd heard it all many times before. "I talked to a nurse, who assured me that the doctor will be stopping in to see you this afternoon."

"He'll probably see me for all of five minutes," her mother said, then proceeded to list all her complaints about various members of the nursing home staff.

I was relieved when Charlotte indicated that it was time for us to leave.

"So soon?" her mother pouted.

"Yes, I'm sorry, dear, but we have to get back so Molly can pack."

"It was very nice to see you, Grandmother, after all these years," I lied.

"Yes," she said, looking tired. "I don't understand why your mother kept you away from me. But then Katherine always was my difficult child. She was like her father, and Charlotte is like me."

My aunt raised her eyebrows, but she merely kissed her mother goodbye and said she'd come again in a few days.

As we descended the curving staircase, Charlotte asked, "Did Mother interrogate you while I was gone?"

I shrugged. "She wanted to know who I'd seen while I was here, and I ended up telling her about visiting Miss O'Ryan. Then she told me how unstable Miss O'Ryan was."

Charlotte shook her head. "The two of them hated each other. Miss O'Ryan thought Mother was an empty-headed socialite and Mother thought she was a crazy bookworm. Mother would have fired her if Father had let her."

"She mentioned that." I hesitated. "She also said that your father was weak and couldn't face life."

Charlotte stopped on the stairs and turned to look at me. "She thinks Father killed himself."

"Why would she think that?"

When she spoke again Charlotte sounded terribly tired. "There was an empty bottle of Scotch and a half-empty bottle of sleeping pills next to Father's bed when he died. Mother came after the maid found his body—they had separate bedrooms by then. Mother got rid of the bottles and the letters Father left before the doctor arrived."

"The letters said he'd committed suicide?"

"No, they didn't say that. But they sounded like farewell messages to Katherine and me, telling both of us that he loved us, advising Katherine to study hard in college and to keep writing, telling me to focus more on my studies and less on boys."

Suddenly I felt sick to my stomach. The parallels to Mother's Christmas letters were unmistakable. Could I just be fooling myself when I insisted that my mother hadn't committed suicide? "But why would he have killed himself?"

"I'm not sure that he did," Charlotte said. "All I'm saying is that Mother believed he did. Because she refused to have an autopsy, we'll never know how much Scotch or how many pills he took. He might have had one drink and, hours later, one sleeping pill. Most probably he did die from a heart attack. He'd had an attack a few months earlier and he wasn't taking good care of himself."

"So you can't think of any reason he might have wanted to die?" I asked again, hoping she'd say "no." I wanted my own mother to have no family pattern of suicide to emulate.

Charlotte seemed to sense the urgency behind my question. "I don't know," she said as we walked outside. "I've thought about it hundreds of times and I'm still not sure of anything. Father did seem a little depressed after his first heart attack and I think it bothered him that he was turning fifty. And at his birthday party I saw him arguing with the woman he supposedly was having an affair with, a pretty young editor. But who knows? Maybe his letters meant he was going to move out and divorce Mother, but he had a heart attack before he could act on it. No one in my family ever talked about what happened."

"What about Mother? Did she know about the liquor and the pills?"

"I assume so, even though Katherine never said anything to

me. I always thought she believed that Father died from a heart attack. It would have devastated her to think he took his own life."

So instead she'd written a novel claiming that someone else— her mother—had been responsible for her father's death.

As we got into Charlotte's Mercedes, I shivered. I was glad that tomorrow I was going home.

CHAPTER SEVENTEEN

Alex had left me a note on the kitchen counter: Hope you had good trip. Detective called. Lab tests showed Stelazine in syringe, no fingerprints except yours. Suzanne Lang has alibi— was visiting sister in Fredericksburg.

Damn! I'd expected those lab results, but I'd nevertheless hoped that Suzanne's fingerprints might have showed up on the syringe. The out-of-town visit was also unfortunate. I wondered if Detective Martinez had interviewed Suzanne's sister in Fredericksburg. I certainly hoped he'd realized how easy it would have been for Suzanne to tell her sister that she was going to spend the afternoon shopping, and then instead made the hour drive to Austin, killed my mother, and still got home in time for dinner in Fredericksburg.

I needed to discuss the matter with the detective, to see what in fact he was thinking about all this new evidence. But when I phoned he wasn't in and I had to settle for leaving a message on his voice mail. I was too edgy to just sit around and wait for his phone call or to do any of the more practical household tasks that needed to be done. The only thing that I figured would make me feel better was doing a little detective work of my own.

I poured myself another cup of coffee and dialed Mrs. Benjamin's phone number in Austin. I hoped Mother's neighbor had returned from her visit with her daughter.

This time she answered. "Yes, dear, I was expecting your

call," she said when I identified myself. "Sarah said you'd talked to her about the day poor Katherine died, and then a policeman came to ask me questions. How can I help?"

"I'm wondering if you remember who you saw at Mother's on the afternoon of December twelfth, the day she died."

"At first I was a little confused about what day it was when I saw the people at Katherine's house—she had a lot of visitors that week. But once I realized that was the day I had my doctor's appointment, then I remembered. One man came just before I left for the doctor's. That must have been around two. And when I got back—it must have been around four-thirty; the doctor kept me waiting and I stopped for groceries—the first man's car was gone. Another man was knocking on Katherine's front door. He was driving a van from the ABC Electrical Company. Katherine didn't answer and the man left. I thought at the time that she just wasn't home, but later I realized that poor Katherine must have already been dead."

Mrs. Benjamin suddenly stopped talking. I imagined her rush of words suddenly colliding with an image of the gruesome reality behind her neighbor's front door.

"Can you tell me what the first man looked like?"

Mrs. Benjamin sniffed audibly. "I never saw him before. A gray-haired man in a tan sports coat and brown pants."

"Did you see him go inside the house?"

"Yes, Katherine let him in. She seemed to know who he was, but I got the idea that she was surprised to see him."

"Surprised?"

"Now I might be wrong about that. I didn't tell that to the policeman because I wasn't certain and, frankly, dear, I wasn't very comfortable talking to the officer."

"Tell me what you thought you saw," I said in what I hoped was a gently coaxing voice.

"Well, of course, I only saw them briefly. Katherine stood in

the doorway talking to him. She looked, well, annoyed that he
was there. I thought maybe the man had shown up at the wrong
time."

I started jotting notes on a yellow legal pad. "Do you
remember anything else about this man?"

"Well, he was a little overweight with a pleasant face, very
friendly looking and not very tall. When he stood next to Katherine he was almost exactly the same height as she."

I felt suddenly cold. No, it couldn't be. There were hundreds—no, thousands—of short, plump, friendly-looking men
with gray hair.

"That's great," I said weakly. "Did—did you see anyone else
the rest of the day?"

"Oh, yes. After the electrician left I saw Helen Lewis. But
that was quite a bit later. I went to take a little nap before dinner. I don't think I even glanced out the window again until I
started cooking. That must have been around six or six-fifteen."

That was when Helen had come to the house to see why
Mother wasn't answering her phone. "I appreciate your talking
to me," I said. What was the old saying: Be careful what you
wish for? So here I was with credible information on who was at
my mother's house on the day she'd died—and I fervently
wished I didn't know it.

"You might also want to talk to the Franks from across the
street," Mrs. Benjamin said. "The police talked to them too. Let
me give you their phone number."

I jotted it down, thanked her again and then, gratefully, hung
up the phone. I glanced at the notes covering my legal pad. The
description certainly sounded like my father, and Ginny had
mentioned that Dad had been in Texas for a job interview in
December. Austin, Texas? I remembered the photo I had of my
mother and father standing together, holding me as a baby.
When I was a child I'd thought, But they're the same height.

Isn't the man supposed to be taller?

If Dad had visited Mother on December twelfth, that would explain his strange message to Mother that I'd heard on her answering machine: "I'm sorry we quarreled, Katherine."

In any case this man—who might or might not be my father— had been long gone before Mother died. Mrs. Benjamin had said that his car wasn't there when she got home at four-thirty.

Next to me the phone rang. I picked it up.

"Ms. Patterson, this is John Martinez."

I stared at the receiver. "Oh, yes, thank you for returning my call. I just wanted to find out what you'd learned about my mother's death. Alex told me about the Stelazine in the syringe, but I was interested in anything else you learned." I felt as if I was babbling, telegraphing my anxiety to him. Abruptly I shut up and took a deep breath.

"I talked to your mother's neighbors and to Suzanne Lang," he said, a bit stiffly. "Ms. Lang was visiting her sister in Fredericksburg on December twelfth. I talked to the sister, who verified her story. Ms. Lang was there from Wednesday night through Sunday afternoon."

I thought I heard something in his voice, some uncertainty about Suzanne's alibi. "But you didn't believe everything the sister said?" I asked. At this point what did I have to lose for making an off-base guess?

The detective didn't answer my question. "None of your mother's neighbors saw Ms. Lang at her house that day," he said. "One of them saw a gray-haired man early in the afternoon and then later Helen Lewis, the woman who reported finding the body."

"Yes, Helen was the person who phoned me." I was fighting two opposing desires: to end this conversation immediately and, conversely, to find out who, if anyone, Detective Martinez viewed as suspects. But I couldn't very well ask, "So what are you thinking about this gray-haired man?" Instead I said, "I talked to Mrs. Benjamin myself this morning, but I haven't talked to the Franks."

Martinez, to my surprise, seemed happy to volunteer information. "They weren't as observant as Mrs. Benjamin. Mr. Frank said he saw a woman go into your mother's house around four, and Mrs. Frank said she saw a woman go in around six. But neither of them could give a very good description of the persons they saw."

"Mrs. Benjamin saw Helen Lewis go into Mother's house around six too," I said before the implications of what he'd said hit me. I sat up straighter, suddenly not tired at all. At four Mrs. Benjamin had not yet returned from her doctor's appointment. Perhaps Mr. Frank had witnessed the killer entering Mother's house. "Could the woman who Mr. Frank saw be Suzanne Lang?"

"Nope. The woman he saw was tall and thin and wearing a black coat. I'd guess Ms. Lang weighs about two hundred pounds. Nothing could make that woman look thin."

I felt a sharp stab of disappointment. "Did Mr. Frank see this woman's face?"

"No, he said she was wearing a big hat that covered her face and hair. He saw your mother let the woman in the front door, and that was all he recalled." He paused. "I talked to Helen Lewis too. She says the only time she was at the house was around six-twenty. Said she got in with her own key."

"Mother gave it to her so Helen could look after the place when she was out of town. They were old friends."

"And she entered the house because your mother wasn't answering the phone." He made the action sound like an illegal activity.

"Helen and Mother were supposed to go out to dinner that night. When Mother didn't answer her phone, Helen was concerned that something might have happened to her."

"She was concerned about your mother's health?"

"Yes, she said Mother had been looking ill. We know now that she had cancer."

"Ms. Lewis said she called nine-one-one, then she phoned you. Do you remember what time that was?"

"Around seven, I think. We'd just finished dinner."

"She said she phoned you earlier than that."

"Maybe she did. I wasn't paying attention to the time. It might have been earlier."

I felt as if a part of me had detached and was observing this conversation with the cool professionalism I brought to my work. I knew exactly what Martinez was thinking: What had this woman, with her key to my mother's house, been doing in there from six o'clock—when two neighbors had observed her entering—until seven when she phoned me? I knew the next question the detective was going to ask before he voiced it: "I understand your mother left Ms. Lewis quite a sum of money. Was she aware that she was in your mother's will?"

"Helen seemed very surprised to learn how much she'd inherited. We both were." But I also remembered what else Helen told me: "I knew that Katherine was going to leave me some money, but I had no idea it was so much."

"You didn't wonder why your mother would leave her a million dollars?"

"No. Helen was Mother's closest friend."

"So you would say that Ms. Lewis was genuinely concerned about your mother?"

"Yes."

"So concerned that she would have wanted to end your mother's suffering from her cancer?"

"I don't think Helen even knew Mother had cancer. Mother didn't tell anybody about it."

"Perhaps Ms. Lewis was willing to help her close, long-time friend to kill herself—and your mother paid her generously for her assistance."

"No, Mother's lawyer said she made her new will on July third, the day after her cancer was diagnosed. So she decided in July to leave that money to Helen."

"Maybe your mother got everything set up so when she became sicker—and decided it was time to die—all her affairs would be in order. And then she asked Ms. Lewis to do this one last favor for her."

"But I don't see her involving Helen. Mother was a very self-sufficient woman. And I also don't think she wanted to commit suicide."

"Which leads me to my other theory."

He wanted me to ask, "What's that?" but I didn't.

After a pause, the detective asked, "Was Ms. Lewis familiar with your mother's novels?"

When I said yes, he asked, "So she would have been aware that in one of your mother's books, a character killed a man with an injection of Stelazine, making it look like the man had died of a heart attack?"

So clearly that it might have been yesterday I remembered Helen telling me that Brenda Stein had said that Stelazine had been the drug the villainous psychiatrist had used to kill his patient in *With Malice Towards One*. But could she have already known about Stelazine before Brenda mentioned it? "I don't know. You'll have to ask Helen."

Feeling numb, I heard the detective ask me to call him if anything else occurred to me. He'd be in touch, he said.

The minute he hung up I dialed my father's number. Surely there was some innocent explanation. In all the turmoil after Mother's death, Dad had just forgotten to mention that he'd visited Mother on the day she died.

On the sixth ring my stepmother's perky voice announced, "We're not home right now, but we'd love to talk to you. Just leave your name and number and we'll call you right back."

My voice sounded strained to me as I asked them to get back to me as soon as possible.

CHAPTER EIGHTEEN

The phone rang Monday morning as I was getting ready to leave for school.

"Molly, hi!" It was my stepmother. "Sorry we weren't here when you called, but we spent a few days with Ethan."

"That sounds like fun." Ethan was their son, who lived in Milwaukee.

"It was fun. And good for your dad. The job hunting has really been getting him down."

"No luck yet?"

"No," she said glumly. "Not even a bite."

"I'm really sorry to hear that." I couldn't think of any tactful way to bring up the reason for my phone call, so I just blurted it out. "Mother's neighbor in Austin mentioned that she saw a man who sounded a lot like Dad going into Mother's house on the afternoon she died. And I remember you said he was in Texas for a job interview."

"That's right. He was in Austin in December for an interview. It probably was Ned who she saw. He dropped by to see Katherine."

Why? I wanted to ask. Instead I said, "Mrs. Benjamin said it was around two."

"That sounds about right. As I recall, his appointment was at three-thirty." She sighed. "Unfortunately, that job didn't work out. Ned said they wanted a younger man."

So Dad was gone before the earliest time—three-thirty, the

pathologist had estimated—that Mother could have died. And if the police ever asked, he had his job interview to prove where he was.

"He flew home that night, right after the interview," Ginny said. "That's why he didn't come to visit you."

Was that why Dad hadn't mentioned seeing Mother when I'd asked about his message on Mother's answering machine—he was afraid he'd hurt my feelings if I knew he'd been in Austin but hadn't come to visit? "Oh, I wouldn't have expected him to drive that far—it's more than a six-hour round trip."

"Well, he certainly would have if he'd had more time," Ginny said. "You know how he loves seeing all of you."

"And we love seeing both of you. But I was kind of surprised, Ginny, that Dad went to see Mother at all."

Silence.

Had I offended her? "I just mean that I didn't think he'd even want to see her," I added lamely.

"Ned didn't want to see her," Ginny snapped. "He went there to ask her to lend us some money."

It was my turn to be speechless. "What—what did Mother say?" I finally managed to ask.

"She said 'no.' It was a very brief meeting."

"I'm sorry about that." Suddenly I understood why my father hadn't wanted to tell me what his phone apology to Mother was about. The fact that he'd been so desperate for money that he had had to ask his ex-wife for a loan must have been deeply humiliating for him.

"I don't mean to speak ill of the dead, honey, but your mother was an incredible bitch to Ned when he asked her for help. With all of her millions, would it have hurt Katherine to loan some of it to the man who supported and encouraged her when she was getting started in her career?"

Her question stunned me. Why would Ginny expect my

mother to lend money to a man she'd divorced over thirty years ago—a man she hadn't laid eyes on since Alex's and my wedding? And how had Ginny known about Mother's wealth when I hadn't? Suddenly I remembered how Ginny had glared at Mother's coffin at the funeral and how angry she'd been that Dad had cried. Her animosity made more sense now.

The whole chain of events—Dad being forced to ask his successful ex-wife for money, her abrupt refusal, Ginny's anger that her husband could grieve for such a woman—made me feel intensely sad. "I was going to save this as a surprise for Dad's birthday this summer, but maybe it will help to hear it now. I've inherited quite a lot of money from Mother, and I want to give Dad—you and Dad—twenty thousand dollars as a birthday gift."

"Oh, Molly, I don't know what to say."

"The only problem is that it will be a while—at least several months—before I get the money."

"That's okay, honey. We can hold out a little bit longer. And Molly, thank you, sweetheart. You don't know how much this will mean to your father. And not just financially. I always told him that you weren't like your mother, that you had inherited your daddy's kind heart. I knew we could count on you."

"I'm happy I can finally help after all the things you've done for me." I glanced at my watch. "But I need to get going. I have a class in forty-five minutes."

"Give my love to everybody. And Molly, I can't tell you how much your generosity will mean to your father and me."

I grabbed my books and headed for the door. So much for getting to school early on the first day of the new semester. I'd be lucky to make it to class on time.

It was not until I was on the Southwest Freeway that something Ginny had said hit me. I wasn't like my cheapskate mother, she'd said, and "I knew we could count on you." Did that mean she was expecting me to give them the money—the money Mother had refused to loan them? Now that I thought about it, Ginny had sounded delighted by my gift to Dad, but she hadn't really seemed surprised.

I'd just hurried into the classroom when I spotted her. Suzanne Lang sat in the back of the room, grinning at my obvious discomfort. She was dressed once again in the long black cape she'd worn to my mother's funeral, the cape that, with her forbidding height and wild gray hair, made her look like a powerful witch. Her expression now was brazen, taunting: So what do you plan to do about this situation, bitch?

I marched over to her. "What are you doing here?"

"I'm sitting in on your lecture. Your department chair said she thought it would be okay—if I got your permission, of course." She sent me a wide-eyed innocent look. "But when I went to your office, you weren't there."

I considered my options as students drifted into the classroom. I could let her stay and hope she waited until after class to take me on, or I could insist that she leave. And if she refused or caused a scene, I would have to call a security officer to escort her out.

"You can stay if you don't cause trouble," I told Suzanne with my don't-mess-with-me look.

As I turned away I heard her chuckle. "Me cause trouble? Never!" I pretended I hadn't heard her.

From the front of the room I smiled at the class and introduced myself. "I hope you all intend to be in Victimology." I glanced around at the seated students, a good percentage of whom I'd had in previous classes. Several of them, I knew, were already working as police or parole officers. They often contributed an interesting, if often cynical, viewpoint to my courses.

I took roll, adding "and Ms. Lang is sitting in on our class today." As I passed out the syllabus, I was relieved that Suzanne was—for the moment at least—keeping her mouth shut. An hour and a half from now, when the class was over, I'd think about how to deal with her.

I launched into my introductory lecture. "Victimology is the scientific study of the victims of crime. A victimologist, a criminologist who specializes in studying the role and plight of crime victims, might use victim surveys to understand crime through their eyes or to calculate the actual costs of crime to them. Or a victimologist might study the relationship between victim and offender, determine the probability of crime risk, or design services for victims of crime."

From the corner of my eye I saw Suzanne Lang's hand shoot up. I ignored her. "Victimological research, for instance, can help us determine what groups of people are particularly vulnerable to a specific crime."

"Excuse me," Suzanne called out. "I have a question."

"Yes?"

"What about people who are wrongfully accused of a crime? Aren't they victims too?" Before I could answer, she continued, "Being accused of a crime you didn't commit is devastating. It can ruin your life." Her fiery eyes locked on mine.

"Yes," I said, "there are many ways that people are victimized by crime." Take, for example, being the daughter of the victim. "But that's not what we're going to talk about today."

Several students turned around to look at Suzanne, but she seemed oblivious to their stares. She started to say something else, but I cut her off. "If you'd like to continue this discussion, you can see me after class. Right now there are other things we need to cover."

"I'll be there," she said, not taking her eyes off me.

Ignoring all the puzzled expressions, I moved on to my next

topic. Thank God I'd taught this class before. Somehow I delivered the rest of my lecture, operating on auto pilot while I tried to figure out what the hell I was going to do with Suzanne once the class was over.

As soon as students stood to leave, Suzanne moved to the front of the class.

Rita White, a savvy young police officer who'd taken a class from me before, shot me a look: Do you need help?

I shook my head, smiling my thanks. "See you Wednesday, Rita." I could handle this myself—couldn't I?

"Let's go to my office," I told Suzanne. At least I had a phone there, and my good friend Lisa should be in her office right next door.

Suzanne followed me down the hall, not speaking. She was a good four or five inches taller than I and at least seventy pounds heavier. And her extra weight looked like muscle.

I unlocked my office door, wondering if it was a mistake to go alone into a secluded room with this woman. Trying to hide my nervousness, I hurried to barricade myself behind my desk. "Have a seat," I said, indicating the chair across from me.

She didn't. Instead she closed the door and moved closer, glowering down at me. "Where do you get off accusing me of killing your mother? Martinez wouldn't admit it, but I know it was you who sicced him on me. You were the one who got him to investigate where I was on the day Katherine died."

"You're not the only person he's investigating," I said, not bothering to mention that she was the only person I'd accused. My right hand inched closer to the phone. Why hadn't I thought of keeping my office door open?

Suzanne leaned down so her face was only inches from mine. I could feel her breath, hot and sour-smelling, on my face. "Your mother was my hero, damn it! I would never have harmed her."

I sat very still, not moving, the way you're supposed to act when cornered by a dangerous animal. Perhaps she just needed to tell me her story, to explain her position. Perhaps not.

"Katherine accomplished what I only dream of doing someday. Do you know how hard it is to get published? And then, even if you manage that part, how slim the chances are of making any money from your work?"

I nodded. Yes, I did know.

"But your mother was one of only a handful of American novelists who supported themselves entirely through their writing."

She glared at me, the daughter who, she assumed, had never sufficiently appreciated her mother's achievements. I started to protest. Despite my resentment of Mother's workaholism I had always been proud of her writing, and I did not like this loudmouthed stranger lecturing me. But Suzanne cut me off: This was her story, not mine.

"I'd just gone through a divorce," she said. "My husband was dumping me for this twenty-five-year-old bimbo, and I was terribly depressed. Then I heard Katherine speak at a writer's conference, saying essentially, 'You can do this. You can get published too.' And I believed her. I went back to school, wrote my master's thesis on Katherine March so I had an excuse to come talk to her again. I tried to model myself after her. She was my mentor." Suzanne turned blazing eyes on me. "Why would I murder this woman?"

She didn't seem to intend it as a rhetorical question. She wanted an answer. I ventured one. "Because Mother suddenly started avoiding you? Because she refused to see you anymore?"

I was afraid she was going to explode into anger, either denying that my mother ever cut her off, or physically attacking me.

To my surprise, though, Suzanne's response was subdued. "I made a mistake, a terrible mistake," she said in a voice laced with sadness. "I was frustrated with all the rejection slips I was getting, and I took that out on Katherine. It was stupid to ask her to call her editor to get me published. Incredibly naïve—as she told me."

I watched her, wondering if all this contrition was for that single outburst at my mother. Or was it guilt for something much worse than brazenly demanding that Mother call in her chips in the publishing world to get Suzanne's work published?

She seemed to read my thoughts. "You can believe me or not, but I didn't kill your mother. I worshipped Katherine. She was the best thing—the only good thing—in my life."

But what happened when the only good thing in your life didn't want to have anything more to do with you?

Suzanne's too-bright hazel eyes fixed on me. "And your mother didn't write me out of her life. I talked to her in November, after a speech she gave at a writer's conference. She told me she was very busy trying to finish a novel. And she looked as if she'd been sick, though she didn't say that. I apologized for my terrible behavior, for expecting her to hand me a writing career instead of taking the time to learn my craft. She was very nice about accepting my apology, said she had a tendency to shoot her mouth off too. 'Yell first and think later' she called it."

Despite myself, I smiled. I could hear Mother saying those words.

Apparently encouraged by my response, Suzanne rushed on. "I told her that if it was all right with her, I'd like to write her biography. I could use some of the research from my thesis, but of course I'd need more information and I'd have to write the book in a more accessible, less academic style."

"What was Mother's response to that?"

"She'd think about it. Katherine said she never thought she'd feel this way, because she always valued her privacy so much, but recently the idea of a biography had become more appealing to her."

Because she knew she was dying. But wouldn't Mother want someone other than Suzanne Lang as her biographer?

"And she said she knew me and trusted me," Suzanne said proudly.

More like she knew she could wrap you around her finger, I thought. Mother figured Suzanne wouldn't push her to answer any tough questions about her personal life.

"But Katherine didn't have time to be interviewed until after she finished her novel. Her book still needed a lot of revision and she couldn't even think about a biography until that was done."

"Did you see her again after that?" Assuming, of course, that you weren't her killer.

Suzanne shook her head. "I only talked to her on the phone. The last time was a few days before"—her voice cracked—"before she died. She told me she was almost finished revising her book. She wasn't sure how good it was; she felt very uncertain about it. I offered to read it, but she said no, she wanted to try it out on her editor first. Katherine intended to mail her the finished manuscript before she went to your house for Christmas. She said she was really looking forward to that—Christmas with you and your family, I mean."

I could feel the tears well in my eyes. Was Suzanne just telling me this because she thought that flattering me would get me off her back? Or had Mother actually said those words: "I'm really looking forward to spending Christmas with Molly and her family."

"And," Suzanne added, her voice sounding louder, more assertive, "she told me that after the holidays, when she got back to Austin, we would talk about the biography. She didn't promise me anything—she hadn't made her mind up yet—but she said she was seriously considering it. And even if I didn't write a book, she told me she had an idea for an article I might want to write about the novel she'd just written."

My head jerked up. "What kind of article?" The true facts behind a fictional murder story, perhaps? But surely Mother wouldn't have trusted a beginner like Suzanne to write such a story—unless she thought she could manipulate Suzanne into writing exactly what she wanted printed.

"Katherine didn't tell me anything else. I didn't even know what the book was about until Sam Pryor told me about it."

Or until you took matters into your own hands and stole the manuscript from Mother's office?

"I figured that I'd learn everything I needed to know when Katherine and I met. We were going to have lunch together on January second." Suzanne's expression darkened.

I didn't know what to say. If she was telling me the truth, if she actually had had an appointment to see Mother—and I could check that out on Mother's calendar; she'd been meticulous about writing down her meetings—Suzanne would have been a fool to kill the subject of her proposed book or article. Unless, of course, she was lying to me. Or psychotic.

"I thought at first that you killed her," Suzanne said.

"Me?" The words came out as a squeak of incredulity.

"You had the most to gain, didn't you? You inherited most of her money." Before I could say anything, she added, "But I investigated and found out you were teaching that afternoon, with witnesses to attest to it."

I opened my mouth to tell her to get out of my office. How dare she investigate me!

"But I'm going to find out who did kill your mother." Suzanne's pale face was flushed with conviction. "I know—I am confident—that she didn't kill herself."

"How—how can you be so sure?"

"Katherine was making plans for the future. She was looking forward to seeing you at Christmas. She left no note. She was anxious to find out her editor's reaction to her new book."

"But she had cancer," I said, playing devil's advocate. "Maybe the pain suddenly got bad and she decided she couldn't go on."

The look Suzanne shot me was full of disdain. "Can you see your mother giving up before she finished everything she wanted to get done?"

"No," I said softly, "I can't. Mother would not have voluntarily died before everything was completed." If she had decided to commit suicide, she wouldn't have done it then. "So who do you think killed her?"

"I'm not sure yet," Suzanne said. "I have several strong candidates, but I need a few more days to investigate. There are things I still have to check out. I'm going to include my investigation in my book, and I want it to be accurate."

"Won't you tell me who you suspect?"

She shook her head. "When I'm sure of who did it, I'll let you know." Then, without a backward glance, she walked out of my office.

CHAPTER NINETEEN

The first week of February Ginny phoned. She and Dad wanted to come visit "to help you celebrate your birthday."

"Why, that's great," I said, trying to sound more enthusiastic than I felt. "The kids will love having you here." Celebrating my birthday was about the last thing I felt like doing, but telling Ginny that would only hurt her feelings. I knew that she and Dad were worried about me and wanted to show their support.

I hung up the phone, feeling uneasy but not entirely sure why. Usually I loved to have my father and stepmother visit. Even though I wasn't in the mood for company, they were easy guests and would only stay a few days. Was my lack of enthusiasm about their visit in any way connected to my disinclination to think too much about Dad's visit to Mother's house? Ever since Suzanne Lang showed up in my classroom last week, I seemed to spend every free moment brooding about the identities of her candidates for Mother's killer. Trying to convince myself that two of them weren't my father and my mother's best friend.

Dad and Ginny arrived the next Thursday night, honking gaily—"Shave-and-a-haircut-two-bits"—from our driveway. The kids and I ran out to greet them.

My father and stepmother were getting out of their old black Mercedes. Both of them were smiling gamely, Ginny calling to my children, "Look at the two of you! You're so grown-up!"

Standing back a little from the others, I saw Dad wince as he got out of the car, his arthritis apparently flaring up after the long drive. And Ginny, who'd always been slender, tonight seemed achingly fragile, engulfed in a dark winter coat that seemed a couple sizes too large for her. The two of them looked so old!

I hurried to Dad, who enclosed me in a warm hug. I nestled my face in his neck, smelling his familiar, spicy aftershave. "How was the drive?"

"Interminable," he said, "but getting to see you and the kids makes it worth it."

Inside I made cocoa and a pot of decaffeinated coffee while Annie and Will took my parents to the study/guest room. The kids came running into the kitchen a few minutes later. "Look, Mom, look what Grandpa and Grandma Ginny gave me," Will said, holding up a new computer game.

"That's great."

"And I got these cool earrings," Annie said, standing in the doorway with Ginny. She held up delicate silver hoops for me to see.

"They're lovely," I said. They were also extravagant gifts from people who claimed to be broke.

I turned to Ginny. "You didn't have to buy them anything."

"But I wanted to," she said, her chin lifting. "They are, after all, my only grandchildren. It's a grandmother's prerogative to spoil them."

Not if you don't have the money, I thought, but didn't say. Ginny had always teased me about inheriting my mother's tightwad genes. "How about a cup of coffee?"

"I'd love one," Ginny said. "I cannot tell you how exhausting that car trip was."

Annie followed her to the table. "How come you and Grandpa didn't fly here the way you usually do?"

"Oh, your grandfather thought it might be an adventure to try something different," Ginny said, a shade too brightly.

Because it was a school night the children reluctantly got ready for bed. I pretended not to hear Ginny and the kids in the hallway making preparations for my birthday.

By ten-thirty everybody was in his or her bed. But I felt too edgy to sleep. Finally, after almost an hour of trying, I decided to get up.

I was surprised to see that the kitchen light was on. My father sat at the table, reading the newspaper. "You can't sleep either?" he asked with a smile.

I sat down across from him. "Aren't you comfortable in the study? Is there anything I can get you?"

He shook his head. "I was very comfortable. Ginny was fast asleep when I came out. You know I'm a chronic insomniac. But how come you're awake?"

I shrugged. "Just couldn't sleep."

Dad studied me with sympathetic brown eyes. "This has been a tough time for you, with you and Alex separating and then your mother's death on top of that."

I looked at the familiar face, now marred by dark circles under the eyes. "Yes, it has been." I wasn't up to discussing my marriage problems, but my mother's death was another matter. Maybe Dad could offer some insights. "I have all these unanswered questions about Mother: How did she die? Why didn't she tell me that she was sick? She was always so secretive about her life, and now even her death is a secret."

Dad sighed. "Your mother was a very complicated woman. She always had a hard time opening up to people. But Molly, I know this about her. She loved you very much, even if she wasn't always very good at showing it."

I could feel my eyes well with tears. Why did I have such a hard time believing that? "Ginny said you saw Mother when you were in Austin for a job interview," I said hesitantly.

Dad sighed. "It was the very day that she died, if you can believe that."

"How—how did Mother seem?"

Dad thought about it. "She was edgy," he said at last. "I had the sense when she opened the door and saw me that she was expecting someone else."

"Do you know who?"

He shook his head. "She never said anything, but she looked surprised to see me and disappointed, as if I wasn't the visitor she wanted to be talking to."

"But she invited you inside?"

"Yes, but she wasn't in the mood to talk over old times. Katherine was impatient that I cut to the chase. 'So tell me what's prompted you to come visit me for the first time in thirty years,' she said. She didn't want to listen to any of my small talk."

No, she wouldn't have. "What did you tell her?"

Two red blotches spread across my father's tired face. "I told her the truth. That I was in Austin looking for a job. I said Ginny and I were having financial problems and I wondered if she would consider giving me a loan—just until I got back on my feet."

He winced slightly, as if remembering a painful scene. "Katherine wouldn't even consider it, said I'd never been able to manage money and, from everything she'd heard, Ginny was even worse. She suggested that we go to one of those consumer credit places where they help you pay off your creditors and force you to live on a budget. 'That's probably the only thing that will make you come to grips with your problem,' she said."

It was not, I thought, a bad suggestion, but clearly Dad did not share my opinion.

"I left right after that. But later—after I heard Katherine had died—I had the feeling that she'd purposely picked a fight with me just to get me out of the house."

"Because someone else was coming over?"

"I don't know why. She said something about being busy and having work to do. But I don't think it was having her work interrupted that made her so jumpy."

Mother had never been a particularly nervous person. What could have made her react that way? An electrician was scheduled to come later in the afternoon. But why would that make Mother nervous? And she was going to have dinner with Helen, but that was hours away.

Was she expecting the woman who'd arrived that afternoon at four? I'd talked to Mr. Frank, the neighbor who'd glimpsed the mystery woman. But he hadn't seen much: not the woman's face or Mother's expression when she opened the door to her visitor. He also hadn't seen the woman leave.

"I wish now that she'd told me what was bothering her," Dad said. "Maybe I could have helped. But instead I was in and out of there in ten minutes. I know I was back in the hotel room by two-thirty, telling Ginny what had happened."

"Ginny was with you?" I asked, surprised.

Dad nodded. "And she was even madder than I was. I guess I shouldn't have given her the blow-by-blow account. It wasn't fair to upset her then leave for a job interview." He sighed, managing to look even older and more tired than he had before. "And that didn't work out any better than my talk with Katherine, though the guy I spoke to was a bit more tactful in turning me down."

"What a terrible day for you!" I felt the way I did when someone picked on one of my kids, full of helpless fury, wanting to make things better but not knowing how.

He smiled faintly. "Tell me about it."

"So that explains the phone message you left on Mother's answering machine."

He sighed. "After I calmed down, I felt bad about my argument with Katherine. I could understand why she got testy. I hadn't spoken to her in years, and suddenly I show up at her doorstep looking for a loan. But Molly, I hadn't meant for it to come out that way."

"I know you didn't."

"And I would have paid back every dollar. I wouldn't have even thought about asking her for money except that Ginny had just read in *People* about her multimillion dollar book contract. I even intended to congratulate her, to tell her I always knew she'd be a big success, but I never got around to it."

I leaned forward to pat his hand. "I know you meant well. Talking to Mother was difficult sometimes; she could be so brusque."

Dad gazed off into the distance, as if reliving that day. "I called her when we got back that night, but she didn't answer."

"You phoned her from Wisconsin?"

He nodded.

A sound from the doorway made me turn around. Ginny was walking toward us, dressed in a yellow chenille robe, her eyes bright with anger. "Molly, you sound like that awful writer who wanted to know what Ned and I were doing the day Katherine was murdered. Do you suspect him too of killing your mother?"

"Of course she doesn't!" my father said before I could answer. "What a terrible thing to say, Ginny!"

The anger that had flared a few seconds earlier died just as quickly. "I'm sorry, Molly. I guess I'm just overtired."

"What awful writer did you talk to?" I asked.

"Suzanne Lang," she said grimly. "Excuse my French, but that woman is a real bitch. She started out being very sweet, wanting to know how Ned and I met, saying she'd heard how much happier Ned's second marriage was. She just wanted a few background facts from me, like about the visitation arrangements for you. That was the first time we talked. But the next time she called she was nasty, looking for gossip. She said I sounded awfully envious of Katherine and her success. It almost seemed as if she was accusing me of killing Katherine."

"You never told me that," Dad said, looking shocked.

"I didn't want to upset you. But I told that woman a thing or two. The idea that I was jealous of Katherine! Or that I would kill anyone."

"She actually accused you of killing Mother?" I asked.

"Maybe not in so many words, but she sure implied it. I told her that if she thought I killed every person I didn't like, she should start watching her back."

I grinned. I'd forgotten about Ginny's temper. Since it had rarely been directed at me, I'd always found it rather amusing. Ginny got mad fast, erupted, and then was over it.

"I also pointed out to her," Ginny continued, "that since I was over one thousand miles away, in Wisconsin, on the day Katherine died, it would have been extremely difficult for me to murder her."

I opened my mouth to protest, glancing at my father for support. But he was suddenly looking at something in the newspaper, avoiding my eyes.

"Well, I guess I'd better get back to bed," I said instead. "I have to go to work in a few hours."

I didn't look at either of them as I walked out of the kitchen.

CHAPTER TWENTY

"What's wrong, Molly?" From across the table in the Mexican restaurant, Lisa eyed me with concern.

I shrugged. "Just tired, I guess."

I watched a bald man in a pin-striped suit grin appreciatively as he passed Lisa. As usual, she didn't notice.

"How are things between you and Alex? You seemed to be getting along well on New Year's Eve."

"We get along fine when we're together. He's coming over tonight for my birthday dinner and to see Dad and Ginny. But I still want to stay separated."

Fortunately Lisa didn't pursue the subject. I already knew what she thought: I needed to forgive Alex and move on. I was grateful she didn't feel compelled to tell me one more time.

As the waiter put down two plates of chicken fajitas, I glanced at the birthday gift she'd given me, a necklace of multicolored beads. "The necklace is beautiful, Lisa. I'm sorry I'm not better company."

"I'm not complaining. I just want to know what's bothering you. Something's happened, hasn't it?"

I hesitated, trying to push aside my guilt for badmouthing my stepmother. Then I told her how Ginny had lied to me about being in Austin with Dad on the day Mother died.

Lisa whistled. "You think she did go to your mother's house that day? And that's why she lied about it?"

"I don't know. She's such a hothead. It wouldn't surprise me if she had gone to Mother's to tell her off." I thought about all the times I'd seen Ginny go ballistic. "That's what Ginny does when she's mad, rants and raves and tells everyone precisely what she thinks of them. Which"—I looked at Lisa—"is a very far cry from giving Mother a toxic injection of Stelazine."

"That's exactly what I was thinking."

A feeling of relief washed over me. "The way Mother was killed couldn't have been an impulsive crime. No one just happens to have a syringe and a vial of Stelazine with them. This was carefully thought out. Not at all the kind of thing Ginny would have done."

"What about your dad? Maybe Ginny was trying to protect him."

"He wouldn't have done it," I said firmly. Although Dad was certainly smart enough to plan such a crime and I knew he'd read all of Mother's novels.

Lisa looked as if she wanted to say something, but decided not to. "So who do you think did it? I had the impression that you'd ruled out Suzanne Lang."

I sighed. "She's not at the top of my list anymore. Detective Martinez seems to suspect Helen. She had a motive of sorts and was the one who found Mother's body. But it just doesn't make sense to me. Why would Helen kill Mother when she was going to inherit the money soon anyway?"

"Maybe she needed the cash right away. Or she was afraid that your mother would change her mind and leave it to someone else."

I shook my head. "Helen was always a loyal friend, and she never seemed interested in money. She wouldn't have done anything to hurt Mother."

Lisa's expressive eyes bore into mine. "Okay, you don't think Helen could have done it. Who could have?"

I took a large drink of my Margarita as I weighed the possibilities. "Sam Pryor, Mother's agent. He's slippery, manipulative. He certainly was familiar with Mother's books. And he'd recently had some kind of disagreement with her. If she switched agents, he'd lose his biggest client."

"But if she died, he'd lose her too."

"Not really." I explained how Sam wanted me to look for any unpublished manuscripts Mother had left behind.

Lisa grinned. "Now we're getting somewhere."

"Yeah, now all we have to prove is how he did it—without anyone seeing him."

"What does this guy look like?"

"Gray-haired, thin, maybe five-seven or eight."

"You think he could have been your mother's four o'clock visitor?"

"Dressed up as a woman?"

"You said the neighbor didn't see the woman's face or hair and that she was wearing a long black coat. Maybe he only assumed it was a woman because he thought the hat looked feminine or the visitor was too slight to be a man. It's also possible that Pryor arrived after the four o'clock woman left. Just because none of the neighbors saw any other visitor that afternoon doesn't mean no one else came."

There were too many maybes, not enough hard facts for me.

Lisa must have been thinking the same thing. "I wish we had more information—especially where Pryor was the day your mother died. And I'd also love to know what Suzanne and the detective have learned."

"Me too, but Sam is too smart to volunteer any incriminating information about himself. And I'm not sure I'd trust any information Suzanne gave me. As for Martinez, I got the idea that all his investigating right now is directed at building a case against Helen."

Lisa took a sip of Margarita before she responded. "You

might be surprised what you can learn. Maybe it's time to put your criminal justice knowledge to some practical use."

"Right," I said, wishing I felt as optimistic as she. As several police officers in my classes had pointed out, there was a big difference between investigating actual crimes and studying them in a textbook.

Another sleepless night. Irritably I peered at the alarm clock: two-fifteen. All through the elaborate birthday dinner that Ginny and the kids had prepared I'd fought to stay awake. So why couldn't I sleep now?

Finally I gave up trying. The light in the kitchen indicated that I wasn't the only one up.

"Ginny!" She was sitting at the kitchen table reading. "I was expecting to see Dad. I thought you were the good sleeper in the family."

She sent me a wan smile. "Lately we've all had a lot of sleepless nights. But tonight at least your father is fast asleep."

"Good." He'd looked as if he needed the rest. I sat across from my stepmother. "The birthday party you gave me was wonderful." Even though I hadn't been in the mood to celebrate, all of the work Ginny had done touched me. "And I love the afghan you crocheted."

She smiled, a genuine smile this time. "The party was fun. And Annie and Will—and Alex too—were a big help."

I poured myself a glass of milk. "How about another piece of cake?" She'd baked a devil's food cake with vanilla frosting, my long-time favorite.

"Go ahead. I'm not really hungry." She waited until I settled across from her at the table, then said, "Molly, I wanted to explain why I lied to you last night."

"You don't have to explain anything to me."

"I want to." She took a deep breath. "I was only repeating

what I said to Suzanne. It was none of her damn business where I was or what I was doing that day. But I didn't mean to lie to you about being in Austin with Ned."

I believed her.

"But I've thought a lot about it, and there's more to it than that. I started thinking about everything that Lang woman said, trying to figure out why it upset me so much."

"Most people would be upset if she accused them of murder."

My stepmother waved her hand dismissively. "But that's not the part I'm talking about. What really made me furious was when she accused me of being envious of Katherine and her success. She seemed to imply that I was spiteful about Katherine because I was angry that my own life seemed so inconsequential in comparison."

"You can't take Suzanne seriously, Ginny. Mother was her idol. Suzanne certainly doesn't have a clear-eyed perspective on Mother and her life. And, more to the point, she was probably just trying to goad you into giving her some juicy quote for her book."

"That may well be. But what I realized today—what I should have realized a long time ago—is that Suzanne was right about my feelings toward Katherine. I was envious of her, Molly. If I had a successful career like that—if I had any career—we wouldn't have these terrible financial problems. If your father were still married to someone like Katherine, he wouldn't be applying for a job as a hardware store clerk."

"He was married to Mother, and she didn't make him happy. But you did. You brought a lot more to the marriage than high-paying job skills. You helped him create the kind of close-knit family life he'd always wanted."

Ginny looked at her glass, her cheeks red. "It's sweet of you to say that."

"It's all true."

Her small chin jutted out. "Well, I'm going to get a job now. I used to be a nurse's aide at a nursing home before I married Ned. I'm going to apply for some jobs like that when I get home."

"That's great. You'd be terrific working with older people."

"There's one other thing," Ginny said, more hesitantly. "Something else I need to tell you. I was there—at your mother's house—that afternoon. I took a cab to her house after Ned left for his job interview."

I stared at her.

"I intended to tell Katherine a thing or two about the kind of man Ned was. A man who'd never said a mean word about her in all the years I knew him. A man who was proud of her success as a writer and was the father of her only child. A man who deserved her respect." Ginny's eyes were now bright with remembered anger. "I didn't think I could get her to lend him the money, but I sure as hell intended to get an apology out of her."

"So what—what happened?"

"Nothing happened."

"Nothing?"

"She never opened the door. I rang the doorbell over and over, banged on the door, but she never let me in."

I thought about what she was telling me. "What time was that?"

"A little after four, maybe four-fifteen."

Did that mean that Mother was already dead? Had the four o'clock woman already come and gone? Or was Ginny the woman in black who Mr. Frank had seen? Ginny, after all, was thin and had a black winter coat. While she wasn't exactly tall, she wasn't short either. But that woman, Mr. Frank said, had gone into Mother's house.

Ginny glared into space. "Katherine made me so mad that

day. I couldn't believe that after everything else she'd pulled, she wouldn't even listen to what I had to say."

I felt as if I was missing something. "What do you mean?"

"I just knew that Katherine was right there watching me bang on her door."

"Why? Did you see some movement? Or hear something?"

"No—I don't know." She seemed to hesitate. "Maybe I just imagined hearing a noise. I guess it's possible that Katherine wasn't even there. Or maybe she was already dead. But I certainly had the feeling that someone was watching me from the peephole and snickering. I could almost hear her breathe."

CHAPTER TWENTY-ONE

"I want to go with you to Austin," Annie announced to my back.

I turned from the kitchen counter. "Are you sure? I'm only going for one night. Dad will stay with you and Will."

"I don't care. I—I'd just like to get out of town for a while."

Today Annie was wearing Mother's silver hoop earrings with her jeans and sweater. Either the earrings were more suited to her than Mother's other jewelry or I was getting used to Annie's new look. I was more concerned about the dark circles under her eyes and the nervous intensity she seemed to bring to every conversation.

Alex and I both had tried to talk to her about what was bothering her, even inquiring gently if she might like to see a therapist. "I'm just sad about Grandma dying," Annie had snapped. "There's nothing abnormal about that."

It seemed like a good sign that she was now showing an interest in doing something, even taking a short trip to Austin. "Sure, I'd be happy to have your company," I said. Maybe when the two of us were alone together she'd give me a clue to what was going on in her head.

We left the next morning. I'd had to call Annie's school to say she would be missing class, but I figured that Annie was a good student who was seldom absent and she needed some special attention right now. I also was flattered that she actually wanted to spend some time with me; in the last two years I'd definitely moved off the list of people Annie wanted to hang out with.

I even thought she looked better today: less tense, less overtly miserable. "I'm glad you decided to come with me," I told her with a smile. "It won't be such a long, boring drive with you along."

Annie leaned forward, fiddling with the radio until she found a rock station. "So have you talked to Suzanne Lang since the day she came to your class?"

"No, I haven't heard from her."

"I hope the police have got something on her by now. Have you heard from that Austin detective?"

"Not lately. But the last time I spoke to him, Annie, I had the impression that he'd pretty much ruled out Suzanne as a suspect. Remember? She was out of town the day Grandma died." I'd told her this part, but I hadn't mentioned who Detective Martinez did suspect: Helen.

"Yeah, but her sister could have lied about Suzanne being with her on that day just to give her an alibi."

"I thought that too at first. But when I talked to Suzanne last week she convinced me that she had no reason to kill Grandma. She said she was going to meet with Grandma in early January to discuss Suzanne's writing her biography. I checked her calendar, and Suzanne did have an appointment."

"Maybe the appointment was about something else. Maybe Grandma wanted to see Suzanne to tell her to get lost."

"That's possible. But I think Suzanne would still have been hoping that Grandma would cooperate with her on the book. This was Suzanne's big chance to get published—something she wanted desperately. She'd be a fool, Annie, to kill the source for her book."

My daughter shot me a malevolent look. "How come you're suddenly on her side?"

"I'm not on her side. I don't even like her. But I don't believe that she killed my mother."

"Then who do you think did it?"

I sighed. "I'm not sure yet."

"So whoever did it is going to get away with it," Annie said angrily.

"Not if I can help it," I snapped back. "And if you want to find out who actually did kill your grandmother, maybe you should stop blowing up all the time and use your head." Stop acting like an adolescent.

Annie looked pointedly away from me. So much for our mother–daughter bonding. We drove the rest of the way in chilly silence.

By the time we pulled into Mother's driveway, I fervently wished I could take back my angry words. Who was I to bite off my daughter's head over excessive emotionalism? I had barely spoken to my mother throughout my own adolescence.

Even walking into this house depressed me. There were too many emotions locked within these four walls that I wasn't yet ready to confront.

Annie followed me inside. I turned to her. "It makes me feel sad to be here," I said, hoping to make up for my outburst, trying to reconnect.

She didn't answer for a minute. Then she looked at me with burning eyes. "That's funny. It makes me feel close to Grandma."

I sighed. So it was going to be one of *those* weekends.

Fortunately there were things I needed to do. "I have to go to the bank and the lawyer's office. Do you want to come with me?"

Annie shook her head. "Could I go to Aunt Helen's?"

"I'll have to phone her," I said, trying to hide my surprise. In recent years Annie seemed to barely tolerate my old teacher. Helen tended to treat all children—and most adults—as if they were in early elementary school.

"Bring her over," Helen said when I called. "I'd love to see you both."

We were at her door twenty minutes later. Helen gave each of us a hug. "How wonderful to see you two."

I hugged her back. How tired she looked! Were Detective Martinez's questions getting to her? Or was something else the matter?

"Would you like a cup of coffee or some iced tea?"

"Mom has a lot of errands she has to run," Annie said.

I glanced at her. Was Annie trying to get rid of me? She turned an innocent-looking face towards me. Yes, indeed, she was trying to push me out the door.

"I do need to get to the bank before it closes," I told Helen. "Could I have that coffee later?"

"Of course, dear." But there was something in the way she said it that didn't sound like the Helen I knew.

"I'll try to get back as quickly as I can," I said, darting an anxious look at my mother's old friend.

"Take your time," Annie said.

Too bad, I thought as I hurried out the door, that I hadn't had enough sense to leave her in Houston.

My errands took less time than I'd expected. At Mother's bank I inspected the contents of her safe-deposit box. There wasn't much inside. She'd kept her insurance policy and most official papers in a vault at her house but continued to keep the backup computer disks of her most recent novels in the bank: For Mother her only real valuables were her writing.

I placed the disks in a padded envelope then drove to the attorney's office to sign some papers. I had twenty minutes to kill before I had to meet a Realtor at Mother's house. On impulse, I pulled out my cell phone and punched in the number I'd written on a scrap of paper.

"Yes?" The belligerent tone of the woman who answered tempted me to hang up. Instead I took a deep breath and identified myself. "I'm in Austin for the day and thought I'd give you a call," I ended lamely.

To my surprise, Suzanne's gravelly voice grew more friendly. "I've been wanting to talk to you too. I have some important things to tell you."

I could feel my heart beat faster. "Have you"—I searched for the right words—"made progress in your investigation?" Such a polite way to say what I wanted to shout: Tell me who you think killed my mother!

"I have. Do you have time to come over now?"

Could she possibly have uncovered something that the police hadn't? "I can't right now. Why don't you tell me over the phone?"

"I don't want to do that. Can you come tonight?"

I hesitated. "I'm not sure."

"Come as late as you want. I'm a night owl."

"I'll have to let you know when I can make it." Was it wise for me to go alone at night to the home of a woman who might very well be mentally unstable? There was also the problem of Annie. If she knew where I was going, she'd want to come along. But bringing her to meet the woman she'd designated as her grandmother's killer seemed like an invitation to disaster.

"Sure, I'm here all day writing. I just got back from a trip where I uncovered some fascinating information." She sounded like a saleswoman making her pitch.

"Well, I need to get going. Talk to you later." I hung up, feeling that I was venturing into dangerous territory.

It was starting to get dark by the time I got back to Helen's. I'd shown the real estate agent the house and made arrangements to put it on the market, all the while wondering who Suzanne had decided had murdered my mother.

"What have the two of you been up to?" I asked Helen.

"Oh, we've just been chatting." Helen nodded at Annie who sat with what looked like a cup of herbal tea.

Chatting for over two hours? I glanced at Annie, who sent me a smug look. "Aunt Helen thinks that Suzanne Lang is up to something too."

"You do?" I asked, turning to her. Wasn't Helen the person who'd told me, after Suzanne had interviewed her, that Suzanne wasn't as bad as she'd originally thought?

"Suzanne Lang is exploiting your mother's death to sell her book," Helen said. "She's making up a murder mystery and inventing conflicts where there were none, just like those tabloid journalists do."

"What kind of conflicts are you talking about?" I wondered if Suzanne had hit a nerve in her interview with Helen, as she had with Ginny.

Helen glanced at Annie. "All kinds," she said stiffly.

"But you're not saying that Suzanne killed Mother," I asked, more for Annie's benefit than my own.

Helen looked shocked. "No, of course not."

"So who do you think killed Grandma?" Annie asked.

"I have no idea. I am not a police officer," Helen said in her grade school teacher voice.

A few minutes later Annie left for the bathroom. Helen said, "Molly, I don't think anyone killed Katherine. I didn't want to say this in front of the girl, but I really believe that Katherine killed herself. Think about it. Those lavish Christmas gifts and appreciative notes. When had she ever done anything like that? It was her final gesture."

"She knew she was dying, Helen. She gave us those gifts because she knew this would probably be her last Christmas, and the notes said what she couldn't say to our faces."

"But look at the way she died: an injection of Stelazine—a technique straight out of her fiction. She told me once that dying from a Stelazine overdose would be fast and relatively painless. I've been giving this a lot of thought. The only explanation that makes sense is that your mother was feeling increasingly ill, but held on until she finished her book. Maybe the book wasn't as polished as she'd have liked, but she'd completed a draft of it.

"I'm sure Katherine intended to make it through Christmas, but she just couldn't. She didn't want anyone to see that she was so sick. You know how she was; she couldn't bear for anyone to see her in distress. She'd been drawing away from me too, coming up with excuses not to see me. And if I expressed concern about her health she practically bit my head off."

I stared at her. "You're saying you think Mother agreed to go out to dinner in order for you to find her body?"

Helen looked uncomfortable. "Maybe. I'm sure the idea of someone not finding her for days—the cleaning lady came on Tuesdays." She swallowed, then began again. "Or maybe she wasn't planning it like that at all. Dinner was my idea, not hers. Maybe Katherine had the Stelazine on hand for when she felt she couldn't go on anymore, and then she decided that time had arrived."

Helen's face softened as she studied me. I knew that what she told me next was going to be very bad news.

"I called the car dealer to see when Katherine bought my car and made the arrangements to have it delivered to me. She signed the papers on December eleventh, the day before she died. And—"

Abruptly she stopped talking as the sounds of Annie's footsteps on her hardwood floor echoed in the hallway.

★ ★ ★ ★ ★

I ended up calling Suzanne at ten-thirty, whispering—in case Annie was awake in the next bedroom—that I could come now, if it wasn't too late.

"Fine," Suzanne said, giving me directions to a tiny stone bungalow near the UT campus.

I tried to convince myself, as I got out of my car, that even though the house looked disreputable, it wasn't a bad neighborhood. Tried not to remember that no one had any idea where I was. In case Annie woke up and found me missing I'd left her a note saying I had to go out for a while. She could call my cell if she needed to get hold of me. Still I didn't feel good about leaving her alone at night in the house where her grandmother had died. She was a heavy sleeper and probably would never realize I was gone, but sometimes the most likely things don't happen.

Suzanne came to the door, dressed in a baggy black sweat suit, her bushy hair tied back in a ponytail. She ushered me into a smoky-smelling dining room where she'd obviously been writing. A laptop computer was surrounded by piles of papers. Suzanne moved a stack from one of the chairs. "Have a seat."

I sat. "I can only stay for a little while," I said. "I left my daughter at Mother's house."

Her lips formed a smile that wasn't quite malicious, but seemed close. "It's your house now."

I shrugged. "Tell me what you wanted to tell me."

She raised an eyebrow. "A cut-to-the-chase woman."

"You might say that." I was already starting to regret my impulse to come alone at night to talk to this strange, angry woman.

"You want to know who killed your mother."

"Yes."

"I've narrowed it down to three suspects."

In other words, you don't know who did it. "Who?"

She lifted tobacco-stained fingers. She touched her left index finger. "Let me give them to you in chronological order. The person I suspected first was your stepmother."

She waited for me to react. When I didn't, she gave that grimace-smile, then continued. "Ginny has a quick temper, a deep-seated dislike of Katherine, and a bad shopping problem. When her husband lost his job, they started having serious financial difficulties."

"I know all that," I said coldly.

"I bet you didn't know that your father and stepmother were both at your mother's house the afternoon she died."

"Ginny told me that Mother never answered the door."

"She would say that, wouldn't she? It's not likely that she'd say, 'Oh, Molly dear, did I mention that I murdered your mother?' "

"Ginny didn't have to tell me anything at all, but she did."

"Did she tell you that her husband was still half in love with Katherine?" she said, watching my face. "After all these years apart, he was still in awe of her—her drive, her talent, her passion. I could see it in his face when I interviewed him for my book."

Why, I wondered, hadn't Dad mentioned to me that he'd talked to Suzanne?

Suzanne leaned back in her chair, enjoying my discomfort. "Jealousy, anger at Katherine's refusal to bail them out of their financial problems, a calculated guess that Katherine's heir—you—would probably be a lot more generous with them: Those are pretty good motives for murder."

I glared at her. "Tell me your other candidates."

Suzanne's eyes narrowed. "Helen Lewis. She's the most obvious suspect, the person who found the body, the one who benefits the most financially—next to you, of course—by Katherine's death."

Tell me something I don't know, I thought. But there was no point in antagonizing her now—not, at least, until I'd heard everything she had to say.

"But the question I always asked myself about Helen," Suzanne added, "was why. If she was going to inherit the money anyway, why kill Katherine now?"

She stared at me, an unblinking, disconcerting appraisal. "Then I found out something intriguing. Did you know that Helen was having serious financial problems?"

I shook my head. "Are you sure about that?"

"Yup. She depleted her savings paying off her mother's hospital bills. Then she invested the rest in her brother's business, and last year the business went belly up. She couldn't afford to lose that money. She'd earned only a modest salary all her life as a teacher. Also"—she smiled that grimace again—"I learned that Helen wasn't getting along so well with her old friend Katherine. She hadn't, in fact, even seen Katherine for over a month. What if Katherine was having second thoughts about the money she'd promised to leave to Helen? All of which gives Helen a pretty strong motive."

I felt a sudden wave of queasiness wash over me. Yes, I thought, it gave her a very good motive indeed.

"And this leads us to our third candidate," Suzanne announced. "Can you guess who it is?"

"Sam Pryor?" My own favorite suspect.

"No. I considered him, but he was in New York that day, with witnesses to verify it. I checked. And I don't think he really believed that Katherine was going to switch agents. Apparently she'd threatened to leave before, but she never did." She looked at me. "Want another guess?"

"Just tell me." It was too late for playing games.

"What would you say if I said I think your grandmother killed your mother?"

"I'd say you'd lost your mind. My grandmother is eighty-two, in poor health, and, from what I saw, hardly ever leaves her nursing home."

"I've met your grandmother—just a few weeks ago, in fact. She was eager to give her version of Katherine's family life for my book. While she may be old, she has the money to hire a hit man. And the ruthlessness to do it without a qualm. It took me a while, but I finally figured out a motive: She knew about Katherine's new book."

"How—how could she know? Certainly Mother wouldn't have told her."

"She didn't. Sam Pryor did." She raised an eyebrow. "So maybe your guess about him as the killer wasn't so off base after all."

I stared at her. "Sam Pryor knows Grandmother?"

Suzanne chuckled. "Luckily for him, he doesn't. But when a *People* reporter contacted Sam for a quote about Katherine's writing career, Sam talked about her 'exciting new book, a coming-of-age mystery novel set in the fifties.' I suspect that your grandmother read that and all the pieces fell into place: why Katherine, after all these years, suddenly decided to visit her last summer, why she was asking so many questions about the past."

"You think she hired a hit man because of what she assumed Mother's new book was about? The book could have been about anything. Mother was never a remotely autobiographical writer."

Suzanne shrugged. "All I'm saying is that a few days after the *People* story came out, your mother was dead."

I still didn't believe it. Hire a hit man to stop publication of a novel? "It would have been a lot easier to hire a lawyer."

"True. But think of the publicity when it got out that Katherine's mother was accusing her of libel in a novel about a social climber who murders her husband when she discovers he's leaving her for a younger woman. Your grandmother spent her whole life trying to look good in other people's eyes. I think she would prefer a more discreet—and more permanent—solution than a lawyer could work out. The only problem with her plan was that she didn't realize Katherine had already finished the book. If she'd killed Katherine a few months earlier, she would have accomplished what she'd intended: to kill the book too."

I tried to sort through everything she'd told me. "But the Stelazine. That isn't what a hit man would choose."

"I'm sure it was your grandmother's idea. She probably hoped that it would look like Katherine had had a heart attack. That was why the psychiatrist in Katherine's novel used the Stelazine injection."

"But Grandmother told me she'd never read an entire book of Mother's."

"Then she lied to you. When we talked she was very knowledgeable about Katherine's work. The nurse told me that Mrs. March liked to read her daughter's novels in front of the other residents."

I sat back, trying to take it all in. "You actually think a hit man hired by my grandmother is the killer?"

Suzanne shrugged. "Unfortunately, I don't know. I do think that one of these three murdered your mother. I'm just not sure which one. That's why I asked you here. You know all three of them. Who do you think did it?"

"I don't know," I said, truthfully. And if I did know, would I tell Suzanne Lang?

"I don't expect you to know for sure who killed her. I'm just asking you to take a guess."

"I'd rule out Ginny."

"Why? Because you like her?"

"No, because I know Ginny. I realize she disliked Mother,

and she does have a bad temper. But she's a yeller, not at all a violent person. She wouldn't murder anyone."

Suzanne nodded. "I'm leaning towards the same conclusion. Which leaves the other two candidates."

"I can't say about them." I wanted to rise to the defense of Helen, my mother's old friend, but for some reason I couldn't. Helen had been acting strangely this weekend, egging Annie on in her hatred of Suzanne, appearing tense and unlike herself. Even her new willingness to believe that Mother committed suicide suddenly seemed suspicious.

And my grandmother? I didn't have a clue. The logistics sounded almost unbelievably complex. Did Grandmother just happen to have the phone number of a hit man—or hit woman, if Mother's four o'clock visitor was a hired assassin? Did one of the nursing home's physicians obligingly write her a prescription for Stelazine when she requested it? Yet she was probably ruthless enough to kill. She was the kind of person who'd do almost anything to get what she wanted.

"I talked to your mother's former nanny when I was in New York," Suzanne said. "Actually, I talked more to her sister. She said you'd been there too."

"Oh, how was Miss O'Ryan? The day when I went out there she seemed quite confused."

"She was pretty disoriented when I saw her too," Suzanne admitted. "It was her sister, Mary Casey, who gave me most of the background information I needed. Now *there* is a woman who really hates your grandmother."

Before I could inquire about Mary's hostility my cell phone rang. I answered it.

"Where are you?" Annie said, sounding furious. "Why did you leave me alone like this?"

I hesitated. This wasn't a conversation I wanted to have now, certainly not with Suzanne a few feet away. "Is something wrong?"

"You left me here by myself. I . . . I'm scared. When are you coming home?"

I knew I shouldn't have left her. "I'll be there in about fifteen minutes, honey. I'm leaving now."

"I have to go," I told Suzanne, starting for the door.

"Stay in touch," she yelled after me with what sounded like a snicker.

CHAPTER TWENTY-TWO

"You left me all alone," Annie screamed when I walked in the door. "In the house where Grandma was killed!"

"Honey, I'm so sorry," I said, moving toward her. "I was only gone for a little while. You were asleep and perfectly safe. I had the locks changed after Grandma died." It was a feeble defense, and I knew it. She had every right to be angry with me.

I started to give her a hug, but she crossed her arms over her chest and glared at me. "So where were you?"

I took a deep breath. "I went to Suzanne Lang's house. She said she needed to talk to me."

"In the middle of the night?"

"Suzanne didn't want to tell me on the phone, and it was the only time I could get away."

"Don't you mean the only time you could get away *without me?*" Annie asked, her voice harsh.

"Since you didn't want to come with me on any of my other errands today, I didn't imagine you'd want to come to Suzanne's either." Which was not entirely true, but I was getting tired of my daughter's love of melodrama.

"What did Suzanne have to say that was so important?"

It was the question I was dreading. Annie deserved an explanation. Her sense of drama might be acute, but her concern about finding her grandmother's killer was genuine. Still there seemed no point in telling her that Suzanne suspected her "Aunt" Helen and Grandma Ginny of being murderers—

not, at least, until there was something more than Suzanne's hunches behind the accusations.

"She wanted to tell me about her efforts to find Grandma's killer," I said. "And no, she doesn't know yet who that is. She's interviewed a lot of people, but she hasn't singled out one of them." She'd singled out three, but we wouldn't go into that.

Annie's large blue eyes narrowed as she considered what I'd said. "Do you still believe she didn't kill Grandma herself?" Her tone was less defiant, more simply curious.

I shook my head. "I don't think she did it." But I could be wrong.

"You think she'll figure out who the real murderer is?"

Our eyes met. "She very well might. Suzanne is a very persistent woman."

What looked like the hint of a smile crossed her face. "Aunt Helen said Suzanne Lang is a real pit bull."

I grinned at her. "On that point Aunt Helen and I are in total agreement."

The moment was gone as quickly as it had come. "I still think she probably killed Grandma herself," she said, once again belligerent.

"You're entitled to your opinion," I said lightly. "But let's go to bed now. We can talk in the morning."

But in the morning Annie was gone.

I had awoken late for me, nine-fifteen. After two cups of coffee I padded to the back door to see what kind of day it was and found it unlocked. But I had locked it last night; I could remember turning the key while Annie railed at me.

Maybe Annie was right outside. I poked my head out the door. No one in sight.

Maybe she came downstairs, stuck her head outside to check out the weather, then decided she needed some more sleep. I hurried up the stairs to her bedroom.

She wasn't there. She also wasn't anywhere else in the house. Her bed had been slept in, her coat and purse were gone, but she'd left no note of explanation.

Think! I told myself, furious and frightened and trying to talk myself out of it. Annie knew practically no one in Austin, didn't drive yet, and wasn't very familiar with the city. Where could she have gone?

I phoned Helen. She lived three or four miles away, but Annie might have decided to walk to her house.

No one answered the phone. Only Helen's recorded voice urged me to leave a message. I did. "Helen, it's Molly. Please call me as soon as you get in."

I threw on a pair of jeans and a sweatshirt and hurried to the car. I would launch my own search. Probably Annie was somewhere nearby, hoping to give her inconsiderate mother a taste of her own medicine—except *I* had left her a note.

After circling the block without seeing her, I drove to Helen's house. Perhaps Annie had just now arrived there, and Helen, home from wherever she'd been, was inviting her in for a cup of herbal tea.

But no one was home when I knocked on Helen's door, and Annie was nowhere in sight.

Where could she be? Maybe Helen was driving her home. Or perhaps Annie had returned on her own.

I drove back to Mother's house, my palms sweating. Annie wasn't there.

With the motor running, I sat in my car, trying to remember everything Annie had said last night—anything that would give me a clue as to where she'd gone.

Suzanne Lang's house! Could Annie have decided to find out for herself what Suzanne had to say? Or maybe she wanted to confront Suzanne. It would have been easy enough to looked up Suzanne's address in the phone book.

I put the car in reverse and drove, well over the speed limit, to Suzanne's. I didn't see Annie, but a great number of other people were there, including three police officers and two paramedics who were carrying a body out of the house on a stretcher.

I parked my car and hurried up to a group of people on the sidewalk. They were watching the covered body being placed in the back of an ambulance. "What's going on?" I asked a tall woman dressed in a jogging suit.

"The woman who lived there died," she said, barely looking at me. "Her sister—the heavy woman standing on the porch—found the body this morning."

I could feel my heart racing. "Died? How did she die?"

This time the woman turned to inspect me. "It should be on the news tonight. Did you know that woman?"

"Not really," I said and hurried to my car.

Annie was back, sitting on the front steps, when I pulled into Mother's driveway. Whatever smart-ass remark she had ready died unspoken when she caught sight of my face. "What's wrong?" she asked. Then "I didn't think you'd be *this* worried."

"Suzanne Lang is dead."

Annie's face turned ashen. "Did somebody kill her?"

"I don't know. I drove to her house looking for you and saw the paramedics taking out her body. Speaking of which—where were you?"

"I went to the Drag, to that UT bookstore you and Dad took us to. I bought some books and stuff." Sheepishly she held up a bag with the University Coop's logo on it.

I stalked past her and went into the house. I'd deal with Annie later. How could Suzanne be dead? Less than twelve hours ago I'd been talking to her. She seemed fine, high-strung and obsessive, perhaps, but healthy enough, enthusiastic about her book, not visibly frightened. What could have happened to her after I left last night?

The phone was ringing. Annie answered it. "It's for you. It's Aunt Helen."

I barely heard what Helen was saying. "I phoned because I was looking for Annie," I said, hoping that was what she'd asked. "But she's home now."

"I must have been at the grocery store when you called. Is something wrong, Molly? You don't sound like yourself."

"Suzanne Lang is dead."

"Oh," Helen said in a flat voice. After a minute she added, "How do you know that?"

"I drove over to her house when I was looking for Annie." The doorbell rang. "I need to go, Helen. Someone's at the door. I'll talk to you later."

Annie had opened the door by the time I got there. Standing in the doorway was Detective Martinez.

"Could I come in?" he asked. "I phoned you in Houston. Your husband told me you were here for the weekend."

I led him to the kitchen and poured us coffee before we settled around the table. From my peripheral vision I could see Annie hovering in the doorway, hoping we wouldn't notice her eavesdropping.

"You're here because of Suzanne Lang's death, aren't you?" I blurted.

Detective Martinez was adept at not displaying his emotions, but I could still see traces of surprise in his eyes. "Yes, but how do you know that?"

I told him about being at Suzanne's last night and driving to her house this morning. "What happened? How did she die?"

Martinez had taken out a small notebook and was jotting down notes. "It looks like suicide."

"What?" I hadn't even considered that possibility.

He looked up and studied me. "She left a note admitting that she'd killed your mother because she tried to stop Ms. Lang from writing a book about her. There was a syringe by her body. It appears that Ms. Lang also died from an injection of Stelazine, although we can't be sure until we get the results of the lab tests and autopsy."

I stared at him, too dumbstruck to speak.

Annie, however, burst into the room proclaiming, "I told you! I knew she was the one who killed Grandma!"

I tried very hard to focus. I'd been chatting last night with the woman who'd cold-bloodedly murdered my mother? "You feel sure Suzanne committed suicide?" I managed to ask the detective.

I could see him hesitate. "Not yet," he finally said. "There was no sign of a break-in or a struggle. No one we talked to seems to have heard anything unusual."

"But?" I ventured.

His thin lips moved into the faintest of smiles. "But the suicide note was typed on her laptop—anyone could have written it. Her sister, who found the body this morning, was certain she didn't kill herself. Said she and Suzanne made plans last night to go shopping and to lunch today."

"For what it's worth, Suzanne didn't seem suicidal to me either when I talked to her. She appeared very involved in writing her book, quite excited about it." I considered telling him about Suzanne's own investigation into my mother's murder, but decided against it. What was the point of maligning three women—two of whom I liked very much?

The detective asked the predictable questions. Had Suzanne expressed any guilt over Mother's death or seemed depressed last night? Had I noticed anything unusual, anyone lurking about when I'd left Suzanne's house?

My answer to all his questions was no. Perhaps I'd been too intent on rushing home to Annie to spot something sinister, but

I didn't think so.

Detective Martinez left a few minutes later, saying he'd phone me when he learned the lab results.

I went back to the kitchen table and sat there, staring at the striped wallpaper I'd always hated.

Annie sat down across from me. "Aren't you glad that they found Grandma's killer?"

I looked at her. She was practically jumping up and down with pent-up excitement. "I just want to make sure she *is* the killer. Then maybe I'll feel glad." Or relieved, or vindicated, or something other than how I was feeling now. "Let's go home, Annie. It's time to leave."

We didn't talk much on the drive home, which was fine with me. Finally around Columbus, Annie said, "I'm really sorry I didn't tell you where I was going this morning. I was trying to make you nervous like you made me."

"It's okay." To show her that I wasn't mad, I asked, "Did you walk to the Drag? That's an awfully long walk."

"No, I took the bus. I phoned Aunt Helen when I got up this morning. It was really early, but I knew she'd be up. I asked her about the bus schedule."

Such a source of information, our Helen, I thought.

"I told her you'd gone to see Suzanne last night," Annie said, sounding relieved that I was finally talking.

I jerked my head toward her. "What did Helen say about that?"

"She wanted to know why you went. I said it had something to do with Suzanne trying to find out who killed Grandma. Then Aunt Helen said Suzanne was making a big mistake."

A big mistake in assuming that Mother had been murdered? Or a mistake in involving me in her schemes? "Did Helen say what kind of mistake she was talking about?"

Annie shook her head. "I asked her that. But she said she had to go. She had an appointment she had to get to."

An appointment to buy groceries? Despite the balmy weather, I felt a sudden chill.

CHAPTER TWENTY-THREE

Alex and Will were sitting at our kitchen table working on the poster for Will's science fair project when Annie and I walked in the door. "Aunt Helen is very worried about you," Will said in the sanctimonious tone I hoped he'd outgrow. "She keeps calling here to see if we know where you are."

"You're not going to believe what happened," Annie announced excitedly, for once more than happy to talk to her little brother. "Suzanne Lang committed suicide, and she left a note admitting that she killed Grandma."

"She killed Grandma?" Will asked, wide-eyed.

"Suicide?" Alex said, turning to me. Apparently Detective Martinez hadn't given him the news.

I told him what I knew, admittedly not much.

Will said, "I wish the police had caught her instead, and she'd had to go to prison."

Annie looked at him. "Me too." After a pause, she added, "Mom went to Suzanne's house last night to talk to her."

"Did she try to kill you too?" Will asked, looking scared.

"No," I assured him. "I was only there a little while, and all she did was talk about the book she was writing."

Alex raised his eyebrows. I could see he was practically bursting with questions that I was too tired to answer.

"I have a terrible headache," I said. "I'm going to take some Advil and lie down for a while. Would you do me a big favor, Alex, and phone Helen? Tell her I'm sorry I didn't call her back to let her know we decided to leave early, but right now I'm not up to talking."

"Sure," Alex said, looking puzzled, probably wondering why I couldn't phone Helen myself.

It was a question I needed to think about later: why the very idea of talking to my mother's old friend was suddenly so repellent to me. But first I needed a nap.

An hour later I awoke, hoping that Alex hadn't left. I really needed to talk to him, to get his take on everything that had happened.

He was sitting in the kitchen, grading papers. "How's your headache?"

"Better. Now I can tell you about Suzanne Lang."

He waited expectantly, his head cocked to one side. It was one of the things I'd always loved about Alex: his genuine interest in what I was thinking and his patience when it took me a while to articulate it.

I told him how Suzanne had insisted I come to her house to talk to her and what she'd said about Ginny, Helen, and Grandmother.

Alex whistled. "Those are some theories. How did you react when she told you all this?"

"I told her I didn't believe Ginny did it, but I didn't say anything about the other two. I wasn't there very long. I had to get back to Annie."

"Maybe Suzanne was trying out her accusations on you—to see if you'd buy them. And when you didn't, she might have decided that nobody else would believe them either."

I considered what he was saying. "I just can't believe that Suzanne killed herself because of my lack of enthusiasm for her suspect list. Martinez had no evidence on her. It wasn't as if Suzanne had to prove that someone else was the murderer to get herself off the hook."

Alex shrugged. "Maybe being around you made her feel guilty about killing your mother."

"She didn't act guilty. For that matter, she didn't seem suicidal either."

Alex stared at me. "Are you saying you think she didn't commit suicide?"

"I don't know," I said miserably. "She was the person I suspected from the very beginning. And the suicide note gave her a motive. Suzanne would see Mother's refusal to cooperate with her biography as destroying her only real chance to get a book published. I never could believe that Mother, with her privacy fetish, would agree to let Suzanne write her life story. I could even see Suzanne finding it amusing to use a technique straight from Mother's novel to kill her. It's like saying 'See what a Katherine March expert I am.' "

"You sound as if you're trying to convince yourself," Alex said.

I sighed. "I don't know, Alex. It just doesn't feel right. Maybe I need some time for it all to sink in."

He walked to the kitchen counter and returned with a small package. "This came in the mail for you."

The return address said the box was from Mary Casey, the sister of Mother's old nanny. I cut open the brown paper and found a letter for me inside the box.

"Margaret O'Ryan died last week. She had a heart attack," I told Alex after I read it. "Her sister says that after I came to visit, Miss O'Ryan told her that she wanted 'Katherine's daughter to have my journals from the years I was teaching the March girls.' "

There were six hard-covered composition notebooks in the box. I opened the top one. The pages had yellowed and the ink faded, but the handwriting was impeccable. I read the first few pages. "This is interesting," I told Alex. "She's describing meeting Mother's family for the first time. She likes Mother—'a bright, likeable girl with an inquiring mind and a love of books.' She doesn't have a lot of use for Charlotte—'pretty, skittish, and not much of a student.' And she really doesn't like Grandmother, says she's a 'vain, brittle socialite, and an indifferent mother.' Grandfather, though, is 'kind and cultivated' and 'a passionate reader.' "

I read a few pages further. Mother, to Miss O'Ryan's delight, was breezing through all the Dickens novels. Charlotte was bright enough but had a short attention span. Grandmother had informed the nanny that it didn't make any difference if Charlotte was a poor student. She was going to be a great beauty and marry brilliantly.

"Well, she was right about the marriage part," Alex said, reading over my shoulder. He picked up another journal and we both read in silence.

Two years later my mother was still the model student, Charlotte a bratty underachiever, and Grandmother had left everyone behind while she traveled in Europe. In her absence Margaret got better acquainted with my grandfather. One Saturday after the girls were in bed, they had a "long, heated conversation" about their favorite authors. And the next afternoon they took the girls for a "delightful picnic in the country."

"Margaret clearly was enamored of your grandfather," Alex said, "but I'm not sure if he was even aware of her feelings. He may have been just a book lover eager to discuss literature with another passionate reader."

I skimmed a few more pages. "I can't imagine why she wanted me to have these journals. Aside from the part about her crush on Grandfather, it's pretty tedious reading."

He shrugged. "Maybe they were her only mementos of your mother, and she wanted you to have them. And who knows? Maybe the later journals are more intriguing."

"They might be." I wanted to read further but right now there were too many other things I needed to do. "Speaking of reading," I told Alex, "I brought back some computer disks from Mother's safe-deposit box that I think are the backups for her latest writing. I need to take a look at them. Sam Pryor wants to know if Mother left any unpublished manuscripts."

"That sounds a lot more interesting than Miss O'Ryan's journals," Alex said. "Maybe I'll look at them when we're out of school next week. Oh, by the way, Helen said you should call her when you're feeling better."

"I'll do that, but not today."

Or not the next five days either. Somehow I always forgot to phone Helen or found excuses not to return her calls.

I tried to figure out why I was so unwilling to even speak to Helen, a woman I'd known and liked for years. Did I honestly think she'd had anything to do with Suzanne Lang's death or—I could scarcely bear to even think it—my mother's? Certainly I had no proof of anything. Helen could have had a hairdresser's appointment before she went to the grocery store last Saturday morning. And while she certainly had not seemed upset when I told her Suzanne was dead, I hadn't really talked to her long enough to have an accurate idea of her feelings. Helen probably was guilty of nothing more than disliking Suzanne Lang.

I wondered if some strange, misplaced pride was fueling my belief that Suzanne had not killed herself. Wouldn't I have picked up on any suicidal thoughts Suzanne was having—me, smart, sensitive Molly Patterson? Of course I hadn't known Suzanne well and I was with her only a few minutes. And maybe the impulse to kill herself had gripped her suddenly hours after I left.

Tomorrow afternoon, when I had no classes, I would call Helen. Even if I didn't want to, even if my instincts told me that she knew more about Suzanne Lang's death than she was admitting.

Detective Martinez phoned as I was getting ready to go to school the next morning. "We got the reports back from the lab," he said. "It was Stelazine in the syringe we found next to Ms. Lang's body."

"So now do you think it was suicide?" I asked.

"No, I don't."

I could feel my heart racing. "You think she was murdered?"

"That's what it's beginning to look like. The autopsy showed she had a skull fracture. Either she hit her head after the shot took effect or someone purposely knocked her out. My own guess is that somebody hit her. She was probably unconscious when she got the shot of Stelazine."

It was what I'd been expecting all along: murder, not suicide. But now, when my suspicions were corroborated, I was suddenly speechless.

"I just wanted to ask you a few questions about your conversation with Ms. Lang," the detective said. "Did she happen to mention anything to you about Helen Lewis?"

"Helen?" I squeaked. Idiotically, my knee-jerk reaction was to try to protect her. But then the full force of what Detective Martinez had just said hit me. The kind, blunt, gray-haired woman I'd known most of my life, the loyal friend to whom my mother had left a car and a million dollars: This woman had likely murdered at least one woman—and very possibly two.

"Yes," I said firmly, "Suzanne told me she thought Helen Lewis could have killed my mother. She said Helen was having serious financial problems and was afraid that Mother would write her out of her will. Mother hadn't seen her for weeks."

I could hear the detective expel a breath. When he spoke again, he sounded as if he was making an effort to sound calm.

"Did you mention this conversation to Ms. Lewis?"

"No."

"Did Suzanne Lang say if she told Ms. Lewis her suspicions?"

"No. I didn't talk to her for very long. I had to get back to my daughter. And, to be fair, Helen wasn't the only person who Suzanne suspected. She told me she also thought my stepmother or my grandmother might have killed Mother."

"Your grandmother?" Despite himself, Martinez could not hide his incredulity. "How old is she?"

"She's in her eighties, but Suzanne thought she'd hired a hit man."

"She mention any motive?"

"Grandmother didn't like her portrayal in the book Mother was writing." I suddenly noticed the time. My class was starting in twenty-five minutes. "I'm sorry, I'm late for work."

"I'll let you go," he said. "I just wanted to let you know that a jogger saw Helen Lewis leave Ms. Lang's house on the morning she was killed. I'm bringing Ms. Lewis in for questioning."

CHAPTER TWENTY-FOUR

The insistent ringing of the phone roused me out of a deep sleep. "Molly?" The voice on the phone seemed far away, part of my dream of walking into Suzanne Lang's house and once again encountering the abrasive woman with the wild gray hair. "Molly, is that you? This is Charlotte."

The urgency in my aunt's voice jolted me awake. "Yes," I mumbled, "what's wrong?" The illuminated numbers on the alarm clock said it was one-fifteen in the morning.

"Mother's dead," she said, sounding on the verge of tears. "The home just called me."

"Oh, no, Charlotte. I'm so sorry," I said. Still half asleep, I barely heard all the details.

"Apparent heart attack . . . died in her sleep . . . Molly, I'm so upset even though I knew this was coming," Charlotte was saying.

"I know what a shock it is," I said, remembering the phone call about Mother's death, a call I hadn't expected for a good twenty years. "If there's anything I can do . . ."

"Yes, there is something. Please come to the funeral. I want you to be here with me, Molly. We're the last of the March women."

Oh, God. I was awake enough now to remember that I'd be out of town, on spring break, next week. I explained this to Charlotte, leaving unspoken the other part of my objection to coming: I barely knew my grandmother and, on the few occasions I'd been around her, I hadn't liked her at all.

But my aunt wasn't going to let me off the hook. "Oh, please come. You don't have to stay long, just a day or two."

Reluctantly I agreed. I'd go for Charlotte's sake, I told myself, not for Grandmother's.

"Thank you, Molly!" my aunt said. "It means so much to have your family with you at times like this."

I hung up, knowing that sleep was going to elude me. Not for the first time I wished Alex was back at home, lying beside me. Ever since Suzanne Lang's death, I seemed to crave his warmth, his calming presence, and his wry sense of humor. Missed having him wrap his arms around me when someone phoned in the middle of the night with bad news. And somehow, without me really noticing the change, I'd stopped being angry at him.

When Alex had suggested that the whole family go to a friend's cabin for spring break, I'd enthusiastically agreed. Although we were advertising it as a family vacation, it was also, we decided, a tentative try at getting back together—a "trial reconciliation," as Alex joked.

Except now would I be in New York when the rest of the family went fishing and hiked through the woods?

Three nights later I was on the plane to New York. I'd managed to whittle the visit down to the bare bones: I'd spend the nights before and after the funeral with Aunt Charlotte and still would be able to go with my family for a few days at the cabin.

But I still couldn't shake my conviction that I should be home with my family instead. My children were acting like the walking wounded. Will pounded me with questions I wasn't able to answer about Helen's guilt or innocence while Annie hardly talked at all. She'd overheard me tell Alex that the police were questioning Helen about Suzanne's death and burst into tears. "It's all my fault," she'd sobbed. "If I hadn't told Aunt

Helen about you talking to Suzanne Lang, she would never have gone to Suzanne's house that morning."

"That's just not true, Annie," I said, wrapping an arm around her thin shoulders. "Did you tell Helen to go over to Suzanne's?"

Sniffing, she shook her head. "No." She dabbed at her eyes with a tissue. "You think she killed Suzanne Lang, don't you?" she asked, shaking free of my arm.

I sighed. "I don't know. But I do know that whatever Helen did is not remotely your fault. That I am sure of."

"Well I think that Suzanne Lang killed Grandma and then killed herself in the same way," Annie announced, her eyes glistening. "Maybe she was feeling guilty for what she did. Or maybe she was afraid someone would find out that she killed Grandma."

"Maybe you're right," I said mildly. Maybe not.

She gave me a suspicious look, then marched to her room. Which was, more or less, where she stayed these days when she wasn't at school.

But there was nothing I could do right now to help my children. I settled back in my seat, trying to read the boring airline magazine. I rummaged through my oversized purse; usually I could find something in there to read. What I discovered was the last book of Margaret O'Ryan's journal. I'd tossed it in my purse on a day I was taking Will to the orthodontist and then promptly forgot about it.

I sighed as I started to skim the first pages. Mother must have been in high school at this point. Her old nanny affectionately described her "heated discussions with Katherine on the marvelous Brontë sisters." Miss O'Ryan by that time was officially only working as Charlotte's tutor, a job she found frustrating at best. At thirteen, Charlotte, she wrote, was "totally unmotivated and interested only in boys." Obviously her unpaid discussions with Mother were what kept her coming back to the house.

I skimmed a few entries about rebellious, boy-crazy Charlotte, suddenly a "belligerent, headstrong girl," a "defiant child who is blatantly rude to me." Welcome to adolescence, I thought, recalling the rude, headstrong daughter I'd left at home. I closed the journal, deciding to catch a quick nap before the plane landed. I'd read about what a bratty teenager my aunt was some other time.

Charlotte herself was waiting for me when I got off the plane. She was dressed all in black: wool slacks, cashmere sweater and wool blazer, which on her looked more like a fashion statement than mourning clothes. "I'm so glad you're here, Molly," she said, giving me a hug.

I studied Charlotte's expertly made-up face. She looked tired, but she seemed to be coping with her loss.

"I feel terrible about interrupting your vacation," she said as we walked to her car.

"Oh, we're still going to the cabin for a few days." Alex had insisted that they couldn't go without me. "We'll leave as soon as I get home."

Charlotte asked polite questions. What kind of place were we staying in? Was it far from Houston?

I told her what I knew. The cabin was going to eventually be the retirement home of a friend of Alex's, so I was hoping it wouldn't be too primitive. It was on Lake Conroe, less than an hour from our house. "Supposedly it's surrounded by forest, on a road called—if you can believe this—Leading Nowhere Drive. There's supposed to be a boat we can use; Alex and Will love to fish. I, on the other hand, will probably just sit on the dock and read."

"Sounds like a very relaxing vacation," Charlotte said as she tossed my suitcase into her Mercedes.

"So how are you holding up?" I asked as she pulled the car into the line of traffic. It was the question, I remembered, that she'd asked me when I'd first come to visit her, barely two months ago.

My aunt considered the question. "I knew this was coming, of course. But nothing ever really prepares you for that phone call in the middle of the night. I'd just visited Mother that afternoon, and she didn't seem worse than any other day. In fact she seemed a little better."

I glanced at her and saw a tear trickle down her cheek. "I'm glad you had a chance to visit her."

"Me too." She took a deep breath. "Mother was actually in a good mood. She kept talking about the conversation she'd had a few weeks ago with that woman who's writing a biography about Katherine, Suzanne Lang. Amazingly the two of them really got along well together. I think Suzanne just let Mother talk and show her family photos."

A slight smile curved Charlotte's thin lips. "Suzanne saved all the touchy questions about Mother's relationship with Katherine for me. But she assured me she wouldn't do a hatchet job on Mother. If she does what she says, her book should have a much more sympathetic portrayal of the family than Katherine's novel."

I stared at her. She didn't know about Suzanne. But then how would she know? "I'm not sure how to tell you this," I began tentatively. "There will be no Suzanne Lang biography of Mother. Suzanne is dead."

"Dead?" Charlotte turned to stare at me.

"Watch out!" I yelled as she almost sideswiped the taxi in the lane next to us.

Charlotte veered back into her lane, ignoring the honking. Thank God the woman had good reflexes.

"How did she die?" Charlotte asked. "And when? Why it was

only a few weeks ago that she was here talking to Mother and me."

I took several deep calming breaths before I answered. "She died a little over a week ago. Annie and I were in Austin for that weekend, and I saw Suzanne the night before. She died from an injection of Stelazine, the same thing that killed Mother. At first the police thought she'd committed suicide, but now they've arrested Helen Lewis on suspicion of murdering her."

"Helen Lewis, Katherine's friend?" Charlotte asked, looking astonished, but—I was glad to see—keeping her eyes on the road.

"Yes."

"But why would she murder Suzanne Lang?"

I hesitated, then settled for the answer I'd given Will when he'd asked the same question. "I don't know that Helen *did* murder Suzanne. A neighbor saw her leaving Suzanne's house shortly before Suzanne's sister discovered the body." I shrugged. "But maybe Helen was just at the wrong place at the wrong time." Except the police detective investigating the case didn't seem to think so.

Charlotte, unlike my son, didn't pursue the topic. We drove in silence for a few minutes. Then my aunt sighed. "I was just thinking," she said sadly, "how many people I know who have died this winter: first Katherine, then Suzanne, and now Mother."

"And Miss O'Ryan too," I said. "Her sister sent me a note that she'd had a heart attack last month."

Charlotte shook her head. "I didn't know that." Silence, like the darkness outside, seemed to envelope us once again. "I'll be happy," my aunt said, "when it's finally spring."

The funeral the next day was a stiff, solemn affair. I sat in the front pew of the lovely old Episcopal church between Charlotte and her son, Andrew, the cousin who I'd just met minutes earlier, while a nasal, white-haired priest eulogized my grandmother. He listed all the organizations she had belonged to, the accomplishments of her publisher husband and of her two daughters, Katherine, "the well-known suspense novelist," and Charlotte, "a philanthropist whose work has benefited dozens of charities." Grandmother, I thought, would have been pleased by the service: the eulogy covered only the glossy surface she wanted to display to the world, and a lot of well-dressed people were there to hear it.

Next to me Charlotte sobbed quietly into a lace handkerchief. Andrew, on my other side, looked on the verge of sleep. I glanced back at the assembled mourners. Most of the group seemed to be Charlotte's contemporaries, but I also spotted a few elderly people, possibly friends of Grandmother's, and I recognized two nurses I'd met at her nursing home. No one except Charlotte, I thought, seemed especially upset by Grandmother's death.

The whole funeral ordeal was over by early evening, after a steady stream of Grandmother's and Charlotte's friends had come to my aunt's apartment to pay their respects. The day had exhausted me. I was tired of making conversation with total strangers, fed up with pretending that I had any emotional connection at all with the deceased. I wished I could think of some excuse to get on an earlier plane, to leave tonight rather than tomorrow morning. I'd done my duty and now all I wanted was to go home to my real family.

"A good turnout," Andrew said to his mother and me after everyone had left. He was a thin, jittery man who had his mother's coloring but not her good looks. He'd been swilling Scotch throughout the afternoon, his shrill laughter growing louder with his increasing alcohol consumption.

"Yes, Mother would have been pleased," Charlotte said.

"I think it had more to do with people's feelings towards you than towards Grandmother," Andrew said.

"Whatever do you mean?" Charlotte asked.

Andrew looked at me and winked. "They know what Molly and I know: It's smart to stay on Charlotte Todd's good side."

"Oh, Andrew, you're ridiculous," Charlotte said. But I thought she looked secretly pleased by the remark.

I could hear the phone ringing somewhere in the apartment. The maid who'd been cleaning up in the kitchen must have answered it because a minute later she appeared in the living room. "Phone's for you, Mrs. Patterson. It's your husband."

I stood up. "Thanks. I'll take the call in my bedroom."

I hurried to the guest room and picked up the phone. "Alex, is anything wrong?"

"No, everything's fine. I wanted to let you know what I just found: a new ending to your mother's novel! A much stronger version. She must have rewritten the book after all."

"Another ending?" I asked, trying to take it all in. "Where did you find it?"

"On the computer disks you got from her safe-deposit box. I had some free time so I decided to see what was on them. The beginning of the book seemed exactly like the manuscript you brought home, but I was curious to see if Katherine worked on the last chapters, the section you thought was so weak. And she had. The last seventy pages or so of the book are totally different."

"That's terrific." And incredible.

"Your mother even changed the person who's the killer," Alex said.

"You're kidding."

"No, but I'll let you read it for yourself. I think the book works better this way, and the writing is infinitely superior to the earlier draft."

"I can't wait to read it. Why don't you print out the new pages, and I'll read them tomorrow at the cabin."

"I already have."

We chatted for a few minutes more. I told him about the funeral and he talked about the preparations for our trip.

"Well, I'll see you tomorrow morning then," Alex said. "I love you."

I grinned. "And I love you too." Once again.

I held the phone for a few seconds after Alex had hung up, thinking over what he'd just told me. Amazing! So Mother had revised her book after all.

The sound of another phone hanging up clicked in my ear. I stared, open-mouthed, at the receiver I was still holding. How long had someone else been on the line?

CHAPTER TWENTY-FIVE

Charlotte drove me to the airport. "I can't tell you how much I appreciate your coming to the funeral," she said, giving me a hug. "And I know it would have meant a great deal to Mother too."

I had almost an hour to kill before my flight left. Brenda Stein had told me that she liked to get to the office before everyone else arrived. I dug through my purse for my address book and walked to a pay phone.

"Brenda Stein," the familiar voice answered.

"Brenda, it's Molly Patterson. I'm so glad you're there. I have the most exciting news."

"Tell me. I could use some excitement."

"Alex, my husband, just found another version of Mother's book—apparently a later draft. He said the final section is much stronger in this one."

"Why, that's wonderful. Where did Alex find this new manuscript?"

"It was on computer disks in Mother's safe-deposit box. I assumed that they were a backup of the manuscript I'd sent you and didn't bother to take a look at them. Fortunately Alex did."

"That's incredible," Brenda said. "I've tried to work on those last chapters, but the ending still isn't good. I kept thinking, If only Katherine had had more time, she could have revised it, breathed some life into it. I can't wait to read this new version. When can you get it to me?"

"Soon. I want to read it first myself."

"Call me the minute you finish. I want to hear all about it."

I laughed. "You will—I promise. Oh, Brenda, I need to go. They're calling my flight now."

"You've made my day, Molly. Talk to you soon."

I hurried to the plane, wishing I could be so enthusiastic. Instead all I felt was anxious. Of course I'd already been worried—about how my kids were doing, about Helen's guilt or innocence—when I arrived. And this short visit, with the glossy funeral for a mean-spirited woman who'd been a terrible parent to my mother and nothing at all to me, had only added to my sense of unease.

And who had been eavesdropping on my phone conversation with Alex last night? And why? When I'd returned to the living room after the call, my aunt was walking Andrew to the door. Could it have been the maid who'd merely lifted another phone to make a call—an innocent mistake? I didn't know, after all, how long the other person had been on the line; I'd only heard someone hang up.

On the other hand, it wouldn't have surprised me at all if my drunken, obnoxious cousin had sneaked away to the extension in one of the bedrooms for the sole purpose of eavesdropping on my conversation. If he'd hurried, he would have had time to get back to the living room before I rejoined the group. The man was just the kind of spiteful gossip who'd get a kick out of listening in on other people's conversations.

And then there were all of my questions about Helen. After questioning her, had Detective Martinez decided that she wasn't involved in Suzanne's death? Or had their discussion only made him more eager to press charges against Helen? And what about my mother? Could Helen have murdered her old friend before she "discovered" Mother's body?

I took several deep breaths, willing myself to relax. I couldn't answer any of these questions right now, and I was only upsetting myself by thinking about them. My sense of foreboding was ridiculous, I told myself. Snap out of it, Molly! You're going on a vacation with your intact, newly reconciled family.

I felt a rush of pleasure when I got off the plane and spotted Alex and the kids. I gave each of them an extra-long hug.

"I thought we'd skip going home and just leave for the cabin from here," Alex said. "They're predicting rain this afternoon. Maybe we can get in a few good hours on the water before the bad weather rolls in."

"I told him that we should just stay home," Annie interjected. She was dressed in blue jeans and an oversized black T-shirt, accessorized by Mother's huge turquoise and silver pendant and dangling turquoise earrings. "That way if it's pouring down rain I can at least go to the mall or watch TV."

"And I told her that she could go to the mall any weekend," Alex said.

"You packed my clothes?" I asked my husband, hoping I wasn't going to have to spend the next few days in the tailored pants suit I was now wearing.

"Yup," Alex said. "Annie helped too."

"I told him to pack that grungy navy sweat suit you practically live in on the weekends," Annie said. "And that ratty white sweater you like and those gross old tennis shoes."

"Thanks a lot," I said, trying not to sound sarcastic. I could tell from Annie's expression she thought I should be pleased that she'd been so observant about my clothes.

"I talked to Aunt Helen on the phone," Annie said as she climbed into the back seat. "She wanted to talk to you, Mom, but I said you were out of town."

I shot a quick, inquiring look at Alex. He shrugged. "Did Aunt Helen have anything else to say?"

"She said the whole thing was a terrible mistake and she really, really needs to talk to you. Right away. Why don't you call her now on Dad's cell phone?"

Alex glanced over his shoulder at his daughter. "Give your mother a break, Annie. She's barely been back fifteen minutes. And I'm sure she might appreciate a little privacy for her phone call."

"Whatever." From the visor mirror I could see Annie scowl. "But you do need to call her today."

I sighed. Whatever.

"The weather channel said we could be getting a big storm," Will was saying when, finally, we turned down the gravel road marked Leading Nowhere Drive. He peered out the window at the already darkening sky. "Wouldn't it be cool if we had to climb on the roof of the cabin and be picked up by a helicopter or a rescue boat? I saw that on TV once."

"Don't get your hopes up, Will," Alex said, sounding amused. "I don't think your helicopter rescue is slated for today."

"People drown in those floods!" Annie said. When I turned around she too was peering out the window, though, unlike her brother, she looked anxious. "Why are we risking our lives to go to a boring cabin that nobody wants to go to anyway?"

"I want to go there," Will said.

"Me too," Alex said.

"You would," Annie said, crossing her arms across her chest and lapsing into sullen silence.

At least the cabin was easy to find. It was a small, squat stone house that overlooked the lake. Inside was one large, multipurpose room—kitchen, living room/dining room—three small bedrooms, and a bathroom. The large room had a great view of the river but the furniture—what there was of it—looked as if it had come from someone's attic.

Ignoring Annie's dramatic sighs, I got to work unpacking the supplies that Alex and Will were bringing in from the car. "I think we're going to need more food," I told Alex. "I'll drive back to that convenience store we passed to pick up some supplies."

"Do you mind if I stay here?" Alex asked. "I promised Will we'd go exploring before it starts to rain."

"Go ahead. I certainly can go grocery shopping by myself."

"I'll come with you," Annie offered.

"Great," I said, trying to hide my surprise.

The minute we got in the car, Annie said, "I really need to talk to you."

I backed onto the road, then glanced at her. "I'm listening."

"It's about Aunt Helen. I'm really worried about her. When she called yesterday, she just didn't sound like herself."

"What do you mean?"

Annie hesitated, then said, "You know how she's always so in charge, like 'I'm the teacher and you better listen to me'?"

I nodded.

"Well she's not like that anymore. She's just very quiet and depressed-sounding. I told her you'd gone to New York and then we all were coming to this cabin. She said it was very important that you phone her."

I glanced at my daughter's anxious face. "I'll call her the minute we get back to the cabin, honey," I said as I pulled the Explorer into a parking space in front of the convenience store.

Annie and I left the store half an hour later, loaded down with considerably more groceries than I'd intended to buy. A chatty, grandfatherly clerk had advised us to stock up on candles, flashlights, and bottled water. "It seems like every time a bad storm comes, the electricity goes out. I wouldn't like to think of you folks sitting there in the dark. Y'all staying around here?"

"We're in a cabin at the end of Leading Nowhere Drive," Annie said. "Does that road flood bad when it rains?"

"No worse than any other of those old gravel roads," he said cheerfully.

The sky was looking more ominous by the time we got back to the cabin. "I thought you said you were only going to pick up a few supplies," Alex said as he helped us carry the bags into the house.

"Let's just say that we have enough nonperishable food, flashlights, and magazines to withstand a siege."

"You said you were going to call Aunt Helen when we got here," Annie reminded me.

I might as well get it over with, I thought, taking the cell phone into the bedroom. At least I owed it to Helen to hear what she had to say. But when I dialed her number, the answering machine played its recorded message.

"Helen, it's Molly. I'd like to talk to you. You can call me here"—I left my cell phone number—"or I'll try you again tomorrow."

I walked into the living room where the rest of my family was peering out the window as lightning arced across the now-black sky. "It looks as if we got back in the nick of time," I said as the rain began in earnest. "Helen isn't home, Annie, but I left a message."

"Okay." Annie was turning her attention to the stack of magazines that she'd insisted we buy.

The idea of settling down for a good read seemed suddenly appealing to me too. "Alex, you did think to pack the ending to Mother's novel, didn't you?"

He pointed to a bulky folder that was sitting on the kitchen table. "I printed out the whole manuscript for you."

"Thanks." I curled up at one end of the old couch and started reading. I skimmed the early chapters to keep the story straight in my head: Jane Page, a bright college-bound eighteen-year-old and the book's narrator, is devastated when her beloved father dies suddenly of an apparent heart attack immediately after his fiftieth birthday party. She is furious to see how little the rest of her family mourns his death. Her mother, Anne, enraged that her husband had been about to leave her for another woman, finds widowhood preferable to divorce, while her younger sister, Emily, a boy-crazy fourteen-year-old, barely seems to notice that her father is gone.

These chapters, as far as I could recall, seemed identical to the manuscript I'd read. But today I picked up nuances I'd missed the first time. Jane—the character who seemed to be based on Mother—was more prickly than I'd remembered, a petulant daddy's girl who starts her investigation into her father's death more from a desire to embarrass her vacuous, socialite mother than from any real conviction that her father had actually been murdered.

I breezed through the middle chapters. No one is buying Jane's claim that her father's death was a murder: not the local police or the doctor who pronounced his death due to a heart attack. The only person who is starting to believe her story is Jane herself, who realizes, as she assembles the pieces of evidence, that the scenario which had begun as a vengeful what-if game now looks more and more like an account of what actually happened. And suddenly her mother is looking like an actual murderer.

I stopped reading long enough to make myself a cup of instant coffee and watch sheets of rain cross the sky. Then I returned to the story.

With sanctimonious, teenaged certainty, Jane confronts her mother. "I know you killed Father, even if no one else believes it."

Her mother leaps up and slaps Jane hard across the face. "How dare you accuse me! Get out of my house! And don't come back until you're ready to apologize."

This scene had also been in the manuscript I'd read. But that novel had ended—quite abruptly, I thought—in the next chapter when Jane, disillusioned and unable to convince anyone of her mother's guilt, went off to college, determined to never again return to her childhood home. Her new life as an independent and rather cynical adult had begun.

This version, however, was considerably different. A day after the confrontation with her mother Jane is at home packing. Her mother is vacationing with friends, while Jane and her younger sister stay home with the housekeeper. Jane has the weekend to pack and move out.

Throughout the summer Jane has paid little attention to Emily. They'd never been close, and with Jane's obsession with investigating her father's death and Emily's focus on her latest boyfriend, the two of them had barely laid eyes on each other. But now Emily has broken up with the boyfriend and is spending the weekend sulking at home.

Jane answers a phone call from the mother of Emily's former boyfriend. Someone has poisoned her son's dog; he is convinced that Emily did it.

Emily denies the accusation. "If I wanted to poison anyone, I would have poisoned Bob!" she tells Jane. "Why bother with his dumb dog?"

Jane suddenly notices how the housekeeper hurries away whenever Emily enters the room. A teacher who has been tutoring Emily on Saturdays falls down the stairs, breaking her ankle. Emily is amused by the accident. "I guess she won't be tutoring me anymore this summer," she chuckles.

Over dinner Emily casually tells Jane about her recent visit to their diabetic grandmother's house. "Mother was too much of a sissy to give Grandmother her insulin shot. She says needles make her faint. I had to give the shot while Mother looked away."

Jane stares at her sister. She feels confident that their father's heart failure was caused by an air bubble injected, via an empty hypodermic syringe, into a main artery—a simple but fatal technique described in a Dorothy Sayers novel that Jane found in the drawer of her mother's nightstand. Her search through their house also uncovered a package of hypodermic syringes in a bathroom medicine cabinet.

But Jane has been wrong about the identity of the murderer. Her sister, not her mother, killed Father. Anne may have wished her husband dead, but she hasn't the stomach for murder. Only Emily, cold and utterly ruthless, does.

A clap of thunder behind me made me jump. There was more to the book, several more chapters, in fact, but that wasn't what I wanted to read now. Jane's conviction that something was very wrong with her pretty younger sister was triggering a strange response in me. I had read this before! Not as well written an account nor such dramatic incidents, but just a list of small cruelties and a tutor's uneasiness over her student's growing deviance.

I hurried to the bedroom to find my purse. I dug around until I found Margaret O'Ryan's last journal—the reading I'd thought so tedious on the plane. With shaking hands I turned to the page where I'd left off and read steadily for the next half hour.

When I returned to the main room, Alex sent me a quizzical look. "Is something wrong, Molly?"

"I'm not sure," I said, feeling dazed. Was it significant that my mother's portrayal of the amoral adolescent murderer in her novel was almost exactly the way that Margaret O'Ryan had described the young Charlotte March in her journal? Both Miss O'Ryan and the novel's young narrator—the character based on

Mother—had realized, with horror, that there was a psychopath in their midst.

As I turned to watch a bolt of lightning slice across the dark sky I felt the same horror. And fear.

CHAPTER TWENTY-SIX

"You can't possibly think that Charlotte actually killed your grandfather," Alex said. He hesitated. "I mean, Molly, in Katherine's earlier draft her mother was the killer."

"I know," I said miserably. "I'm not sure what to think anymore." We'd moved to our bedroom—about the only place in the cabin where the kids wouldn't hear us—to have this conversation. I glanced out the window in time to see a bolt of lightning slice across the sky above the water. The rain was letting up a bit but the weather still seemed threatening.

I wanted to believe that *The Summer That Changed Everything* was pure fiction. Other writers used real-life situations and characters based on actual people and then built a make-believe plot around them. Wasn't that, in all likelihood, what my mother had done? If Mother had wanted to expose her father's killer, wouldn't she have written a true-crime book? So maybe this was just another of her suspense novels.

A sound from the front of the cabin made me turn. "Alex, did you just hear somebody knocking on the door?" Who in their right mind would be out in such terrible weather?

Alex and I made it to the front room just as Annie and Will were opening the door. "Hey, Aunt Helen," Will said to the figure in the doorway. "Come in. You sure look wet."

Helen? What was she doing here? I hurried over to the bedraggled-looking woman in the dripping cardigan, her gray hair plastered flat to her head. "Helen, you must be freezing!

225

Take off your sweater and let me get you some dry clothes."

She turned to me, her expression strange, as if she was not sure of who I was. Her eyes, I thought, looked bright, feverish. Was she ill? "I need to talk to you, Molly," she said in a too-loud voice. "Right away."

"You can talk to me in the bedroom while you change your clothes," I said firmly, shaking my head when Annie started to follow us.

The minute I closed the bedroom door Helen grabbed my arm. "You have to listen to me!"

Her hands were icy. The woman would catch pneumonia if she didn't get out of those wet clothes immediately. Had I driven her to this—this frenzied desperation—by refusing to talk to her on the phone? "I will give you my complete, undivided attention as soon as you dry off and change your clothes." Urgency and guilt made my voice harsh. "Helen, I can't deal with your death too."

She dropped her hands and, reluctantly, peeled off her dripping cardigan. "You need to hear this, Molly. You're in grave danger here. You and your family."

I stared at her. Was what she was telling me true? Or was Helen now envisioning imaginary threats? Or maybe—the thought came unbidden and decidedly unwelcome—this threat to me and my family was coming from Helen herself.

I pulled my sweat suit and thick wool socks from the suitcase and handed them to her.

"I was so worried about you that I violated Detective Martinez's rules to come here," Helen said as she took off her shoes. "I'm not supposed to leave the city, he said. But since you wouldn't answer my phone calls, driving here seemed the only way I could talk to you."

I could feel my face grow hot. "I called you this afternoon when I got back from New York, but you weren't home," I said, sounding defensive. Never mind why I hadn't called the week before that. "Why are you so worried about us?"

She pulled my sweatshirt over her head. The pants were too long for her, but at least the clothes were dry.

"You're not safe here. Someone—I'm not sure who—is stalking people who are looking into Katherine's death. That's why Suzanne Lang died—because she was trying to figure out who killed Katherine." Helen's eyes burned with an intensity that was almost frightening.

I sat down heavily on the edge of the bed. "But what makes you think we're in danger? I'm not writing a book about Mother's death like Suzanne was."

"But you *are* asking questions. You've been questioning Katherine's neighbors, Suzanne, and the police. And the last person who asked so many questions is now dead. This killer will obviously do anything to avoid being exposed."

Involuntarily I shivered. I had been asking a lot of questions. And each of Suzanne's prime suspects—Ginny, Helen, and my late grandmother—was aware of it. As was my Aunt Charlotte. Had the killer decided that I too was getting too close? Was I the next intended victim?

"I've spent hours and hours thinking about this," Helen said, "thinking about who could have committed these terrible murders. Obviously it's someone who's very clever. Someone who's read Katherine's books and then was resourceful enough to obtain the Stelazine. Someone who, after Katherine's death, was talking with Suzanne. A person who's totally amoral, ruthless, and evil."

Evil: a word that had been used before to describe the person I now suspected. A word that Margaret O'Ryan had used when she also had tried to warn me.

Helen, I suddenly noticed, was shaking. With cold or pent-up tension or fear, I wasn't sure which.

I leaned forward and clasped an arm around her shoulders. "Helen, it's okay. We're safe for now. We're all safe." I wanted very much to believe it.

She pulled free from my embrace. "Safe? Out here alone? No other houses in sight?" Her voice had an almost hysterical ring to it. "When Annie told me on the phone where you were going, I was terrified. That's why I drove all the way out here in this horrible weather. You're perfect targets out here, sitting ducks."

I jumped when Alex knocked on the door. "Everything okay?" he asked.

I motioned for him to come inside. "Helen thinks we're in danger from the person who killed Mother and Suzanne."

"It's so remote out here—no one for miles," Helen started to explain.

Alex sat down on the bed. "You might be right," he said, to my surprise. "It *is* very isolated. I'm sure we're fine for tonight, but I think I might feel a lot safer back home where there are some other people nearby."

Of course both my mother and Suzanne Lang had been killed in a large city, surrounded by neighbors, I suddenly wanted to point out. Urban amenities hadn't helped either one of them. But I was glad that Alex, with his soothing voice and his aura of reasonableness, seemed to be having a calming effect on Helen.

My husband glanced at me. "I think we should go home tomorrow. We'll just tell the kids the weather is too bad to stay here."

I nodded. "Annie, for one, will be thrilled to leave." For now, I decided, I'd keep my reservations to myself. If someone was after us, would we really be any safer at home? If Helen was right and I was the killer's next designated victim, would we be safe anywhere?

Helen, though, looked relieved by our decision to leave. "Of course the other problem," she said in a tired voice, "is that Detective Martinez is convinced that I am the killer who Suzanne discovered. He thinks I murdered my best friend in order to get some inheritance money." She shook her head in disbelief. "Why would an old lady like me need all that money? What am I supposed to do with it—build a mansion, travel around the world, buy myself a BMW?"

"Suzanne Lang," I said carefully, "thought you were about to go bankrupt because you'd invested in your brother's business."

"Bankrupt?" she asked, looking incredulous. "I did lose money investing in my brother's business. I invested ten thousand dollars and I lost all of it, but I certainly was not about to go bankrupt. My house is paid for, I have my teacher retirement pension, and my savings. I certainly wasn't rich, but I wasn't impoverished either."

A look of anger crossed her face. "That woman never once mentioned this lame-brained bankruptcy idea to me. I always thought that she was suspicious of me because I found Katherine's body. Suzanne should have used her vivid imagination for writing fiction, instead of trying to twist the truth to fit her latest story. I went over to her house that Saturday to tell her that if she insisted on spreading lies about me in her book, I would take legal action. But she never answered the door. Unfortunately, one of her neighbors saw me leave, which apparently made the police conclude that I killed Suzanne."

I thought for a moment she was going to break down into tears. How could I ever have imagined that this decent, honest woman, my mother's loyal friend for almost thirty years, had killed Mother?

"Oh, Helen, I'm so sorry." Sorry she'd been at the wrong place at the wrong time, sorry that I hadn't believed all along in her innocence.

With an obvious effort, she regained her composure. Glancing out the bedroom window, she said, "I see it's finally stopped raining. I need to get started for home."

"I won't hear of you leaving," I said. "I don't want you driving these roads in the dark. We have extra beds and lots of food, and we'd all love to have your company."

"Of course you'll stay," Alex chimed in. "The kids will think it's a real treat to have you spend the night. And tomorrow morning we'll all leave."

"I never intended to impose on you like this," Helen said.

"You're not imposing at all," I assured her. "You risked a lot to drive all the way out here to warn us." A trip which wouldn't have been necessary if I had been courteous enough to return her phone calls. "It will make me feel much better if you stay with us tonight."

"Well then, maybe I will," Helen said.

The kids were both pleased that Helen had agreed to stay over. "I told Mom to phone you," Annie said to Helen.

"Well, your mother and I have had our conversation now," Helen said briskly. "And this way I get a chance to see all of you as well."

I glanced at my watch. "Annie, why don't you come help me with dinner. You can make a salad, while I start the spaghetti sauce."

"Can I help?" Helen asked.

"No, thanks, it's going to be a quick throw-together dinner. Sit down and relax for a while. You certainly deserve it."

"First I need to get my purse from the car. I was in such a hurry to talk to you I think I left it out there."

"Want me to come with you?" Will asked.

"No, stay inside and keep dry," Helen said, affectionately mussing his hair. "I'll be right back."

I filled a pot with water to cook the pasta and was browning ground round and onions for the spaghetti sauce when Annie said, "Hey, Mom, shouldn't Aunt Helen be back by now?"

Will walked over to the kitchen window and peered outside. "Her car's still out there, but I don't see her."

Alex, who'd been reading a magazine at the kitchen table, stood up. "I'm going out to check on her."

"I want to come too," Will said.

"Not this time," Alex said. "I'll be right back. Helen is probably just taking a little walk."

Alex had just opened the kitchen door when I heard his sharp intake of breath.

"Didn't mean to startle you," a familiar voice said.

I turned in time to see my husband back slowly into the kitchen. "Alex, what's going on?"

Aunt Charlotte stepped into the kitchen. She was smiling, but it was a hard, unfamiliar smile. "It was a good thing you mentioned that Leading Nowhere Drive, Molly. Otherwise it would have been impossible to find you."

I gasped as I caught sight of the gun she was pointing at my husband's chest.

CHAPTER TWENTY-SEVEN

I stared, transfixed, at the revolver.

Will walked into the kitchen. "Hey, where's Aunt Helen?"

The smile that crossed Charlotte's face was chilling. "Aunt Helen," she said, "has had a little accident."

In my mind Helen's trembling voice once again warned me: "Get out of here, Molly. You and your family are in terrible danger."

I grabbed Will on his way to the door to find Helen. "Stay with me," I whispered, wrapping an arm around him. I didn't want him to have a "little accident" too.

Charlotte nodded. "If you do exactly as I say, Will, nothing bad will happen to you, to any of you."

I knew she was lying.

"What do you want?" Alex asked her. "Why are you here?"

My aunt's blue eyes narrowed. She was dressed all in black: slacks, sweater, high leather boots. Where once I'd thought her all-black outfits the height of sophistication, now I knew otherwise. They were the clothes of a terrorist intent on blending into the darkness.

"I want you to sit down over there with your wife and son." She pointed the barrel of her handgun toward the kitchen table. "Where's our little Annie?"

I prayed that she was on my cell phone right this second calling the police. Had she heard Charlotte come in and slipped away to summon help?

"Annie!" Charlotte called.

"I was in the bathroom—" My daughter stopped talking as she caught sight of Charlotte. Her eyes widened.

"How nice to see you again, Annie." Charlotte's lips were smiling, but her eyes were ice cold. "Come sit down with the rest of your family. We need to have a little chat."

Trembling, Annie sat next to her father, across the table from Will and me. Unconsciously perhaps, Alex imitated my posture with Will, draping an arm around Annie's shoulder, trying somehow to protect her.

Charlotte moved to the head of the table, keeping her small but deadly-looking revolver trained on Alex. "What I want," she said, answering Alex's question, "is the manuscript to Katherine's latest novel—the new and improved version."

The version in which the protagonist's sister—the character based on Charlotte—was the killer. The manuscript which Charlotte had learned about by eavesdropping on my phone conversation with Alex. I sent Alex a look: Let me handle this. "I have a copy here. I'll go get it."

"No!" Charlotte looked around the table. Her eyes settled on Annie, whose face was now as pale as her father's white sweater. "You go get it for your dear Aunt Charlotte. And if you're harboring any ill-advised heroic fantasies, I want you to know I'll shoot your father if you're not back here with the manuscript in three minutes."

Annie stood up. She was shaking all over.

"Wait!" I said to Charlotte. "She doesn't even know where to look."

"So tell her," Charlotte ordered.

"It's on the table by my bed. Right near my purse." My purse that contained the precious cell phone. But would Annie remember that? And would she take the risk of phoning the police, with the clock ticking and her father's life at stake?

Annie sent me a frightened look then started walking. She was almost to the bedroom when Charlotte called out, "And Annie, bring your mother's purse back with you."

Alex leaned forward. "Charlotte, whatever it is you want—"

"Shut up!" she ordered, moving the muzzle of the revolver closer to his face. "You have two minutes left, Annie!" she called.

Sitting next to me, Will began to whimper. I pulled him tighter. "It's okay, sweetie," I crooned.

"Everything's going to be all right, Will," Alex said. But in his voice I could hear the fraying edges of his control.

"One minute, Annie," Charlotte yelled.

I could feel the sweat trickling down my sides as we all turned toward the hallway. Will had stopped crying, but he clung to me. I could feel his breath, hot and too fast, against my neck.

Annie hurried toward us, carrying the manuscript and my purse. Her eyes looked enormous in her ashen face.

"Good girl," Charlotte said. "Set everything down on the table in front of me. Then go sit down."

Annie did what she was told.

Charlotte waited until Annie was sitting before opening my purse. She chuckled. "Oh, I thought you might have had a little revolver tucked inside. But instead there's only a cell phone." She pulled it out, glancing at me. "How very Molly-like."

Across the table Annie sent me a horrified look: I'm sorry. I didn't know.

I shook my head: Don't blame yourself. Except the phone might have been the only chance for any of us to get out of here alive.

I watched Charlotte leaf through the last pages of the manuscript and nod. "That's not the only copy," I said.

"I didn't think it was," Charlotte said. "I'll get the others too."

And then, with all of the manuscripts in her possession, she'd have to get rid of us. There was no other option.

"We already sent copies to Mother's editor and literary agent," I said quickly. "They'll have the new version too."

Charlotte's look would have stopped any mugger in his tracks. Then she smiled. "You didn't have time to mail them a copy. You hadn't even read the new ending."

But Charlotte had, I realized with a start. She must have. Why else would she have risked coming here, threatening us, in order to retrieve the manuscript? The little information that Alex had given me over the phone wouldn't have brought her here so quickly. But how had she known? Had Mother told her?

Think, Molly! "I—"

Charlotte interrupted me. "You're the very self-important literary executor, after all. You'd want to make sure that this is the better version, the one you approve of. You're just as much of a control freak as Katherine was. Except you don't have your mother's talent for keeping secrets."

I could feel my cheeks grow hot. Then I heard a faint noise from outside. It sounded like a car coming down the road. A police car perhaps, cruising the area? "You've already read the manuscript, haven't you?" I asked, a little too loudly.

"Shut up!" Charlotte had heard the noise too. She turned her head to listen.

It was a car, driving very slowly from the sounds of it, down Leading Nowhere Drive. Would the driver spot Helen lying outside and stop to help? (Where was Helen? And what kind of "little accident" had she had?)

Charlotte glanced toward the kitchen window. It was too small to see much of anything from where she was standing. Keeping her gun still trained on us, she moved sideways to the window.

Damn! The car was not stopping. I could hear it moving down the road.

Charlotte heard it too. Her body visibly relaxed as she glanced out the window.

She was just in front of Alex now. From the corner of my eye, I saw his body tense. He leaped onto her, knocking Charlotte to the floor.

I jumped up, craning to see what was happening in the blur of rolling bodies. Alex was much bigger than Charlotte. And stronger. He seemed to have pinned her to the floor.

"Get back," I yelled to my kids. I rushed forward, intending to pry loose the gun that Charlotte was still gripping in the hand Alex held down.

But before I could get there, Charlotte's head reared up. Alex roared in pain as Charlotte savagely bit his ear.

I heard Annie's scream as I ran forward. But in that split second Alex relaxed his grip and Charlotte wrenched her hand free. She slammed the gun down hard on Alex's head.

I watched in horror as Alex collapsed onto the floor. His body, limp, unconscious, lay on top of Charlotte.

"Stay back or I shoot him," she screamed.

I froze in my place. "Alex!"

He did not answer me.

Charlotte shoved his body onto the floor. When she stood up her face was contorted with rage. Her beauty, her most admired attribute, was gone, shed like an unwanted mask. Her teeth now were bared, like a wild animal's, Alex's blood still on them. She glanced at each of us, looking, I thought, as if she wanted to shoot us all, right this minute.

"You said you want the other copies of the manuscript," I said quietly, trying to keep my voice calm.

Charlotte turned to me. "And I want the computer disks, all of them."

"They're in Houston. We'll have to go there to get them." How quickly my clever strategies had deteriorated into this: All

I could do now was buy us some time. If we were driving to Houston, at least we were alive. For a few hours anyway.

"We?" Charlotte raised her eyebrows. "No, I don't think so."

"But you need us there to get the manuscripts and the disks." I thought fast. No, all she required for that was my house keys. "And you need us to get into our bank safe-deposit box where Alex put the disks," I lied. "You'd never get in there without Alex or me along."

Charlotte studied me, apparently trying to decide if I was telling the truth. I met her eyes, daring her to disbelieve me.

"You probably should come with me to Houston," she finally said. "But the others are staying here."

"What?" I could hear Will, beside me, gasp.

"They'll stay here while you and I make our little trip," Charlotte explained. "There's no reason to drag everyone along. If you do what I tell you, all of your family will be fine."

I stared at her, feeling panic surge through my body like a bolt of electricity. Did she intend to kill my family now, then finish me off in Houston after she possessed the manuscripts and computer disks?

"I'm going to have to tie everyone up, of course," Charlotte continued. She looked at Annie and Will. "To make sure that you don't go running for help the moment I leave. But hopefully you'll go to sleep, and when you wake up tomorrow, your mother and I will be back to untie you."

Yeah, right. Charlotte, of course, had gone to all the trouble of following me here—flying from New York and tracking me down, assaulting Helen and Alex, threatening us at gunpoint—only to end the visit with a cheery goodbye once she had the manuscripts in her possession. Did the woman think we were stupid?

Glancing at my children, I could see how badly they wanted to believe her. They were terrified and grasped at the assurance that we'd come back and untie them—and then bad Aunt Charlotte would leave with her stolen manuscript and everything would go back to normal.

Charlotte moved to the window and looked out. "We're all going to go outside now. We have to move Helen into the house."

"What about Dad?" Annie said, glancing down at him.

"We'll worry about him when we get back." Charlotte pointed the gun toward the back door. "Now get going."

I shot a quick look at Alex as I walked by. He lay perfectly still, his ear dripping blood. Would he regain consciousness soon? Did he have a concussion? With a sudden wave of nausea I remembered Suzanne Lang. Suzanne whose skull had been fractured before she was injected with Stelazine.

"Move!" Charlotte ordered.

I took a deep breath and followed my children out the door.

Outside the rain had finally stopped, but the gravel driveway was filled with puddles of water. I squinted in the darkness. Where was Helen?

"She's in her car," Charlotte said, inches behind me. "In the backseat."

We found my mother's old friend there, crumpled on the floor of her Volvo. Charlotte must have sneaked up behind her when Helen was reaching into her car.

At Charlotte's instruction, I climbed into the backseat. I felt for Helen's pulse. At least she was still alive. With me lifting her shoulders and the children each holding one of her legs, the three of us managed to carry her into the house. Charlotte held the cabin door open for us, making sure that we saw the gun trained on us.

"Put her on the couch," she ordered.

We did. I gently placed a pillow beneath Helen's head, hoping she would regain consciousness soon. Hoping she would regain consciousness at all. Helen, the most law abiding of women, had violated police orders to not leave town and then driven through torrential rain in order to warn me that my family and I were in grave danger. And for her trouble she'd ended up being attacked herself.

I could feel the tears start to well in my eyes as I touched her wrinkled cheek. Don't die, Helen! I need you. We all need you right now.

When I turned around, Charlotte was pulling a length of rope from her big tote bag. As my children watched in horror she opened a pocket knife and began cutting the rope into smaller pieces. "Be prepared, I always say." She grinned at the expressions on the kids' faces. "You're a Boy Scout, aren't you, Will?"

"Yes, ma'am," he replied, his eyes widening.

"Good. I want you to take this rope and go tie Helen's feet together and then tie her wrists," she said, keeping her gun trained on Annie and me.

Will took the two pieces of rope she was handing him. He stood up, looking achingly young, uncertain of what to do. I nodded reassuringly at him.

"And Will," Charlotte added, "don't try anything tricky. I'm going to be checking your work."

We all watched as Will did what she'd instructed.

Charlotte walked over to where Helen lay and yanked on the knots to make sure they were tight. "You're next, Annie. Take the chair you're sitting on into the other room and put it over there by the couch."

Annie's face was expressionless as she picked up the wooden kitchen chair and carried it into the main room. Charlotte followed her, her revolver trained on Annie's back. She watched attentively as Will tied Annie's feet together and then started to tie her arms behind her back.

Will stopped what he was doing and turned his head toward

the kitchen.

"What is it?" Charlotte asked, her voice sharp.

"Uh, I just thought I heard something," Will said. "But I guess I was wrong."

Charlotte's eyes narrowed. "Keep tying," she told him, then gestured for me to move with her to where Alex was lying on the floor.

Charlotte jabbed the toe of her boot sharply into Alex's side. I flinched, but Alex didn't. "Guess he's still out," she said with a malicious grin.

She was enjoying this, I thought. Relishing our terror. How could I, someone who'd read innumerable studies of psychopaths, not have picked up any warning signs or seen any red flags? This woman was a sadistic murderer who seemed to destroy innocent people with the casualness I used in picking out a movie rental. And I, a professional criminologist, had been totally oblivious! Only today—after I'd read the new ending of my mother's novel and Margaret O'Ryan's last journal—had I suspected that Charlotte was the person who'd killed my mother. A conclusion reached too late to save my family from this grinning monster.

Will had finished tying Annie's hands by the time we got back. Charlotte had had me bring another kitchen chair and set it down next to Annie's. Then she made me tie up my son.

"Tighter," Charlotte ordered, watching over my shoulder.

I swallowed, trying not to sob at the sight of my two children sitting there, with their hands tied behind their backs. Both of them white-faced and terrified.

"Now for their mouths." Charlotte pulled bright red bandannas from her tote bag. "We don't want anyone disturbing the neighbors."

Will's eyes were filling with tears as I tied the kerchief around his mouth. "I'll be back for you," I whispered.

Annie stared straight ahead, her eyes hard, as I tied her gag. "Hang in there, sweetie," I whispered.

Then I moved on to Helen. She was still unconscious as I tied her gag—perhaps a more enviable state for the long hours ahead than my poor children's.

Charlotte turned the television on. A rerun of *Frasier* was playing. "Now don't say I didn't do anything nice for you," she told the children.

Finally Charlotte had me tie and gag Alex, leaving him in the same position on the floor. The sight of my husband's pale face and limp body made me shudder. What violence I had delivered to my family!

Charlotte gave the knots a final yank, then jabbed the revolver into my back. "Get up. We need to get out of here."

As we headed for the door I cast one last look at my bound and gagged children.

"See you soon," Charlotte called merrily as we walked out.

CHAPTER TWENTY-EIGHT

"You drive," Charlotte said. She unlocked the door of her rental car and motioned for me to get in.

I cast one last look at the cabin, envisioning my terrified children, my unconscious husband, and my mother's old friend inside. And all of this trauma, this devastation, was caused by one person, one violent, amoral woman who destroyed everyone who got in her way. A woman who had to be stopped.

My aunt watched as I slid into the driver's seat. Standing in the open doorway, her revolver almost in my face, she said, "There are only two things I want you to be focused on right now: your driving and how distraught your children will be at losing their mother if you try to fuck with me."

I stared straight ahead as she slammed my door shut. Charlotte walked quickly to the passenger side, got in, and handed me her car key.

"Buckle your seat belt," she said as she did the same. "I wouldn't want anything to happen to my favorite niece."

I backed the car out slowly, hoping I might encounter someone on the road. But not even a car was in sight until we reached the convenience store's parking lot.

Charlotte lifted the handgun from her lap. "Keep driving."

I did, driving cautiously on the slick road, trying to beat down my growing panic. Trying to think of a plan. Charlotte seemed jittery to me, on edge. She scanned the road with as much vigilance as a traffic cop, keeping a wary eye on me too.

I needed to get her talking. "I'm curious how you learned about this new ending to Mother's novel. Obviously you knew what was in the book before I did."

At first I thought she wasn't going to answer. But after what seemed like an eternity, she said, "I read about it in the *People* story about Katherine."

"What?" I turned to stare at her. I'd read that interview too, and nowhere did it mention the topic of Mother's novel.

"Keep your eyes on the road," she barked at me.

Looking straight ahead, I said, "All that article said was that Mother was writing a mystery novel that was set in the fifties."

"Right. A coming-of-age novel. And I read that and thought, So this is why Katherine came home to visit her family for the first time in twenty-five years. Why she spent hours with Mother poring over old family photo albums. Suddenly I put two and two together, and had a pretty good idea of what Katherine's mystery novel was about."

It seemed like a big leap to me. What if Mother had been writing some other story altogether, something not even remotely related to her own family?

"But to make sure," Charlotte added, "I phoned Katherine's publisher and pretended to be one of her adoring fans. When was this new book coming out, I asked, and what was it about? The woman I talked to said all she knew was the title of the book, *The Summer That Changed Everything*. The author was finishing the book right now. That was all I needed to hear. I knew exactly what summer my dear sister was writing about."

"So you flew to Austin and killed her," I said. It was not a question, and Charlotte didn't take it as one.

We turned onto the tree-lined road that would take us to the highway. Speaking the words—you killed her—seemed to change me. All of my fear and indecision crystallized into steely resolve. Whatever the cost, this woman needed to be killed. I took a deep breath, gripped the wheel hard, and braced myself.

"I took the manuscript and her computer disks that same day," Charlotte said in a chatty, pleased-with-herself voice.

I eased my foot off the accelerator. In a few more minutes you can do it, I told myself. But I wanted my questions answered before one—or both—of us died.

Now I knew why I hadn't been able to find the novel the first time I'd looked for it in Mother's office and why the manuscript had suddenly reappeared. Charlotte must have returned her version of the novel while Helen and I were at Mother's lawyer's office.

"Unfortunately I didn't know that Katherine also put those computer disks in her safe-deposit box," Charlotte said. "I thought I was being so clever. I rewrote the ending of the novel, you know, picking a more appealing villain. Appealing to me, at least." She chuckled at her own joke. "Wouldn't Katherine have been shocked to learn that she wasn't the only fiction writer in the family?"

"You wanted people to think your mother killed your father?"

Charlotte looked annoyed. "I certainly preferred that they thought Mother was the killer rather than me. But if you're asking if I wanted this novel—my version of the novel—to be published, the answer is no. It's a summer I would prefer be forgotten. Unfortunately the novel was already scheduled to be published and Katherine's editor and agent had seen some of the book, so I couldn't just destroy the manuscript and pretend it never existed. The best I could do was make some revisions to minimize the damage. Though I must admit the idea of Mother—Mrs. Don't-Air-The-Dirty-Linen-In-Public—being so publicly humiliated was rather amusing. It's too bad she died before the book came out."

"Did Grandmother know that you'd killed your father?"

Charlotte shrugged. "We never discussed it. She probably

suspected it, but Mother was very good at not seeing what she didn't want to see. And actually Father's death was convenient for her. He was about to leave her. They'd had a big fight about that right after his birthday party. In Mother's mind, being a widow was a lot more socially acceptable than being a divorcee. You see her family had been quite poor, a terrible embarrassment to her. Marrying up—making it to the upper-middle class—was incredibly important to her. I think all along that was Father's main appeal to her: he was her ticket out of Blue Collar Land."

"I wonder what attracted him to her," I said, remembering the shrewish, book-hating old woman I'd visited.

Charlotte smiled. "She was very beautiful when she was young and she could be charming when she wanted to be. And by the time Father realized they had absolutely nothing in common, Mother was already pregnant with Katherine. So Father did the decent thing and married her—a decision he regretted every day of their married life. He told her that after the party. Said he was starting a new life with the woman he truly loved, his soul mate. Rather sweet, I thought."

"So why did you kill him?"

"Because part of his new life plan involved sending me to an all-girls' boarding school. A strict convent school for rebellious rich girls. I wouldn't have liked it."

"Why did you kill Suzanne?"

"Because she was poking her nose into my business." Charlotte's voice was suddenly harsh. "The last thing in the world I wanted was Katherine's biography—the March family chronicle—published. It was bad enough that Katherine's account of our dysfunctional family was coming out, but at least I could tell everyone that it was only fiction. I should have killed Katherine years ago, you know. But I was too damn sentimental. I wanted to believe that she had enough sisterly loyalty to resist writing about me."

And for years she had resisted it. Out of fear? I wondered. Or denial? Perhaps Mother's illness had convinced her this was her last chance to tell the truth about her monstrous sister, even if she had to present the story as fiction. Her portrayal of Charlotte was chilling, but it didn't begin to touch the nonchalant evil at the heart of this woman who had unrepentantly killed her father, her sister, and her sister's would-be biographer. A woman who, as soon as she got her hands on the computer disks and extra copy of Mother's manuscript, planned to kill me, my family and my mother's old friend as well.

Unless I stopped her.

I spotted a huge oak immediately ahead, at the right side of the road.

"Did you kill Miss O'Ryan too?" I asked.

"Of course," Charlotte said sweetly. "And it was much harder than you would have imagined. That sister of hers hardly ever leaves the house. And, since we're on this true-confession jag, you certainly don't think that my dear, philandering husband's boating accident was accidental, do you?"

Gripping the wheel, I said a silent prayer. I pictured the faces of the people I loved the most: Alex, Annie and Will. Then I slammed my foot on the accelerator.

"Stop! I'll shoot!" Charlotte roared.

I kept my eyes on the target. Felt the car lurch as we veered off the road.

I heard the shot seconds before the impact. What happened next was a long string of sensations, one blurring into the other. The sharp, searing pain in my arm. The sound of screams (mine? Charlotte's?). The crash of metal and glass colliding with a sturdy oak. The jolt of my body hurtling forward, the air bag slamming into me. The taste of blood. An explosion of agony. Loud moaning filling the car.

I managed to lift my head to inspect the damage. My aunt's side of the car had taken a direct hit. The moaning was coming from her. I saw the blood, the strange, distorted angle of her body.

She stared at me, her face bloody, her eyes wild with pain and hatred. "I wanted to take you back to the cabin to see the ashes," she rasped. "I set a bomb."

"Bomb?" I shouted. "When? When will it go off?"

I heard her ragged breath and saw the blood bubbling out of her mouth. "Think of me, lonely Molly, at their funerals."

"No!" I howled, frantically clawing at my seat belt. Finally I managed to shove open my door.

As I pulled myself out, I saw my aunt's revolver next to my seat. Saw her left hand reach painfully for the gun.

With all my might I shoved her into the crushed car door. I picked up the gun.

"Shoot me!" she taunted. "I would have shot you."

How I wanted to! My finger clutched the trigger. I could make sure that the evil ended here.

But at the last second I stopped myself. Shooting her was what she wanted me to do—what she would have done.

With my uninjured left hand I tossed the gun as far as I could into a nearby field, then I limped, sobbing and bleeding, to the road.

I'd walked only a few yards before I spotted car lights moving toward me. "Help me," I sobbed when the driver stopped the car and hurried over to me. "I've got to get to my family. There's a bomb. . . ."

"You look like you need an ambulance," the man said, pulling out a cell phone. "Let me call the police."

"Please," I pleaded, "take me to the cabin. Now! Before it's too late."

I heard it as he phoned the police. Even miles away, the boom of an explosion was unmistakable.

I could feel myself swaying. Then, mercifully, I succumbed to unconsciousness.

CHAPTER TWENTY-NINE

I woke up in the hospital to a world of too-bright lights, too-loud voices, and pain. Incredible pain.

"Did she say who shot her?" someone was asking.

"The guy who found her said all she kept saying was that a bomb was about to go off in some cabin."

I groaned as memory flooded back.

"Lie still, dear," a woman's voice commanded.

"My family . . . a bomb," I moaned.

"Your family is safe," the woman, a heavy-set black nurse, said.

I knew she was lying. I closed my eyes, trying to block everything out: the noise, the glare, the pitiful remnants that remained of my life.

"Molly!" The voice was urgent. Familiar.

I managed to open my eyes. Alex? Was I dreaming? Hallucinating? Or had I died?

"Molly, it's me, Alex." I could feel his warm breath on my face. Could see the sweat on his forehead, the concern in his eyes. "Molly, we're okay. The kids and I are okay."

I reached out to touch him, to make sure he was real, but was engulfed with pain.

"We need to get her into surgery, sir," the nurse said. "We'll let you know as soon as it's over."

"Bomb," I whispered as they pushed me away. But nobody seemed to hear me.

"She looks real bad," said a scared, small voice near my ear.

I opened my eyes and tried to smile at my white-faced son. He was standing beside my hospital bed, shifting his weight from one foot to the other. "Hi, honey."

"Do you feel terrible?" Annie asked. Standing next to Alex, she looked tiny, her eyes huge in her small face.

"Yes, but my doctor says I'll get over it."

Alex smiled and leaned down to kiss my forehead. "You look a lot better than you did yesterday."

I vaguely remembered seeing him as I drifted in and out of sleep in the recovery room. Today I'd been moved to a private room.

At my invitation, Will sat, very tentatively, on the edge of my bed. I watched him inspect me, taking in the dressing, the IV tubes. "Is that where Aunt Charlotte shot you?" he finally asked, pointing at my bandaged arm.

I nodded. "The doctor said I was lucky that the bullet missed my vital organs. I told him I'd feel a lot luckier if the bullet had missed me altogether."

"And Dad said you have cracked ribs too," Annie said.

"Yes, from the car crash." The car crash that I had intentionally caused. "Tell me what happened to Charlotte."

"She's dead," Alex said quietly. "She died on the way to the hospital."

I closed my eyes. So I had killed her.

"I'm glad she's dead," Will said heatedly. "She was going to kill us, all of us."

"She planted a bomb under the cabin, Mom." Annie took over the story. "She intended to blow us up."

"I know." I started to cry. "She told me after the car accident, when she thought I was getting away. She said"—I struggled to stop sobbing, to get the words out—"she said that I should remember her at your funerals."

"My God," Alex said, shaking his head. He moved forward to gently take me into his arms.

"I thought you all were dead," I sobbed into his big shoulder. "When I heard that explosion . . ."

He let me cry myself out. I cried all the tears I hadn't shed before. Cried tears of relief and tears for all our losses. And when I was finished, feeling soggy and empty, my injured ribs screaming their protest, I asked the other question I needed to know. "What about Helen?"

"She's here, in the hospital," Annie said. "She was still unconscious when we got her here, but she came to in the emergency room. The doctor said she doesn't have a skull fracture, but her brain tissue is swelling."

"She's having surgery today to relieve the pressure," Alex said. "I'm going to check on her in a little while." He looked worried, I thought, wondering if there was something he wasn't telling me.

"Aren't you going to ask us how we got out of the cabin?" Will asked, sounding hurt.

"Of course I want to know," I said quickly. "How did you get out of there when all of you were tied up?"

A small smile twisted the corners of Will's mouth. "Remember the magic tricks that Grandma taught me and Annie when she was writing that mystery about the magician?"

I nodded.

"Well, one of the things she showed us was an instant rope escape trick. The secret is that you have to twist the rope to allow enough slack so the person can slip her hand in and out, though it looks as if her hands are tied tight behind her back. Of course you need to tie the rope right. I had to tie a knot on the top of Annie's left wrist, which looks kind of weird, and Annie had to lift her finger to position the rope.

"I was afraid if Aunt Charlotte looked too close she'd know we were trying to trick her. So I pretended to hear Dad move. Aunt Charlotte left to go check on him. By the time she came back, I was done."

"But Charlotte checked your knots," I said. "I saw her."

"That made me really nervous," Annie said. "But I guess she just thought Will had a funny way of tying things. The knots do look tight."

"Aunt Charlotte was a lot more worried that Dad would get loose," Will said. "Remember how she kept looking at Dad and gave his rope a really hard yank?"

"She certainly did," Alex agreed.

"How do you know?" I asked. "You were unconscious."

"I was pretending to be. When I came to I heard Charlotte in the living room giving orders. I figured I had a better chance of surviving if she thought I was still unconscious. That was not a woman I wanted to mess with again."

"A very wise decision," I said.

"After you and Aunt Charlotte left," Annie said, "I pulled my right hand out of the loop just like in the magic trick. But it was harder than when we did it before because this rope wasn't soft clothesline like Grandma's. Finally, though, I got myself and Will untied, and we untied Dad and Aunt Helen and got them to the car."

"You had to carry Helen outside?"

Annie nodded. "Will had her head and I took her feet. Dad was too woozy to help." She sent an appraising look over her father's physique. "It's a good thing we didn't have to carry you out. It was bad enough having you lean on us on the way to the car."

Alex shook his head ruefully. "And I appreciated your support."

Annie ignored him. "Because Dad was so dizzy, I got to drive!" she announced proudly.

"She almost hit a parked car," Will added.

"Shut up! You're just jealous." Annie turned back to me. "I drove us to that convenience store—and Dad said my driving was great. We phoned the police from there. We heard the explosion when the policeman was driving us to the hospital."

I closed my eyes. How easily things could have turned out differently. If it had taken them half an hour longer to get out of the cabin . . .

Alex draped an arm around each of the kids. "Thank God for Katherine's magic lessons," he said. He grinned down at our children. "And thank God the two of you were paying attention."

Two days later a gray-haired police officer came to my hospital room to get my statement on the car accident. I'd been expecting this, worrying about it.

I took a deep breath and told the officer that I'd caused the accident to protect my family.

He nodded, his face expressionless, as he jotted down notes. "Did Mrs. Todd shoot you before or after impact?"

"Before. When she realized I was veering off the road."

"We found the gun quite a distance from the car."

"I threw it out when Charlotte tried to shoot me again, after the crash." When I seriously considered shooting her.

He made a few more notes, then stood up. "I think that's everything I need."

"What—what's going to happen next?"

The officer sent me a level look. "It's clear to me this was self-defense. I don't see us pursuing the matter."

I felt a wave of relief wash over me. "Thank you."

"My pleasure, ma'am." He nodded, then walked out the door.

There was one more question I had to have answered. Gingerly I sat up and, ignoring the protests from various parts of my body, managed to plant my feet on the floor. Alex had called from the motel to say they were coming in about half an hour, after breakfast. But I wanted to make this trip alone.

I could feel my heart pounding as I found the room. No one responded to my knock, but I walked in anyway. Helen Lewis lay on the bed, sleeping. One side of her head was swathed in bandages. Her face looked pale, old, and disconcertingly vulnerable.

I could feel tears start to trickle down my face. "Oh, Helen," I muttered, "what have we done to you?"

I heard a movement. "Molly." Helen reached out a hand to me.

With my left hand—the one not in a sling—I grasped it.

"I am so glad you're all right," she said, the tears starting to well in her eyes too.

"I had to come see you," I said. "To see for myself. How do you feel?"

"Old. Tired. And I have a ferocious headache. But it's better than yesterday. The doctor says that's a good sign."

She studied me for a moment. "I guess that after running into that terrible woman, we should just count ourselves lucky to be alive."

I nodded. "I guess we should."

When Alex stuck his head into the room a few minutes later, Helen and I were wrapped in a tight—and quite painful—hug.

EPILOGUE

Last year, driving home from work on the day my mother died, I'd wanted nothing more than to skip the holidays and fast-forward my life to spring. But now, twelve months later, all I felt was gratitude for the loved ones assembled at my home for Christmas dinner. I'd come too close to losing them.

Affectionately I looked around the table. Sitting on either side of me, Dad and Ginny were chatting with Will and Annie while, at the opposite end of the table, Alex and Helen were discussing the reviews of Mother's new book.

Helen's once-gray hair had grown back in coarse white curls that, she said, made her look as if she'd stuck her finger in an electric socket. But her current expression of prim disapproval— her teacher look—was very familiar. "I read one review which said *The Summer That Changed Everything* was an autobiographical account of a 'talented but dysfunctional family which produced a best-selling mystery novelist and a glamorous serial killer.' Wouldn't Katherine have been appalled to read that?"

"That sounds pretty tame in comparison to some of the tabloid stories," Alex said. "There was one I read about 'the violent rampage of The Socialite Psychopath.' But Katherine did want the truth about Charlotte to get out, even though she wasn't even aware of most of the murders Charlotte committed."

"She knew what her sister was capable of," I said, jumping into the conversation. "And since she had no way of proving anything to the police about her father's death, the only way Mother thought she could stop Charlotte was by exposing her in print."

"You know, Molly," my father said, "I've learned more about your mother's family from the articles I've read in the last few months than I ever did from Katherine during all the years we were married."

Ginny looked up at her husband's mention of his first wife. But even she, I thought, had mellowed on the topic of my mother. Now that Ginny had found a job that she loved as the volunteer coordinator at a nursing home and Dad was working at a new Realtor's office, it seemed easier for her to be generous about Mother.

Ginny turned to me. "Annie has been telling me that she'd like to get a navel ring."

I rolled my eyes. I'd been so pleased when Annie finally started acting like her old self again and stopped wearing Mother's jewelry every day. Little had I realized what was coming next.

"Will must have grown three inches since last year," Ginny said. "He doesn't look like a little boy anymore."

I gazed fondly at my baby, who, almost overnight, it seemed, had suddenly become as tall as I. But the changes I most valued weren't the external ones. After months of working with a counselor, Will was finally sleeping through the night without having terrible nightmares.

Ginny leaned forward and, in a softer voice, said, "And it's wonderful to see you and Alex looking so happy."

I nodded. All of us, I thought, were beginning to heal.

From the end of the table Helen said, "Molly, I was just telling Alex that the last thing your mother told me was how much she was looking forward to having Christmas with you and your family."

I swallowed hard. "I wish that had happened."

"I wish Grandma were here right now," Annie said, looking as if she might cry.

"Me too," Will said. "But I think about her when I use the computer she gave me. I think about how she knew it was exactly what I wanted."

My dad turned to me. "What about you, Molly? Have you used that laptop that Katherine gave you last Christmas?"

"I'm starting to. I'm going to take a sabbatical next year to write a book."

"What kind of book?" Ginny asked.

"Probably a study of unlikely killers." A topic close to home.

"Oh, your mother would be so pleased." Helen beamed at me. "She always said that you'd write a book some day. She was confident of it."

"I know," I said, remembering her Christmas note to me. I smiled, thinking of my know-it-all mother, who'd been right after all.

I'd recently reread Margaret O'Ryan's journal accounts of my mother's childhood. Strangely, what touched me the most was the description of how Mother had adored *Little Women,* the Alcott novel which Miss O'Ryan gave her for her eighth birthday—and which Mother gave me last Christmas. I'd always assumed she was so attached to the book because she identified with Jo, the feisty, tomboyish March sister who wanted to be a writer. But now I could picture little Katherine, who desperately wanted a warm, supportive family like the fictional March family.

But instead of nurturing Marmee, she'd had a social-climbing tyrant who was totally oblivious to her needs. And instead of jolly Meg, Beth, and Amy, she'd had an amoral murderer for a sister. I liked to think that Mother had given me her prized childhood novel so I could better understand the sensitive, bookish little girl she'd once been.

My mental image of her as a child in that disturbed family had somehow shifted my perspective of Mother. Yes, she had been secretive, undemonstrative, and too often preoccupied with her work. But she had allowed me to be who I wanted to be, applauded my successes, and helped me to find a way out of my failures. It was a great deal more than her mother had done for her.

I was still smiling when Alex raised his glass of wine. "Merry Christmas, everyone," he said with a grin. "And may you all have a New Year filled with joyous new ventures."

We all raised our glasses and wished him the same.

ABOUT THE AUTHOR

Karen Hanson Stuyck is the author of four previous mystery novels: *Fit to Die, Cry for Help, Held Accountable,* and *Lethal Lessons.* She has worked as a newspaper reporter, an editor, and a public relations writer for hospitals and a mental health institution. Her short stories have been published in *Redbook, Cosmopolitan, Woman's World,* and other magazines. She lives in Houston.